# TWO
# WAY
# TOLL

ALSO BY ZACHARY KLEIN

**Still Among the Living**

# TWO WAY TOLL

A Matt Jacob Novel
of Suspense

## ZACHARY KLEIN

HarperCollinsPublishers

FIRST EDITION

*Designed by Alma Orenstein*

LIBRARY OF CONGRESS CATALOG CARD NUMBER 90-56364

ISBN 0-06-016420-4

91 92 93 94 95 HC 10 9 8 7 6 5 4 3 2 1

*To Susan, who has seen me through the worst of times.*
*It's my pleasure to share the best.*

# ACKNOWLEDGMENTS

FIRST, TO MY FRIENDS AND AGENTS, Herb and Nancy Katz. Their encouragement, support, and faith in my work helped me through my second-book doubts and questions. Thank you.

And thank you, Herb, for another wonderful title.

No book would be complete without a lineup of the usual suspects—though none are at all usual, and their help not at all suspect. Thank you Sue, Sharon, Bonnie, Bill, Ron, Dr. J, Diane, Eddie, Denise, Nancy, Eric, Jeff. A very special note of gratitude to Tsiv, who kept me alive through my last deadline.

And my publishers. Thank you, Eamon, for your patience, flexibility, and helpful criticism, Larry, for your kind words, and Eve, for your diligence and uncanny ability to sense what I'm driving at.

# TWO
# WAY
# TOLL

# 1

THE ALARM SOUNDED and I awoke already depressed by the day's invitation to brain-death. I reached under the bed, pulled the ashtray onto my stomach, lit a cigarette, and eyed the leftover roach. It was too early for grass; better to shower and give last night's high a fighting chance to dissipate. The cigarette triggered my thirst, so I reluctantly pulled myself out of bed and trudged down the hall past the living room, past the office, and into the kitchen. By the time I arrived I had given up on the shower. I'd need one to slice through the numbness when I returned in the evening. One thing worse than doing something you don't like is doing it twice.

I splashed cold water on my face, returned to the bedroom, and lit the damn roach. I considered calling in sick, but I had turned down this particular mall too many times to fuck with them again. Also, I really didn't want to lay dead at home: before I'd hired Charles, a tenant, to replace me as the building's manager I could always find something to fiddle with or fix, but when I did that now he panicked.

I looked out the window and watched the cold, nasty November rain puddle on the gravel in my back alley. Just beyond, the supermarket was stirring, its amber crime lights bathing the morning delivery trucks with a pale yellow glow. The scene resembled an aging photograph discarded in the street, abused by the elements. Unfortunately, the picture lost its poetry when I remembered I had to join it.

It took a patient explanation and the photostat of my PI license before the mall's exterior security pronounced me fit-and-official. For yet another day I was a Mall-man. The show-and-tell at the mall's back door rain-logged my container of coffee, and I traipsed through the deserted shopping womb sharp-nosing chainlinked doorways, looking to smell something brewing.

My interest in the coffee turned sour after a sip, so I walked upstairs to an out-of-the-way john and dumped the stuff. Enveloped by pastel-tiled lavatory quiet, I squeezed into a stall and sucked on my personal public concession to the raging war on drugs: a single toke, smokeless pipe. Fortified, I ambled toward the detaining room, idly hoping that someone from administration couldn't sleep and was on time, ready with my assignment.

Someone was there but he wasn't from admin. Fat and balding, a tie squeezed up against layers of chins, he sat like a dangling-legged Buddha on the desk at the far end of the room.

"Turning yourself in? I didn't think there was anything open to steal from." He enjoyed his joke and laughed along with my grimace.

"Warren here?" I knew better, but felt uncomfortable just wearing a painted grin.

"Are you kidding? You a new dick?"

"No, but I could use one." I saw him get ready to laugh so I quickly added, "I fill in occasionally."

"Another hired gun?"

"I don't think of it that way, but yeah."

"I call myself a consultant. You?"

"Matt."

I was treated to another ripple of belly, jowls, and chins as I moved across the room and tried to twist my body into the one-armed wood-and-metal elementary school desk.

"Well, Matt, you'll never get comfortable in one of those. They don't want the sticky fingers to relax. That's why I'm parked here."

He was right. I stood up and wandered around the room until I came to the bulletin board.

"Listen, my name is Harry. Check out that board. Lists assignments. They figure if they do it the night before they can sleep guilt-free and we'll be good little drones and take our spots. I say, 'fuck 'em.'"

I read my location and looked back at Harry. "Beats waiting around."

"I suppose." He pushed his way off the desk and waited for his belly to stop bouncing. "How much you getting"—he paused—"if you don't mind the length of my beak?"

"I don't mind," I lied. "Forty."

He looked at me with a little surprise. "Forty, huh?" He winked. "You're either good or you know the Old Man's wife?"

"I know the wife." But I should have known better as his laugh squeezed the air out of the room.

"Matt, huh, you're all right!" He peered at me intently. "You look sort of familiar. You got a face that reminds me of someone."

I nodded. "I get that a lot. Usually it's the Pillsbury Dough Boy."

Everything in his clothes started to shake, and we waited until he caught his breath. "You're a funny guy. Don't usually find a sense of humor in our line of work. You remind me of some dead actor. One of those English guys." His voice dropped and became conspiratorial. "I get paid by the head."

"For every collar?"

"That's right." He puffed out the top half of his belly. "Not many consultants do that. You either, I bet?"

What we had here was a True Believer. "I like to eat."

He walked toward me rubbing his belly. "Hell, does it look like I miss many meals? They didn't hire a one-eyed Dick Tracy when they hired you, did they?"

I smiled at his lousy joke. "Not one-eyed, but not twenty/twenty either."

He chuckled, reached up, and patted me on the shoulder. "That's okay. In this racket no one is." He yanked at his pants in a futile attempt to get them up over his belly. All he got for his effort was a flash of white socks. "Come on," he said, "let's get out of here. I'll see this room enough today." He strode out the door and called over his shoulder, "No one showed you the holes, did they?"

"The holes?"

"I never show 'em either, but hell, I don't usually start my day laughing."

Harry led me to the upper floor. I hoped the dope pipe had worked as advertised since we walked through the same bathroom door. Just in case, I lit a smoke. "Want one?"

"Nah, that shit'll kill you. Finish it and I'll show you the holes."

I threw the cigarette into the toilet, flushed, and watched as Harry opened what looked like a closet door in the back of the bathroom. He motioned for me to follow. "Stay close. There's not much light."

For the next twenty minutes I followed him through a labyrinth of connecting tunnels, pausing occasionally to look through one-way mirrors into the stores. At one stop a clerk was preening in front of the mirror. Harry gave him the finger. "I hope to Christ he don't pop that fucking pimple on my window."

"Let's keep moving, Harry. How come they didn't tell me about this?"

He bellied through the dark corridor past a few more mirrors. "They think it bothers the yuppies to see someone walk out of the wall holding handcuffs. Not classy enough." He yanked on my leather jacket. "Look at this one," and pointed toward another mirror.

I looked, but all I could see were early morning customers browsing around a lingerie shop. "Who are you looking at?"

"That tall lady fingering the panties. She's warming up for someone, and I guarantee it ain't for the little mister at home." He glanced at me from the corner of his eye. "You work the holes long enough you see what life is really like because no one knows you're watching. That's the fun part of this job. The busts are for the money."

His eyes returned to the full-length mirror as the lower part of his body rocked gently back and forth. Dimes to dollars his hand would have had company if I hadn't been there. "Harry, man, I gotta go to my spot. How do I get out of here?"

"Keep going straight until you get to the stairs. Go down and use the door on your right. Takes you into the sporting goods store. Anybody asks, tell 'em you were with the Mole." His eyes never wavered and his mouth never completely closed. Harry was falling in love.

"Thanks for the tour."

"Yeah, sure, no problem. See you later."

I followed his directions and finally stepped into bright fluorescent lighting, took a moment to regain my vision, then looked at a broad-shouldered kid by my side.

"Sir, may I see your identification? No one is allowed back there."

I fumbled for my wallet. "I was with the Mole."

His eyes widened. "The Mole showed you his tunnels?"

"Yeah. I'm a substitute shamus."

The kid shook his head and waved at my wallet. "Don't bother."

Harry the Mole had groupies. I wondered glumly whether I'd eventually have them too if mall work remained the pinnacle of my PI career.

In the concourse I found a bench from where I could see most of my area. Someone had left the *Herald* and I got busy with the sports pages. Hourly rates had certain advantages.

And serious disadvantages. I spent most of the day strolling into stores choking back ennui and its sidekick, lethargy. I never understood why I got repeat mall assignments, since I rarely made any arrests, and the arrests I did make were invariably on some high-priced klepto released before I finished the paperwork. Maybe admin wanted Caucasian bust stats.

It was close to the end of my shift. I was hiding in the bathroom trying to escape the sweaty smell of aftershave and perfumed buying madness, when I decided to sniff around the holes instead. The sharp lighting from the stores fought its way through the irregularly placed, one-way mirrors and the pale glow cast a gloomy, checkered effect into the narrow, twisting passageway—a surrealistic path for a demented Jimmy Durante hat waving farewell.

But I was coming, not going, so I started down the weaving walkway wondering whether I'd find the Mole in a compromising position. I hoped not.

Once I'd gotten over the sneaky thrill of playing lead in *The Invisible Man*, watching people shop became a bore. I was sure Harry saw things I didn't.

I was peering into a record store when someone—I thought it was a he—parked in front of the mirror, catching me unexpectedly. The middle of my view was suddenly blocked by a tall, thin, threadbare peacoat with hair on the top of it. After my initial surprise, the endless day's frustrations caught up with me, and I became irrationally annoyed because Peacoat placed the sole of its shoe on the wall, its heel catching the bottom of the glass. I decided to wait it out.

Twice, I almost quit the game. His/her torn, jeaned butt was no Rubens, and I was near the end of my day. But before I finally decided, the coat, hair, and fanny slid off the mirror just out of my sight. I pressed my cheek against the glass, but all I saw was a shadow pass through the store's doorway.

I raced down the corridor in the direction I'd been moving, pausing briefly at each window for a quick, fruitless search. Then I decided to quit: no reason to work late on an unpaid, quixotic gender identification mission.

Retracing my steps toward the bathroom I stopped three mirrors short of home. Right before the window stood the front of the Peacoat. The top didn't look much different than it had from behind. He, and it was a he, stood staring directly toward me; the slit passing for his mouth opened, displaying brown, cracked teeth in a forest of hair.

It wasn't the teeth that bothered me, nor the look of insolence no amount of hair could cover. What bothered me was the reverberation deep inside my own waste dump of memories.

THE BEARD STARED through the glass as though he knew I stood hidden behind his reflection. It suddenly became important to me to remember how I knew him. When he slowly turned and walked toward the store's exit, I followed.

After some hasty scrambling through the holes I picked him up downstairs in Designer Discounts. Again he stood, hands in pockets, scowling, looking through the glass, and I had the uneasy feeling he'd been waiting. A minute after I spotted him he turned, walked to a sock counter, and fingered the goods.

Tired of my lost cause I had just decided to leave when Peacoat picked up a pair of socks and retreated behind the counter outside my field of vision. Then I noticed Harry enter the store. I watched as he moved his bulk purposefully toward the sock bin, tongue flicking rapidly over his partially open mouth.

When the Mole moved out of my sight I dashed to the nearest

door, opened it, and startled customers in the rear of the adjoining bookstore. I grunted through the staring people, walked down an aisle, and out the door.

The afternoon crowd was thinning into a suppertime lull, but a circle of curious onlookers had gathered in the concourse in front of the department store. Shouldering my way through, I saw the Mole and Peacoat eyeing each other like Bert and Harry Piel. I stopped moving when I heard the Mole's enraged voice.

"You stupid, ugly bastard, you're going down for *socks*? Four stinking dollars' worth! They were on sale, for Christ sake! It's ass-holes like you that make me rich."

I edged closer, but they were so angry that neither noticed me. Two glittering black coals shot sparks from the holes left for his eyes in Peacoat's full-face beard. He looked like a street lamp with hair on the end of it. A red-faced Harry dangled a pair of handcuffs from his fat hands.

"I don't make you rich, you fat slob! The rich make you rich, just like they give their guard dogs steak. You're just a German shepherd that can't see the leash!"

The words dripped with a nasal singsong sarcasm that shook my skull. Twenty years is a long time to remember anything, but I remembered the voice.

"Ain't no way you're going to get them on me, Porker. You try, and I'll bite your fat fucking ear off." He waved long, bony-white, nail-bitten fingers toward the cuffs.

Harry glanced at the growing number of onlookers and tried reason. "Everything will go easier if you just come with me. Then I won't have to use these or call for backup."

"Call your fucking backup. I don't go nowhere with police washouts." His voice had the grind of dry metal twisting against dry metal. I'd hated it twenty years ago, and I'd heard enough to hate it now.

The Mole didn't like being called a washout, but Peacoat always had an instinct for the short hairs. I took a deep breath and stepped through the front row. "Blackhead. Long time no see." He seemed surprised to hear his name, and I waited silently while he tried to make me.

Harry looked relieved; people sensed an end to the confrontation and the circle began to splinter. "You know this smartass?" he asked.

I nudged them to the side of the concourse as I answered. "Years ago. I was a street worker in The End and he was one of the kids."

"Shoulda left him on the street. Asshole was sitting on the floor pulling the damn socks on his feet. They were on sale," the Mole added incredulously.

"Yeah, I heard." I looked at Blackhead and realized he was holding his shoes. He stared at me, oblivious of Harry's comment. I hoped he would stay quiet. He opened his mouth, but I moved between him and the Mole. "Why don't you lay him on me?"

"That'll cost me money."

I looked around and urged the last of the spectators away. "How many did you score today?" I asked over my shoulder.

"Twelve," he said, pride poking through his gruffness.

I looked at him with genuine respect. "Jesus, Harry, you must have eyes behind your head."

A small flattered grin flashed across his round face as he weighed my proposal. "I suppose it wouldn't break me"—he glanced at the clock on the far wall—"I still got time to make up for it." He frowned. "That is, if this skinny turd hasn't hung a sign on me."

I sensed Blackhead start. When I looked his mouth was open, and he was staring at the Mole with amazement. "The fat man is a *bounty hunter*? That's pretty sick shit, Washout."

"Shut up, jerk." I shook my head at Harry. "Maybe I *should* have left him in the damn street. He's an asshole, Mole, but he's an asshole I know. I'll owe you one."

Harry was stuffing the handcuffs back into his pocket. "Don't worry about it. I'll bust two in the time it takes to do this freak's paperwork. You gonna be here tomorrow?"

"I haven't checked."

"Well, maybe I'll see you." Blackhead was already yesterday's news as Harry waddled back toward the department store. Before he disappeared through the entrance he turned and stared. For a second I thought he had changed his mind. But all he said was, "It's someone, but it ain't the Dough Boy."

Blackhead stood shaking his head, a scornful look on his face. "Ain't this a trip? The original bleeding heart social worker doing security for a bourgeois mall. I'da never figured you for a cop, you were always such a big nanny."

I waved my arm toward the center rotunda. "I'm touched you remember me at all, Blackhead, but you have your classes confused. This place is a step up from bourgeois. Why don't you give me the socks and put your shoes back on?"

He looked at me contemptuously. "Give you the fucking socks? Are you crazy? I put up with insulting shit from a fat tub of guts and you want me to give back the socks? You want 'em? Take 'em, cop."

No way I was going to touch his feet. "I'm not a cop."

"What are you then? I didn't think malls hired social workers." A nasty grin crossed his face. "Of course it might be a moneymaker. You might be helping the nervous middle class overcome their spending anxieties?"

It had been a long time since I'd thought about The End, and my memories almost crowded out his sarcasm. "I'm a PI. What do you do when you're not stealing socks?"

Another brown-chipped-tooth grin split his thick beard. "Nothing as exotic as mall security."

He sat on the polished tile floor and pulled on his shoes, over the stolen socks. When he stood back up, I looked at his added inches. "'The more things change, the more they stay the same,' huh, Blackhead."

He started for the mall's exit. "Don't call me Blackhead. I haven't been called that since I was a kid, and I don't like it."

"Is there anything you do like?"

The suppertime shoppers gave way as Blackhead grunted his way through. He leaned his tall frame forward as he walked, moving close enough to create discomfort in anyone he was behind. I kept my eyes on his long, scrawny neck, hustling to follow before the gaps closed. We made it to the exit in record time until I remembered I hadn't punched out.

"Slow down, man. You still didn't tell me what you're called?"

He stopped and turned around. "Emil."

"Emil?"

"Yeah, that's my name. I guess your cop friends all call you 'Flower Child.'"

"I don't have any cop friends. Matt works fine."

"What happened to Jake?"

I grinned. "I dropped the nickname when I went into the detective business. I didn't want anyone to confuse me with Jake Gittes. I like my nose."

He turned toward me. "Who the fuck is Jake Gittes?"

I shrugged. "Never mind."

"Well, Matt, are you leaving or what? I don't feel like jawing in Yuppie World."

I almost felt good about reporting to the detaining room. "Sorry, Emil, I can't leave. You ever see the rest of the gang?"

A dark look crossed his face but all he did was grunt. "What gang?"

"You know, the kids you ran with."

He shrugged. "Some of them."

"Well, say hello for me."

He turned his back without answering and almost ran down a pair of packed jeans pushing a stroller. He started to snarl, then turned back to me with a strange look on his face. "Tell 'em yourself. It wouldn't kill you to visit The End once in a while. You used to say it was the first place that felt like home."

I was surprised to hear my words thrown back at me. "You have a good memory, Emil."

Another strange look crossed his face. "Too good," he said, low.

I watched as he ducked and disappeared through the revolving door. Halfway back to the detaining room I grew annoyed that he hadn't bothered to thank me.

# 3

"LOU, THIS IS THE THIRD TIME in the past two weeks you've *hocked* me about the buildings. Everything here is fine." I was still smarting from Blackhead's final remark, and this telephone call just added to my defensiveness. I suppose it showed. Lou's wheeze worked overtime to keep his exasperation under control.

"You tell me everything is fine but you don't send the details. Boychik, we invested a lot of money in the renovation. I don't think it's asking too much to see some pictures."

I looked at the joint in my fingers. I'd torn the paper, and most of the dope had spilled onto the desk. I felt a wave of guilt thin my irritation. *We* hadn't invested money, *he* had.

"I know Charles does the managing," Lou continued, "but you're my partner. If I can't get the straight dope from you, I'm out in the cold."

Dope he could get. "Listen, I send you all the important information."

"But the pictures. I can't visualize things from here."

The suffocation was starting. Since Lou's wife, Martha, had died, calls from Chicago had come with increased frequency, jammed with increased demands. The unsent snapshots were just the latest.

Resignation replaced my guilt. "As soon as I get the camera from the shop I'll take the pictures."

"You can't borrow a camera?"

"Jesus, Lou, don't you have anything better to do than worry about this?"

"What's to do? I have time to attend to our business now, that's all." His voice suddenly guarded.

"What about friends?" The image of the crowded temple during Martha's funeral crossed my mind. I'd known about Lou's political importance before his retirement, but I had been staggered at the turnout. Half of Chicago had been there.

"Friends," he snorted. "How many times a week can you talk about 'the good old days'?"

"Lou, you're backing yourself into a corner." And into me.

"You're warning me about corners? Mr. Cus DiMato himself? Instead of my corners, worry about your own. If you just took care of what I ask, we wouldn't have a problem. The way you do things makes me feel like you don't care about the buildings."

His combativeness was back, and I started to reroll the dope on my desk. "Look, I'll send the pictures as soon as I can." I felt ashamed of the sharpness in my voice. I didn't want to drive him away, but the more he demanded the less I could deliver. I could only hope the long-standing warmth between us would, whatever his demands, whatever my reactions, remain intact.

And it took remembering those feelings to stay quiet when he said, "Maybe it would be better if I paid a little visit, boychik. Something tells me I'd see the buildings quicker that way."

I tried not to react to the fingers reaching around my throat. I didn't think his "maybe" meant maybe. "That would be nice, Lou, it's been a while."

"Well, I'll think about it," he said, sounding as though I'd done the inviting. "Check with the camera store anyway. They might give you a loaner."

"Sure." Maybe they could throw in a thousand free miles.

I was relieved to be off the phone. A familiar sensation but, until the last few months, not one I'd associated with Lou. I rubbed my eyes and tried to push my reaction away. When Chana and our daughter, Rebecca, died in the accident, Lou and Martha had stood strong as I slowly pulled together the shattered fragments of my life.

I took a long drag of the grass. It couldn't have been easy for them. Chana had been their only child. Now Martha was dead, and I sat in my office, fighting with the guy when he needed me the most. I bit the end of the joint where a seed blocked the smoke's passage and inhaled. As much as I wanted to help, my relational ties were no match for my emotional claustrophobia.

I put my bare feet up on the desk and looked at the forest-green walls and cream woodwork. After the accident Lou had bought this six-flat to give me something to do. When I'd gotten involved in the detective business, he'd bought the six-flat next door and made us partners in both. Lou had even hired Richard, an architect and Charles' live-in lover, to renovate and attach the buildings.

It was through Richard's insistence and craftsmanship that I had an office at all. He stole some cellar and designed a new kitchen at the end of my interior hall. Then he transformed the old kitchen into an office. Somehow, he'd managed to keep the Forties feel of my place intact. Something I appreciated, psychologically unprepared as I was to leapfrog decades.

Unfortunately, the renovation mostly meant a longer walk from the bedroom to refrigerator. Who needs an office when you're malling for work?

The joint had gone out. I relit it and a cigarette. I had never imagined myself a landlord and Lou's reminder served to unleash more memories from the past. Hell, one of my shining moments had come when a group of neighborhood people organized a rent strike and takeover from a usurious landlord: I still remembered the looks on their faces when I got the damn boiler to work.

We'd won the battle, though the war had been lost long before I'd set foot in The End. In a neighborhood ravaged by neglect and poverty, a call for a *minyan* would have gathered newspaper-shoe'd bag ladies, crazies, grifters, and professional do-gooders. A neighborhood where what little money there was flowed in only one direction—out. But The End was the neighborhood where I had fought for Truth, Justice, and what I believed was the American way. A community where I could escape from my own desperate youth. Or so I had imagined.

It had been a long time since I'd thought about The End. Not simply because it was a forgotten part of my city, or because I was no longer involved in social service. Not even because I'd lost most of my faith in *T*, *J*, and *A*. I didn't want to think about The End because it was where I had begun my disastrous marriage with my first wife, Megan. Things ended up so sour between us that it had lemoned damn near any place we'd ever gone. There were restaurants, movie houses, whole sections of town I still avoided. It didn't seem to make any difference that I'd once thought of The End as home.

But Blackhead's remark, and the reminder of my new-found status, threatened my ability to Sherman the past. Or even hopscotch the present. Truth was, I was a naked landlord, sitting in my junk shop–furnished, art deco office, guilty and unhappy about my present life.

I suddenly couldn't stand to stay in the office. Grabbing my stash I flopped onto the living room couch. I flipped on the tube, and waited for the one-two punch of dope and television to work its magic. I kept watching and smoking, but couldn't get rid of the hazy memories swirling inside my head. I hadn't thought of The End or its lost people in so long that I had trouble matching names with faces. At least I hoped it was the passage of time. I didn't want to believe it was the dope.

# 4

SLEEP BROUGHT UNEASY TOSSINGS and jump starts of wakefulness. Eyes open or closed almost didn't matter: there was no escaping the leering image of my first wife. Back then I had imagined that my work in The End signaled the start of a new life, the finish of an abusive past. But hooking onto Megan proved otherwise. Our relationship began with me courting, she regularly rejecting, then finally accepting. Our marriage wasn't any different until after her second lover, when I stopped courting. Then it was over.

I awoke with an unusual sigh of relief. As if to wash the dreams from my eyes I reached for the phone and dialed Boots' number. She picked up the receiver on the second ring and I drawled, "Hey, babe, who's looking at ya?" my voice still thick with leftover memories.

"You're not really asking, are you?" Her low whisper suggested a still sleeping visitor.

"Oh." My eyes got sleep-heavy, and I suddenly wanted to make up for my fitful night.

"Don't sound so defeated, Matt, it's boring. I thought you'd given up on mornings. Is something the matter?"

"No, not really. I thought we could do breakfast. But since you're busy ..."

"Slow down. If you can do mornings, I can do breakfast. It can't be a long one, though."

I suggested Charley's, gave her directions, then hung up the phone. My reaction surprised me, since I wasn't often thrown by Boots' arrangement with Hal. Hell, I rarely even thought about it. By the time I was ready to leave the house, I had assigned the fetid taste to my Megan memories—how easily the unpleasant past infects the everyday present.

She wasn't hard to spot in a deserted restaurant. She wasn't hard to spot in wall-to-wall crowds. In a town where fashion was typically defined by long skirts worn with running shoes, Boots' expensive Soho stylishness invariably caught eyes.

I detoured to the counter where Phil was hunched over the grill. He had to be cooking breakfast for himself, because there was no one else in the place. My lovely didn't do grill.

"Hey, dude, what's happening?"

He turned around, startled. "Well, look here, Matt Jacob. Didn't hear you sneak up."

I smiled. It was nice to see him. "Where's Red?"

He scowled. "Good question." He nodded toward the booth where Boots was looking at us. "The lady with you?"

"Good question. She eat yet?"

"Nah."

I held up a finger, walked over to the booth and took Boots' smile and breakfast order. I returned to the counter and gave both to Phil along with my own. He turned his back and spoke over his shoulder. "Thought you might be eating in more elegant surroundings after that stuff in the newspapers." He was careful to keep any criticism from seeping into his voice.

It startled me to realize I hadn't been there since the shooting. "I've just been laying low. Anyhow, this is my kind of elegant."

Despite his disbelieving grimace, I wasn't lying. Black-and-white tile floor, baked-enamel-topped tables, with old-fashioned sugar bottles and thick heavy china, overhead fans. All the place needed was a train car exterior. And customers. Area gentrification had made winners of some, losers of others. And real estate brokers rich.

Phil grunted and focused on his cooking. I stayed at the counter as long as I could, then walked back to the booth. It surprised me to see how well Boots' chic fitted in with our surroundings; of course, I was often surprised by how well Boots' chic fit in with me.

"Why do I get the impression you regret having called?" She tossed her head and I watched her thick black hair swing wide and settle around her face. Her long-lashed Mediterranean-green eyes glittered and she smiled, but there was no humor in her voice.

"I'm not sorry about calling. I'm sorry about my greeting."

"No, you're not. You're sorry about my answer."

I was too tight to trust a response. Instead, I shrugged, lit a cigarette, and waited quietly while Phil worked on the food. A couple of times Boots started to speak, then stopped. She held out her smartly painted fingers and I handed her the smokes. But before she finished lighting, Phil was piling dishes on a tray. I excused myself and walked over.

He looked at me. "You think I'm too old to work?"

"I needed a break."

He wiped his forehead with a white towel. "Must not be a client."

I nodded. "You charge extra for clairvoyance?"

I placed Boots' low-cal in front of her and unloaded my nitrites and cholesterol onto the table. Boots turned her attention to the food with the same enthusiasm she always did. I forced myself to eat; didn't want to insult Phil and didn't want to talk. Boots finished her cereal, sat back, and watched me toy with my meal.

"You going to eat or play with that?"

"Both."

"Give me another cigarette, will you?"

As soon as he saw us smoking Phil was over, pouring steaming coffee into our mugs. Boots drank, grinned, and sat back smoking contentedly. "This place is a sweet find, Matt."

"How would you know? Your breakfast came out of a box."

"The look, the coffee. Reminds me of your apartment. You didn't invite me here to sulk, did you?"

"I'm not sulking," I sulked.

"Then what are you doing? You have an attitude's a mile wide."

"Isn't that what they said about Nixon?" I deflected. "Support a mile wide but only a half-inch thick?"

"I'm not talking about the good old days, or Richard Nixon, Matt. I'm talking about your telephone call and your attitude right now."

"What attitude? I had a hard time sleeping last night, that's all."

Boots inhaled on her cigarette and smiled sardonically. "You should have listened to the sound of your voice once you realized Hal was there." She looked at me carefully, and I could see the crow's-feet at the corners of her eyes deepen. "I don't expect that shit from you," she added. "It's not part of the bargain."

"The Bargain" wasn't something we talked about, just lived. For Boots, it meant maintaining relationships that did nothing to threaten her independence; for me, it meant keeping romance and friendship separate. That duo had been the part of me Chana occupied, and when she died it went with her.

We were both over the line...my jealous reaction, Boots' demand for an explanation. "Bad dreams," I said. "I ran into some-one I knew from my days in The End."

A question pulled at her neat, thin eyebrows.

"That's where I met Megan," I added. Boots knew who Megan was and, I was sure, what she was. Old friends, Simon and Fran Roth, had introduced me to Boots about a year after Chana died. Simon went back to my days with Megan and, though I was certain he hadn't spared Boots any of the gory details, she and I never spoke about it. Or why I no longer saw Simon or Fran.

"I hadn't realized you met there," Boots said, her jaw rigid.

Despite her usual tolerance, "there" rolled off her tongue like a dead fish. Most people thought of The End that way. If they thought of it at all.

"I lived in The End when I first landed in town. A long time ago, twenty years." It bothered me that I sounded apologetic.

"This person you met, who recognized who?" A small smile played at the corners of her lightly glossed lips.

"I recognized him. It wasn't too hard, his voice makes my skin crawl. An ugly scene at the mall. He was getting busted and I sprung him."

"For old times' sake?"

I nodded.

Boots looked carefully at the ash on her cigarette, then gracefully flicked it into the ashtray. "This morning was just more mall blues?"

"Not really." I hesitated, then pushed myself to speak. "For a moment your relationship with Hal piggybacked onto Megan. I was out of line."

She stubbed the remainder of her cigarette into the ashtray, and shook her head. "You're a piece of work, Matt. Every time I turn around you're bashing your head against some ghost. You don't let go of anything, do you? Divorce, death, it doesn't matter, Matt Jacob never lets go."

She was awfully ferocious about a two-minute telephone conversation. I was sorry I'd said anything, but felt my temper slip. "Lighten up. I never give you shit about Hal."

I punched out my smoke, lit another, and proceeded to give her shit about Hal. "Maybe something's bothering you about him? Christ, you don't need him to pay for your apartment. You got your own money, and you're a veep at Ma Bell. Damn, woman, he's old enough to be your father!" I sat back in my chair and clamped my mouth shut around the cigarette. I didn't know who was more surprised by my tirade.

Whatever Boots' surprise, it did nothing to lessen her anger. She tugged at the collar of her gray silk blouse, her green eyes flashing. "And you say Hal doesn't disturb you? What bullshit!" She yanked her hand away from her shirt. "You're damn right I don't need his money. If I did, I wouldn't touch a nickel. Try to get it through your head, it gives him pleasure to do something for me. It gives *me* pleasure to let him."

Boots stuck out her hand and I rapidly complied. She turned to the side and lit the cigarette. When she turned back she had an odd look in her eyes. "Despite his age Hal is there for me when I need him. Something your damn ghosts could never let you be," she added softly, looking away.

It was a relief to be outside her line of sight. I was still disconcerted by my outburst, and now I had her response for dessert. I wasn't used to this kind of conversation with Boots.

Mercifully, Phil lumbered over with the coffee pot. By the time he left, so had some of our anger. Boots dipped her spoon in her mug, then placed it on the table. We both sipped our coffee in silence, letting more of the tension drain away. Finally she looked up and asked, "Who was it you ran into?"

I smiled at her, grateful to be on somewhat more comfortable ground. "A kid I knew from the old days. After I got the leash off, he insulted me for being a 'cop.'"

"Insulted you?"

"Accused me of selling out."

"Selling out? Better you should be a janitor?"

"It's 'manager,' not 'janitor.' Drag your nose back down to earth." I grinned, though I suspected more than a joke behind her dig and my reaction.

"You sound as if you take this thief seriously?"

"It doesn't matter who throws your past in your face, if it's no longer who you are."

"That's called 'change,' honey." She smiled at me. Both of us felt better on familiar ground, Boots trucking down her path, me limping down mine.

"It's a good thing," she added.

"What's a good thing?"

"Change."

I lifted my mug and finished the last of the coffee. Phil caught my eye, raised the pot, and I nodded. "That depends on the changes, Boots. It's difficult for me to remember a time when so much seemed so important, and compare it to now."

"You imagine things don't mean as much to you now?"

"It's not just me. I'm not the only person who's given up."

Boots grinned and shook her head. "You haven't given up; it's just harder for you to find things to believe in."

"That's my Boots. Glasses are always half full."

"That's why we fit, Matt. You only see half empty."

We sat quietly thinking about the other's vision. I saw her look at the clock and asked, "Do you want something else?"

"No," she answered. "I have to run. But Sweetie, I think you do."

"Do what?"

"Want something. Your hostility about Hal sounds like unfinished business with Megan."

There was no hint of reproach but the comment was too much like the ghost crack. It annoyed me that she kept pressing the envelope. "Megan? I doubt it. The only unfinished business I have is the rest of my life."

I signaled to Phil for the check and slowly stood. "I can't say this has been an unadulterated pleasure."

Boots closed her triangular leather bag. "Was that intended or just Freudian?"

I laughed. "A little touchy, aren't you?"

She flipped the bag's clasp and stood. "Maybe, maybe not."

Boots slipped on her coat while I paid the bill and said goodbye to Phil. I held her arm and walked toward the door, confused and disquieted by our conversation. I felt impatient to see her again, to talk in our old way about the usual things. I was about to ask, but the door to the diner suddenly flew open. Red breezed through, bringing a gust of freezing air. She looked surprised to see me, then more surprised when she eyed Boots and her five-hundred-dollar suit. "I didn't think you had it in you, stranger," she murmured, winking.

I rushed my hello, rushed my goodbye, then quickly followed Boots' tracks outside. I looked up and down the block before I walked back to the car. Boots had disappeared. Red was right, I didn't really "have it in me."

Home is where the telephone is, was, and unfortunately always will be. I grabbed the receiver, hoping it was Boots. It had been almost a week since we'd met for breakfast, and I still hadn't left her completely behind.

It wasn't Boots, or even some administrator with a belated summons to monitor the day's shopping lust. It was that noxious, nasal voice of gloom and doom. Still, I was almost glad to hear from him, a definite testament to the week's three mall blues.

"Is this Jake, I mean Matt Jacobs the gumshoe?" He accented and dragged out the last word.

"Jacob, Blackhead. Without the 's.'"

"Stop calling me Blackhead, will ya? I hate that fucking name."

"Sorry. Emil, right?"

"It's good to see that you're not totally stupid. After you told me you were a cop I wondered."

My streak of glad faded. "I'm not a cop, Blackhead."

"Not much difference in being paid by the State or by the people the State works for, is there?"

"Did you call to lecture me about my role as a running dog lackey for the capitalists?" Despite the bark, my words didn't contain much bite. When I saw past Blackhead and Megan, I realized a lingering affection for The End.

"Some," he admitted without the sarcasm. "I'm sick and tired of everyone who supposedly had principles during the Sixties, chasing the green just as hard as the people they said they hated."

I'd chased a lot of things, but money wasn't one of them. "You got no one else to talk to about this? You want a shrink referral?"

"I don't remember you having a wise mouth."

"Has to do with age." I suddenly wanted off. "What did you call about, Blackhead?"

"Emil. Don't be a shithead."

"Okay, Emil. What is this about?"

His voice dropped into a conspiratorial whisper. "I want you to look into something for me."

"I'm not a social worker anymore," I reminded.

"If I needed a social worker I'd stick a butterfly net out my window and catch half a dozen."

I chuckled. The End had always been locked and loaded with workers. Just graduate from social work school? Work in The End. Want to relate to the tired, poor, and the wretched? Work in The End! Want to play with psychotics? Work in The End!! There used to be constant debate whether there were more workers than clients. But all of us social workers were afraid to count.

"Emil, you call, insult my job, then ask for help." I hesitated, then added, "I don't think you can afford it." I wondered why I'd given him an opening; I didn't want to be a detective "worker" in The End.

"What do you charge?"

When I told him he exploded. "That's what you get paid for catching people with their pants down? Do you get extra for photos or are they included?"

"I don't do divorce work. If that's what you are looking for, I can't help."

"That's not why I called," he said sullenly.

I wasn't surprised. It was hard to imagine Blackhead married. "Emil, I told you what I charge if—and it's a big if—I take the job."

"I can afford it."

It didn't sound like a lie, and my growing curiosity was suddenly spiked with suspicion. "You get nailed stealing socks; now you tell me you can afford my cost. I don't do illegal work, Blackhead. I don't fuck with the law."

"It's got nothing to do with illegal. Anyhow, don't talk shit over the phone."

I knew better than to stay on the line. I knew better than to even consider working for Emil. The last time I'd worked for someone I knew, I had exchanged my best friend for a permanent keepsake—I could feel the bullet wiggle in my thigh.

But something had me hooked. Maybe it was The End, or maybe it was seeing people I'd known twenty years earlier. Maybe it was that unfinished business Boots had talked about.

I did know I was still holding the damn receiver. "So what is it?"

"I don't want to talk on the phone. Where do you live?"

I wasn't that hooked. "No way, Blackhead."

For a moment his sarcasm returned. "Are you afraid I'll trail in End Disease?"

Before I could say goodbye he downshifted his mouth. "Look, I'm sorry, okay? I've been stressed out. We can meet at the Wagon Wheel. I'll be there in an hour."

I was almost willing to be mollified. "Well, I can't. I'll meet you around nine."

"You're so busy I got to wait until nine? My money is green."

"I'm busy enough not to take your mouth."

"I'll watch my mouth. Just meet me there, will you? I need the help."

I looked at my face's reflection in the mirror and counted the creases. "I'll meet you for old times' sake, Emil, but I'm not promising to take the job. I'll listen, that's all."

After he'd hung up I continued to stare into the mirror, until I caught a glimpse of Megan over my shoulder. Whatever lingering affection I had for The End evaporated. I jammed the dead receiver down on the table next to its base. One call a day was enough.

I pulled my stash from the drawer and sat staring at its contents. It was time to prepare for the Wagon Wheel, but I wasn't certain how. Before making any final decision, I walked into the bedroom and dragged my guncase out from under the bed. I carried the .38 and holster back into the kitchen and plunked them down on the table next to the pharmacy. It was mid-month, which meant I could anticipate a visit from Julius. It had taken a little time, but he was finally convinced my new building owner rank didn't threaten our unspoken drugs-for-rent arrangement. He'd even gone back to his practice of breaking in and leaving the package on my kitchen table. To maintain tradition, I instituted frequent lock changes. I didn't really expect to stop him and hadn't. Praise the Lord.

I rolled a city-slicker and poured a double bourbon. No use wasting money trying to get high on bar whiskey; I'd just use that to keep dehydration at bay. I slowed down enough to realize I was anxious, considered a Valium, and settled on a half. Something dragged on my gut but I didn't know if it was The End or the gun. I hadn't worn it since the time it had been fired.

In the old days, if I was forced to retrieve someone from the Wagon Wheel, I carried a length of lead pipe. Now I strapped on the holster, surprised by its familiarity and comfort; along with age had come evolution.

I debated another double, then settled on a small single. I felt excited to be going where I'd been twenty years before. It made me feel young.

I might have believed the feeling a little longer, but the bar had a full-width mirror stretched behind its fancy bottles of fake fancy liquor. Everything in the grim tavern seemed unchanged, with the notable exceptions of my face and a caged, bare-breasted woman shaking mournfully to Hank Williams Jr. The new brass did nothing but add to the old sleaze. The Wagon Wheel remained a tough tavern, rife with the smell of sweat, piss, and unstarted fights. Between the cracks you could feel the hostile frustrations of broken lives.

I added to the gray cloud overhead as I lit a cigarette and ordered a double. At least the bartender didn't ask if I wanted Jack Daniel's. It was reassuring not to be mistaken for a tourist. Then I looked at the other regulars, and reconsidered.

When I faced the crowded tables in the back I saw Blackhead staring at the dancer. As the song ended she squatted like Johnny Bench, and swigged from a beer bottle on the cage floor. I watched Blackhead pull himself from his reverie and look around the room. He spotted me and waved, teeth cracking through the forest on his face. I threaded through the crowd, careful not to brush against anyone. I might be twenty years older and carrying a gun instead of a lead stick, but my apprehension hadn't slackened. Too many drunken customers stumbled out of this bar surprised to discover knife wounds or empty wallet pockets.

I got to the booth, and Blackhead bobbed his head. "I didn't think you were going to show."

I sat and waved to the waitress. "Still without that trusting spirit, huh?"

He grimaced. "Look around. These people been trusting their government for two hundred years and what's it got them? A broad with bouncing silicone. Takes their mind off the fact that none of 'em gets laid."

"You seemed smitten yourself, Emil."

He looked at me out of the corner of his eye. "How long were you spying on me?"

"Looking for you. Looking for you." I turned to the waitress, who'd finally made it through the sea of groping hands. She wore a miniskirt, cowboy boots, a wide, white-lipsticked smile, and blue paint over dead eyes. I ordered a single refill for the dregs in my hand, waited for Blackhead who shook his head, and watched the lady fight her way back to the bar.

Blackhead had no glass. "They let you sit here without drinking?"

"I don't like paying for colored water."

"And they let you stay?"

"I have friends. Let's leave it at that."

"I find it difficult to believe."

He suddenly shook his head. "Why do you keep insulting me?"

I drained the rest of my own colored water. "I don't know. You bring out my best." I grew impatient. "Okay, so what's this all about?"

"Don't you want to wait for your drink?"

"Are you kidding? By the time it shows, the girl will be dancing and you won't be able to talk."

"You weren't always this funny."

"Come on, Emil, I don't like it here."

"What's the matter? You spend all your time in the Rich Man's World? This ain't no fancy mall, but at least there are real people here. Not the phonies who think a hard time is finding a tax shelter."

I started to stand. "I quit college, Blackhead. If I want a political sociology course I'll go to night school."

"Okay, take it easy, will you? Sit down. I don't want to keep fighting, man. Come on, sit. For Christ sake, you haven't been in the neighborhood since dirt, now you want to run right out."

I sat. "Well, make it quick."

He nodded toward my right shoulder. "You got a license for that?"

I threw my hands up. "You don't get it, do you? I don't need new drinking buddies."

His eyes flicked around the room as he leaned across the table, his whisper barely audible over the jukebox and crowd. "Do you remember Peter Knight?"

It took a minute, but I finally nodded. "He had a sister, right?"

He leaned even closer. "Yeah, Melanie. Do you remember how he died?"

I knew he *had* died, but not how. It happened after Megan forced us to move from The End, because she was tired of living thigh-to-thigh with "losers." The same reason she eventually gave for taking lovers.

Blackhead used the silence to fill me in. "He accidentally drowned in a quarry. I don't know whether you were still living here or not. Anyway, I was with him earlier that night, and the pigs hauled my ass over the coals. Stupid fucks wanted to hassle me, so they tried to make it seem like I had something to do with it."

He scowled silently as if remembering the particular night. "Nothing came of it. Everybody knew that I wouldn't hurt Peter.

Hell, if I'd been there when he went in, I woulda died trying to save him." He stopped talking and sat back in his seat. I saw his eyes glisten, but it was probably from the smoke in the room.

"What's this got to do with me?"

"Just hear me out, will you? I got this letter threatening to reopen the whole fucking case. Said there was proof that would put my ass in Walpole. The fucking letter said there was nothing I could do about it, either. I want you to find out who sent the damn thing. I don't want my ass in Walpole."

I shrugged. "I don't think you have much to worry about."

"Well, I'm worrying anyway. What if someone's trying to set me up?"

"You think Peter was murdered?"

He looked frustrated. "No, man, I don't think Peter was murdered."

"Then what are you worried about? The cops have better things to do than run down every crank note that comes their way. Damn, Blackhead, it's been twenty years. They wouldn't give a shit even if you did kill him."

"Stop calling me Blackhead. And don't fuck around! I know how long it's been, but I don't care. I want to know who's fucking with me."

"What do you think I can do?"

"You're a private cop, aren't you? You can investigate."

"The city is filthy with private cops." I decided not to tell him how much they charged: he'd have a heart attack.

"Yeah, but I ran into you. Also, whether you like to admit it or not, you're sorta from the neighborhood. People knew you and I figure they might talk better."

My crap detector was firing. "Blackhead, answer me straight. How are you going to get the money to pay me?"

He looked at me scornfully. "I told you not to worry. You'll get your stinking money."

"That's not good enough. I want to know how *you'll* get it."

"Look, man, I sell a little grass. That's why I don't like to talk on the phone."

I wondered what he meant by a little. "And your dealing has nothing to do with this letter?"

He looked perplexed. "Why should it?"

I motioned him closer. When he moved I circled his skinny neck with my hand, pinned his arms between his body and the table, and squeezed. I didn't want to be obvious; free-for-alls used to happen here with even less provocation. Still, I let my hand stay where it was until I saw his eyes flash with fear and pain.

"Do you think I'm stupid?" I had trouble keeping my voice low. "Every night someone turns up dead because of drug jockeying. You deal, and I'm supposed to think drugs have nothing to do with this bullshit?"

I felt a deep-seated rage but knew enough to push him back into his seat.

"Why'd you do that, man?" he croaked. He massaged his neck and looked at me reproachfully. "I'm not lying. There ain't no turf wars here. Everybody knows everybody. Nobody figures The End is worth the trouble. I'm telling you, I just need to know who's fucking with me." He kept rubbing his Adam's apple. "I even brought money for you," he added.

When he started to reach into his pocket I grabbed his arm. "I'll take your money if I decide to work for you. Right now I haven't decided a damn thing."

"I'm telling you, Matt, this don't have nothing to do with drugs. I just got to know who is messing with me."

"You could be lying. Or you could be wrong."

He began to protest but I waved it off. The ugly of both the bar and my behavior sickened me. I pulled a pen from my leather and handed it to him. "Don't talk. Just give me your address and number and I'll get back to you."

He scratched on a thin cardboard Bud coaster and pushed it to me. I took it, shook my empty glass, and stood. "Give me back the pen. And use your money to pay the waitress if she shows."

He flipped the pen and sat staring into the crowd, rubbing his neck. "I don't understand why you did that, man."

Blackhead had company; I didn't either.

IT TOOK A LONG, HOT SHOWER to scrub the Wagon Wheel's smell off my skin. It took even longer to wash away the stink of my own actions. I didn't do too well in bars; maybe because I'd been brought up in one. At times it had been fun; mostly it involved long boring hours on a stool watching my parents pretend friendly.

Naked and dripping, I ransacked the apartment for sweats. I finally dug them out from the floor of the closet. I dressed, felt my stomach curdle at the thought of a nightcap, and wound up at the kitchen table rolling a joint.

It wasn't the bar, wasn't my childhood. But I still didn't know if the evening's rage had come from my repulsion and suspicion of Blackhead, or the possibility of doing something for a living other than walk on marbleized tile. Had I again, like so many times before, settled into a set of unrewarding habits, frozen by my reluctance to change?

I stood, opened the refrigerator, and looked at the bright white light. I slammed the door when I realized I was staring at the bulb because it was the only thing close to edible. I got a glass of water, wandered back to my seat, and lit the joint.

I hated to do business with Emil, but my past, with a goose from my present, beckoned unnervingly. Megan stood guard like an ugly gargoyle but memories of better times flashed behind her. Times filled with hope and idealism. Times charged with the positive electricity of change. Blackhead's case gave me the chance to see what had become of people I'd known twenty years previously. I knew what had happened to me: I wanted to believe there were other options.

I stood and anxiously gripped the back of my chair. Grass and television weren't gonna do it: I grabbed a whole Valium, retreated to the living room couch, and forced myself to stare at black-and-white reruns. Hooray for cable. I finished the joint, felt the pill kick in, and rested my eyes.

Deep in the back of my pounding mind I heard the creaks of the front door. For a moment I thought I'd passed out in the Wagon Wheel and someone was coming to fetch me. But I knew I'd fallen asleep once I focused and saw Julius' sagging black face and salt-and-pepper hair. He'd never set foot in that cracker gin mill.

I struggled to sit and finally succeeded. Julie watched quietly, his face a mixture of amusement and pity. Once he saw me stabilize, he said, "Stinks like a brewery in here. You lose your cookies?"

"I was at a lousy joint and brought the flavor home."

"Doesn't sound like the best of times, Slumlord."

I started to shake my head but felt the back of it slide, and stopped. "Business. What time is it? I can't read the clock from here."

"You couldn't read the clock if it was right next to you. I find it troubling to think you could get wasted on bar whiskey."

"Keep your faith. I ate a sleeping pill."

A look of disgust crossed his face. "I like getting high, Slumlord, but I'll never understand volunteering for a down."

"What's to understand?"

"Why you would ingest something that tramples what little life you have. One of these days I'm going to walk in here and find you laying on that bathroom floor, a syringe hanging out your arm."

I forced my arm to wave. "No you won't. You don't give me anything I can use with a needle. Lighten up, I've already been lectured once tonight about my failings."

"What's it matter what anyone says? You never listen."

I tried to shrug without moving my head, then realized he was empty-handed. "Where's the medicine bag?"

"Already left it in the other room. You weren't exactly quick to your feet."

Julie was one of the original tenants. In the beginning we'd stalked each other, waiting to declare ourselves friend or foe. We turned the corner when he decided he liked the way I treated Mrs. Sullivan, who was a touch too old to fend for herself. For my part, I enjoyed the air of mystery and knowledge that filled any room Julius entered. I also liked the rent arrangement.

I squinted the clock into focus. "Then why the fuck are you talking to me?"

He grimaced and chuckled. It sounded like a woofer in his throat. "Got a treat for you, Slumlord."

"You've changed your mind about providing me with syringeables?"

He shook his head. "I do not enjoy your sense of humor as it pertains to drugs."

I shrugged. "Neither did Gloria when she was my shrink."

"Perhaps you might consider a return visit or two?"

I grabbed my heart and grinned. "You sure know how to hurt a guy, Julie, but she wouldn't take me back."

He shrugged and settled on the battered Oriental next to the coffee table. He reached into his pocket but stared at me expectantly before taking out his hand. I slipped down from the couch and joined him on the floor. He nodded and pulled out a little round ball of tinfoil. A smile crossed my face and I stood to get a pipe. Julie motioned me back down.

"Don't need nothing fancy. Got us a steamer."

He placed the cardboard cylinder from a toilet paper roll on the table next to the little ball. I leaned over, picked it up and inspected. He had wrapped one hole of the cardboard closed with taped tinfoil, and had neatly cut a pipebowl with a fitted screen on the top. "I haven't seen one of these in a long time."

"I like the hit," he said.

"Do we need a knife?"

He looked at me. "Still as white as your skin, eh? You got a silver spoon for coke? Or maybe one of those machines that rolls joints?" He cackled as he bent over the table and unwrapped the hash.

"Got to be nasty, don't you? Just can't stand your own generosity?"

Julie glanced up at me. "You said you don't see your shrink no more."

He lifted a ball of very black hash between his thumb and forefinger and sniffed. He fished a disposable lighter from his shirt pocket and, for a second or two, held a flame under the hash. He nodded to me and I took the lighter from his hand and gave him the steamer. He rubbed his finger on the heated section and we both watched as pieces crumpled into the makeshift bowl. He started to hand it to me, but I shook my head. Julius shrugged and lit the dope. I watched the tinfoil quiver with his inhale.

He passed me the steamer and I lit up. Suddenly my lungs were burning, my eyes watering. Billowing smoke exploded from my mouth along with a hacking cough. Julius grabbed the toilet paper roll and waited silently for my gasping to subside.

"I guess I overtoked." I could barely squeeze the words past the tremors in my lungs. "Is there anything left?" I hissed.

He kept his face impassive as he handed me back the steamer. I relit and carefully inhaled, mindful of the pounding in my chest.

A look of amusement crossed Julie's face. "You might have waited a moment."

I handed back his pipe and struggled to keep the smoke down. He dumped the ashes and rubbed more hash in. I felt my fingertips grow airy and everything begin to slow. Julie finished his toke and I took another. I held my breath and felt the dope trail its way around my body, massaging as it burrowed into my nerves. I thought about protesting when he put the pipe on the table, but it didn't look like he was going anywhere. I pushed the table out of the way, lay down on my side, and leaned on my elbow. The room seemed a tone brighter.

Julie rested back on his hands. "Don't like your humor about drugs," he repeated. "Reminds me of when you first moved in."

I tried to recapture that era, then didn't want to. "Nah. I'm not depressed, just quiet. Working the malls, all that bullshit."

His head shook almost imperceptibly. "I beg to differ, Slumlord. It's one thing to be quiet, another to be dead."

As if to prove I was still breathing, I sat upright, reached onto the coffee table, lit two cigarettes, and passed him one. While I was there I took a small hit off the steamer. Finally I said, "The malls can do that to you." I put it back on the table as I thought of my meeting with Blackhead. "Anyway, my meet in the Wagon Wheel may have brought me something different to do."

His half-mast eyelids lifted a fraction. "What can The End bring besides trouble?"

"It's not so bad. I worked there when I first got to town."

"The Wagon Wheel?"

"Hell, no, The End."

"How long ago was that?"

"About twenty."

"Shit man, you weren't no older than a kid. What the hell were you doing in the Wagon Wheel tonight?"

He seemed surprised I'd made it out of the bar intact. I felt my stomach growl and tasted the Wheel's whiskey. Sort of intact. I ran down Emil's request. But, by the time I finished, my earlier suspicions of Blackhead and his job nipped at the elastic in my sweat cuffs.

Julius' response didn't make it any easier to shake them off. "This here case sounds like bullshit. And you ain't too stupid not to smell it."

I thought of doing another day at another mall, drinking another twelve cups of bad coffee, and felt a dose of annoyance cloud my high. "Easy enough for you to say 'Go spend your days playing guard dog on the swells side of the track.'" Then I felt silly paraphrasing Blackhead, and reached for the pipe.

Julie waited quietly then helped himself to the dope. I lay back down on the floor and felt my petulance dissipate. "The story doesn't feel right to me either, but the thought of more malls is ugly. On top of that, Lou may visit."

"Since when is Bhwana Lou a bummer?"

"Since the fucking reno was finished. He's been picking at me like I was a scab."

"Since the renovation, or since you be in Chi for the funeral?"

"I don't know, man. If he comes you can ask him." I didn't want to know. The whole subject made me feel bad.

Julie took another pull at the steamer as I rolled to my side and reached toward him. He handed me the pipe; but he didn't let go until he said, "You don't want to be forgetting your roots, Matt."

By now my lungs had no problem with the size of my appetite. I exhaled another long drag, and said, "I had weeds, not roots. It's taken me a lifetime to pull 'em out."

Julius shook his head. "You're not getting it down, are you?"

"Getting what down?" But my mind was already drifting. I suddenly saw Bhwana Lou's bulky body squeezed into every inch of my apartment.

I came back to the last echo of his words. "What did you say?" I asked.

It took a long time for him to answer. "I said you don't seem bothered by that idea."

"What idea?"

"Damn."

I watched as he stood. "What's the matter, Julie?"

"You be too high to talk."

"I am not! I'm not that high. I just didn't hear what you said."

"I said The End is a helluva place to try and hide."

I stood, felt a little dizzy, and sat down on the couch. "I'll probably just look up some old acquaintances to see how they made out."

Julius frowned down at me. "You'll surely find them. That place is a one-way ticket."

"Hey, I got out."

"If you call you out," he said, watching me hold on to the arm of the couch. "Anyway, you weren't born there."

Julius leaned over the table, lifted the steamer, and inspected it to see if anything was still alive. With a shrug he tapped the dottle into the ashtray and started toward the door.

He was halfway out when I said, "You forgot the hash, man."

He turned back to me. "You keep it, Slumlord. Something tells me you're going to need it."

# 7

THE NEXT DAY BEGAN LATER THAN USUAL. It tried to start at its regular hour, but I pulled the couch's pillow over my head to block out the telephone's morning wake-up call. By the time the phone tried again, I was up and moving—albeit slowly.

"Were you taking a shit or something?" Blackhead's whining grate clanged through my brain. "I tried calling you earlier but there was no answer."

Had I known it was him there would have been no answer this time either. "I was sleeping."

"Sleeping? I didn't know detectives kept executive hours."

I flashed on consulting detective Harry the Mole. "I'm an executive detective, Emil. What're you calling for? I said I'd ring you." I reached for my cigarettes and lit one. "What time is it anyway?" I asked.

"It's 'Miller Time.'"

"What are you talking about?"

"I'll tell you what I'm talking about. We're fucking finished. I was out of my mind to ask you for help in the first place. You don't ask no one for help that kicks you in the ass."

I started to interrupt, but his words sizzled like steam escaping from a broken pipe. "From the moment we ran into each other you been pissing on me. You fucking choked me! Forget I asked you for anything! Just stay on your damn side of the street. We got enough assholes here."

I heard him gulp, waited for an added assault, but all he said was, "I ain't gonna pay for another."

I couldn't blame him but still felt disappointed. "Last night you seemed pretty eager for my help."

"That was last night. I can't believe I threw my money at you."

I almost offered to do his job on the house, but reeled it in before it hit air. No way I was going to beg. "You're sure, man?" Well, I wasn't going to grovel, anyway.

"What's the matter with you? Of course I'm fucking sure."

I started to talk, but he stepped on my words. "I don't want you messing in my business. Do you understand?"

I hid my chagrin. "Yeah, I understand. But don't I get a thanks?"

"Thanks? For what? For insulting me, grabbing my neck?"

I felt myself get stubborn. "How about for cutting the deal in the mall?"

"That fat fuck." He caught himself and lowered his voice. "Okay, asshole, thanks."

I stared at the dead telephone. I'd gotten my thanks; ain't I special? I felt my stomach growl, remembered the empty refrigerator, and stood cursing. I was antsy, hungry, and felt like I'd just missed my bus. I walked over to a window and thought about going out to eat, but it looked too raw. Or was it me who was too raw?

I heard my stomach complain again and caught myself staring at the wall that used to hold Mrs. S's call contraption, missing her repeated intrusions. There were times when taking care of her took me out of my skin. And into some home-cooked food.

I found something presentable to wear, grabbed my toolcase, and hiked upstairs. I could always pretend it was the old days and fix something of hers in exchange for a meal.

Later that evening, I realized my visit with Mrs. S was a moment of idealized nostalgia for my pre-detective days. So was the entire afternoon tinkering with my Bakelite radios, something I hadn't done for a year. The problem was, it wasn't the old days. Mrs. S, though feeding me, had nothing for me to fix, and I couldn't get any of the plastics to work.

I stood, flicked on the television, turned it off, and anxiously prowled the house. I looked out my office window, past the alley and into the parking lot. I kept staring, until I saw a down coat trot by, breath steaming from nose and mouth. I retreated to the closet and zipped the lining into my leather jacket. I pulled it on, grabbed a pack of cigarettes and a joint, and went out to my car. It was difficult to start but, with a little gentle encouragement and a nasty slap on the dash, the engine turned over.

Driving around aimlessly and watching the city's lights shimmer behind the languid movement of traffic and the carbon monoxide haze, I lit the joint but it did little to alleviate my anxiety. A grieving, live-in Lou, with only malls for escape, was too much for even dope to offset.

I had nowhere to go, including home, a feeling that reminded me of my marriage to Megan. During its stretch run we lived on the second floor of a converted coffin factory. I hated to return from work and begin the long march up the stairs. Didn't want to go there, but didn't have anywhere else to go either.

A loud squawk from the snout of a space-age van shook me from my drift. I turned at the next corner and aimed the car toward The End. I had no job or reason, but my curiosity made a visit seem better than nothing. When I got to the neighborhood's edge I looked around until I found a parking space under a street lamp. The car was old but, hell, it was paid for.

Even at night you could see people on the street talking to themselves. We used to bet on the number per block, and the head count always topped our predictions. But, as I walked down Wilson, I was staggered by the number of people curled in entranceways. A substantial portion of The End's population had always squatted in abandoned buildings, but I didn't recall this many sidewalk sleepers.

It was impossible to walk a block without being aggressively accosted for money. After the first three or four encounters, I found myself growing hostile. My surprise about the homeless—and my hostility—told me I was more integrated into the Nineties than I cared to admit.

I walked past block after block of substandard housing. Twenty years ago I'd seen living space as a challenge—the literal battleground between good and evil, rich and poor. Now it all just looked like dilapidated buildings. I turned left onto Rutledge and was surprised by an oasis of middle-class tranquility. If housing stock was indeed a battleground, the well-to-do had gotten themselves another toehold.

I felt less comfortable staring at fancy rehabs than rundowns. I turned, walked back to Wilson, and automatically gravitated toward the building that had headquartered most of my community organizing. When I got to the block I stopped, lit a cigarette, and paused on the corner. I was a little surprised to see the storefront standing, much less lit.

A group of teenagers were pushing their way out of my old building. They didn't appear strung out, or even particularly intent on shit-kicking; they actually flashed a spark of healthy life in the middle of dark, dead concrete. I flipped my butt and moved slowly toward the storefront. By the time I was directly across the street, the group had rambled away. There was a bus-stop bench and, despite the cold, I hunkered down and watched the storefront door.

Every once in a while a couple of kids would leave, usually laughing, looking as if they were enjoying themselves. Often they carried books. It seemed like an anomaly; I tried to remember if I'd ever seen anyone in The End carry a book.

I lit another cigarette, rushed a beggar on his way, and let myself float back in time. These were the corners on which I had stood, the buildings in which I had organized. This was the neighborhood where I had looked for people to help. Looking in some unconscious way for myself.

I stood, ground the cigarette under my heel, and headed toward the storefront. Twenty years later, a little more conscious, I was back.

The door swung open before I had a chance to grab the handle and I stood facing a dark-skinned teenager. Although he held the door and nodded, his gaunt face looked defensive, as if I was about to hit him. As I entered, I tried to relax his fear and my own discomfort. "I was walking around and saw the lights."

He closed the door, but gazed at me with the same stricken eyes. I tried again, "I used to work here, a real long time ago ..."

He looked over my shoulder, and I turned to see a medium-sized woman with blonde hair and wire-rim glasses walk down the long thin hall. Although her arms swung loosely at her sides, she conveyed an undercurrent of determination. She nodded to the kid, and he slid behind the large desk by the storefront's plate-glass window.

Despite her severely pulled-back hair, there was a softness to her face. She barely glanced at me as she politely launched into a memorized monotone. "You don't have to explain. You're new to the precinct and are wondering what we do here? Every week another new policeman is assigned to The End. And every week they are around here asking about us. Why doesn't the Captain put up a sign?"

There was nothing hostile in her manner, just automatic. I stuck up my hands. "Whoa, I am interested in what happens here, but I'm not from the police. I worked out of this storefront about a hundred years ago and got curious."

She took off her glasses and dropped them into the breast pocket of her dark blue chamois work shirt. She wore no makeup, but then, she didn't need to; her skin was smooth and, even under the harsh fluorescent light, lovely. Lines suddenly creased her forehead, but her voice stayed pleasant. "We are an alternative learning center for dropouts who won't go near traditional schools. Perhaps you've heard of Hope House? We're part of it."

Hope House had been the largest and most conservative social agency in The End. "I'm surprised. I thought the only thing that interested Hope House was training case workers."

She began to look closely at my face. "You really haven't been here for a while. Things are very different these days." She grimaced and raised her eyebrows. "It's unusual to suddenly get curious after how many years, really?"

"Twenty." I smiled. "Really."

She shook her head. "That's long enough, but you do look familiar."

"Probably not, my name is Matt Jacob."

Her blue eyes widened and the worry lines deepened. "Jake," she gasped.

I had this crazy thought that fear crossed her face, but the moment passed as soon as my embarrassment for not remembering who she was caught hold. "I use Matt these days," I said sheepishly. "I'm sorry, but my memory is lousy and I don't recognize you."

A small resigned smile played at the corners of her full lips. "Melanie," she said, "Melanie Knight."

# 8

THOUGH THE NAME KNIGHT had danced through my head since my conversation with Blackhead, I hadn't conjured up a clear image of Peter, much less his sister. Melanie noticed my difficulty because she said, "You probably remember my brother, Peter Knight."

"Not really, twenty years is a long time," I replied lamely.

"But you remember him better than you remember me, I'm sure." Her smile seemed forced.

"Maybe a little," I admitted.

"You left just before he died."

I was surprised by her clear memory.

"You knew he was dead, didn't you?" Melanie's voice was tight, and she rubbed her hand across her face wiping away the smile. "He drowned in Quarry's End."

"Yes," I said, "I knew that." But I really hadn't. I'd known about a "dead body" whose name was Peter Knight. Standing there, faced with someone to whom the loss meant something, put a real person in the quarry. Just like I had a real wife and a real daughter twisted in the torn metal remains of an automobile. "I'm sorry." There was more to say, but these were the things I wouldn't say to myself. "I'm sorry," I repeated.

"So was I."

The air between us grew tense. Before I lifted my eyes from our shoes, a voice from the rear of the storefront asked people to return to their seats. I looked toward the back where some teenagers stood in the doorway of the large open room that flared out at the end of the hall. A couple of them wore "fuck you" looks. It bothered me that people mistook me for a cop.

I turned my attention back to Melanie. "You've grown up."

"I don't ever remember not being grown up," she said quietly. A small frown crossed her face and she looked back at the group of kids. "Come on, guys," she said in a friendly but firm manner. "He's not a cop. Why don't you get back to work?"

As the kids disappeared into the back room, Melanie turned toward me with a rueful smile. "Why don't we reminisce in my office?"

I nodded, glad for the privacy, and followed her into the first of the row of partitioned stalls on the left-hand side of the long corridor. There was barely enough room in the cubicle for a desk, filing cabinet, and two folding chairs. Melanie sat in one chair and motioned me to the other. A small glass-framed diploma hung on the otherwise bare, institutional, green walls. Melanie took her glasses from her pocket, reached over to the desk, and placed them on a stack of forms. Our knees almost touched and, despite her thick shirt, her breasts attracted my attention. I quickly shifted my eyes to her face. "Is this a bad time to be here?"

"Why would it be a bad time?" Her voice was quiet, her face neutral.

"I don't know. There's a lot going on."

"There's always a lot going on. Don't you remember what The End is like?"

The mention of The End generated a force of its own and, though she sat there calmly, I had an image of someone inside beating on a glass enclosure. I didn't know whether that someone was Melanie trying to escape The End, or me still trying to get away from my death pictures.

Nervously I broke the silence. "I thought I remembered The End. But I've been in the neighborhood for about an hour, and now I'm not so sure."

Her eyes narrowed. "What do you mean?"

"I don't know. Things seem worse, if that's possible. Do you mind if I smoke?"

She pointed to an ashtray overflowing with stubbed-out filter-less cigarettes. "Does it look as if I'd mind?" Melanie raised her eyebrows. "And what made you think it wouldn't be worse? Nothing's trickled down to this part of town. Including people," she said pointedly.

I lit two cigarettes, gave her one, and reached for the ashtray. "Twenty years is a long time, isn't it?"

She stared at me and folded her arms. Instead of shielding her chest, the posture just made it more difficult for me to keep my eyes on her face. "I mean, hell, the last time we saw each other we were still kids. Like them." I poked my thumb toward the back room.

"I never thought of myself as a kid," she said again. "You always thought of me that way."

We sat through another strained silence while I thought about what she said. It was true; I had thought of her as Peter Knight's shy kid sister. I watched her lips circle the cigarette and felt something stir. She didn't look like anyone's baby sister now.

Melanie broke the quiet. "What are you doing here?"

"I don't really know," I finally answered. "I was walking around the neighborhood and wound up at the scene of the crime." I saw her startled look and added, "I mean here, where I used to work. Is the storefront only used as a school?"

"During the day we provide advocacy services for community people fighting with bureaucracies. At night we become a school." She appeared relieved by my question.

But there was a resolute note in her voice. I was glad I wasn't one of those bureaucrats. "High school kids?" I asked.

"Most, but not all. We have kids who dropped out long before high school and older people as well."

I nodded absently, and a look of annoyance darted across her face. "You aren't interested in the school, are you?"

I smiled stupidly. "I don't know what I'm interested in. It's as if I know who I'm talking to, but it's been so long that I don't know you at all. It seems very strange. When we knew each other I didn't have to shave and you barely had breasts."

I wanted to carve out my tongue and eat it alive. My face grew hot and I quickly stubbed the cigarette into the ashtray. Unfortunately, the motion toppled the ashtray onto the floor, spreading ashes and butts around our feet. Both of us bent over and we bumped heads. I avoided looking at her as I dropped to my knees, wondering whether to sweep up the mess with my hand or just crawl out the door.

A shrill, reedy voice wafted over the stall's eight-foot wall and through the space extending up to the building's twelve-foot ceiling. "Are you all right, M? Is everything okay?" I looked up well past Melanie's corduroyed legs to her smile. I hoped it was the question she found amusing.

Melanie stepped back a couple of inches and gave my face more room to look dumb. "Therin, please get a broom and dustpan from the closet." She motioned for me to rise.

We stood quietly while I prayed that my earlier subconscious lunacy had scattered with the ashes. At the sound of a tentative tap, Melanie opened the door, and I saw the same kid I'd met out front. This time I took a closer look. Despite the cold weather, he was wearing torn jeans and a dirty short-sleeved tee shirt. I hoped he had a warm coat. His hair was very straight, very long, with a very black gloss. He pushed his way into the tight space, whacking at my toes as he swept. I backed over to the filing cabinet and swung onto it to get my feet off the floor. Melanie moved to her desk.

Without looking at either of us the kid swept furiously, and was about to disappear with the broom, dustpan, and ashtray when I reached toward the ashtray, only to have him pull it away.

"Leave that here, will you?" I asked.

He ignored me but glanced at Melanie, who nodded and said,

"It's okay, Therin, leave it. This is Matt Jacob, an old friend who used to live in the neighborhood. Matt, Therin Whitehawk, a student at the school and a more recent friend."

The kid handed me the ashtray, but kept his eyes on the dustpan as he backed out of the office. "M," he said, "if you need me for anything, call."

"Therin." There was a hint of sharpness in her voice. "I'm perfectly fine. Why don't you work on your GED with everybody else?" His head shook an emphatic "no" and Melanie suggested, "Well, you could cover the front door and answer the phones." Therin shrugged, and backed the rest of the way out of the cubicle.

I stayed perched on the metal cabinet and lit another cigarette. "An Indian?" The End was a hidden reservation for the Northeast Indian poor.

Melanie put her glasses back on her face. "He's half Native American." She rummaged under the pile of papers on the desk, pulled out a pack of Camels, lit one, and looked up at me. "He's spent his entire life in The End, raised by his mother to dislike almost everything about Native Americans." Her mouth snapped shut.

"You like him, don't you?"

She said quietly, "I identify with him."

I wanted her to say more, but we sat silent while the office filled with smoke. "What about you?" I finally asked. "Have you been here all this time?" Julius' words about never getting out whispered in my memory.

Melanie gave me a guarded look. "This is my home," she said simply.

"Where did you get the degree?"

"The University opened a community program and Jonathan helped get me in."

"Jonathan?" Damn, she was pretty.

Another tight smile and a quick shake of her head. "You really haven't kept up, have you?"

"I told you, I have a lousy memory."

Melanie put her cigarette out and turned her face away. "Memory has nothing to do with it. You got married and left before Jonathan moved into the neighborhood. He's my stepfather. He's also the

Director of Hope House. He had quite a bit of influence with the University program." She nervously poked at the cigarette stub in the ashtray and switched subjects. "How is Megan? I've neglected to ask."

Again I was surprised by her ability to recall ancient details. "I don't have a clue. She walked out on me a long time ago."

Melanie scratched her cheek with unpolished nails. "I'm sorry," she said, still not meeting my eyes.

I let myself drop down from the cabinet. "Don't be. It was one of my luckier breaks."

"I'm sorry about that too," she said carefully.

I zipped up my jacket. "We've spent a lot of time apologizing, haven't we?"

"Are you leaving?"

I couldn't think of an excuse to stay. "Well, it's late ..."

She pulled another smoke from her pack and lit it. "I suppose I'll see you in another hundred years?"

I smiled. "Sooner than that."

Melanie's eyes focused on a spot somewhere over my shoulder. "Twenty years is a long time." Her voice sounded as if she was talking to herself.

I felt bad that my presence recalled a painful period in her life. In both our lives. I put my hand over my heart and tried to skate past my discomfort. "I swear to god I'll be back sooner than that."

"I only believe in the devil, Matt," Melanie said with a small smile.

"Then I'll definitely keep my promise."

The inches between us leaped alive with a sudden taut sensuality. I found myself appreciating the richness of her looks, the comfortableness of her clothes, even her lack of makeup. It was an exciting contrast to Boots' sleek fashions. I almost asked if she was married, bit back the words, and opened the office door.

Therin shot us a suspicious glance from behind the front desk as we walked into the hall. The sensuality disappeared, leaving in its place a sudden distance. Melanie reached out and grasped my elbow. "Do you remember the Harrigan sisters?"

I was too aware of her fingers to remember anything clearly, though vague faces drifted into my head. "I don't know, the name sounds familiar."

She pulled me toward the back room. "You'll recognize the fights. Why don't you say hello?" Melanie's voice was inviting, as if reluctant to part.

As we walked through the open door Melanie pointed toward the back of the room. Two middle-aged women flanking a card table looked up as we entered. They did look familiar—just a generation older than I'd imagined.

"Janice is on the left, Margaret the right."

I nodded gratefully. The Harrigans either remembered me or were just plain curious, because they immediately walked in our direction. Janice, the larger of the two, got to us first.

"Look what the end of Indian summer brought." Her face was open and friendly.

Margaret arrived and Janice lost some of her friendly when she glanced at her sister and saw an unspoken criticism. "Stop looking like that, okay?"

She pointedly turned her back to Margaret and went on, "I saw your picture in the paper a while ago. I thought it was you but the name was wrong."

Margaret started to chime in but Melanie interrupted, "What paper?"

By now the few remaining kids were paying attention. "Can we get out of here?" I asked.

The four of us crowded into the skinny hall. Margaret turned to Melanie. "It's that rag she reads. Janice devours anything that has gossip in it."

"Marge thinks reading anything other than the *New York Times* is déclassé. Don't you, dear?"

"You two never stop, do you?" Melanie said wearily. "Just tell me what you're talking about."

Janice waved at me. "You're that Matt Jacob, no doubt about it?" She didn't wait for a response. "He was in the paper about a year ago. He tried to prevent a suicide. The story had you with a different name, but I never forget a pretty face." She leaned closer and poked my side. "A little softer than in the old days, huh?"

"I use my first name now. Matt," I said uncomfortably.

"I don't care what name you use," Janice said. "I never met a private detective before." She grinned. "I love reading them, though."

Melanie looked at me with clouded blue eyes. "You didn't mention you were a detective, Matt."

Margaret looked scornfully at Janice. "You see, Jan. You just don't know how to keep quiet. Maybe he doesn't want anyone to know he's on a case."

"Is that true?" Melanie asked.

I shook my head. "No, of course not."

"Did you hear him, Marge? You always think I screw up. Get with it girl," Janice said.

"Will you two stop this? I'm sick of it!" Melanie's voice was suddenly harsh, and the words burst out in rapid-fire staccato. "I brought Matt back here to say hello, not to witness your constant bickering."

The two sisters looked at each other, before Margaret said, "You're right, Mel. Our quibbles are quite a bore." Janice nodded, struggling to keep down a smile. Margaret pursed her lips and took her sister's hand. "Come on Jan, let's finish up."

Melanie turned on her heel and took a step toward the front of the store. "Will we see you again?" Janice asked me.

"I hope so." I smiled at the two women and hurried to catch Melanie at her office door. But when she looked at me, there was no mistaking the suspicion in her eyes. Her lips were drawn across her teeth as she said coldly, "I'm glad you dropped by, but I have work to finish before I can leave. It's been good to see you."

Therin sat at the front desk biting his lower lip, openly watching the two of us. I considered telling her that my detective work consisted of protecting designer finery, but the idea embarrassed me. I pulled my leather tight around my body. "Listen, Melanie, if it's possible, I really would like to see you again."

She had her hand on the door to the partition. She hesitated, then looked back at me and conceded somberly, "Anything is possible, Matt. If you work in The End, you have to believe that."

"ANYTHING IS POSSIBLE." I didn't feel the nasty November on my walk to the car, during the ride home, or in the alley by my apartment. Though we'd ended off-key, my meeting with Mel left me exhilarated. And the Harrigans, their fighting unchanged since the old days, were a fireman's pole to the past. I didn't feel the bitter wind until the key was in my apartment door, and I thought of Boots. Then I felt iced. I shouldered the door open, then slammed it on the cold.

I left my jacket on and sat at the desk in the quiet dark of my office. I lit a cigarette and dragged deeply. Before I exhaled I drew a circle in the air with the glowing red tip. Inside the bull's eye I placed an image of Hal's wrinkled face. Boots and I had no papers on each other.

I retreated to the living room couch and channel-surfed with the remote. Ten minutes later, frustrated, I settled on a paid half-hour stain remover infomercial and promptly fell asleep.

*The night was city hot and sweaty humid, heat that made you drip even when you were still. We sat on the fire escape that overlooked the small concrete park with the parched red brick fountain. Music blared from slowly snaking cars along the street beneath us, every other song the theme from Shaft. We sat quietly listening as Isaac Hayes filled the summer night.*

*Melanie rested her head on my knee and her fingers danced on my calf. It seemed odd for us to be naked but unconcerned about being seen. I reached down between my legs, stroked her heavy breast, and saw her nipple stiffen. The heat created a damp salty pool where our skin touched.*

*"We shouldn't be doing this," I said.*

*"Why not?" She nuzzled her face on top of my thigh, and her loose blonde hair tickled my erection.*

*"You're a kid and I'm supposed to be a social worker."*

*I could feel her lips move on my skin. "That's why you didn't notice me twenty years ago."*

*"It is twenty years ago." I raised my arm and pointed to the street. I tried to show her the cars, billboards, stores, even the clothes the pedestrians wore. I tried to show her that everything was the same as it had been, but she kept her face buried. None of it mattered.*

*Finally she lifted her head and slowly stood up. "Do I look like twenty years ago?"*

*She lifted her breasts, then slid painted fingers down her hips. She stepped forward between my spread and naked legs. My face was level with her round, soft stomach, and I watched it move with her breathing. Her navel was surrounded by a light film of perspiration I desperately wanted to lick. I heard myself groan and tried to keep from looking up or down, but the top of her pubic hair kept crawling into my line of vision and pulled at my head until I stopped fighting.*

*The humid air exploded with the cacophony of sirens … sirens organic to The End's summer nights. I followed a bead of belly sweat crawling through her thin, light brown patch while we waited for the*

*noise to quiet and the music to resume. But the shriek refused to die,*
*and instead changed into an insistent bell. Melanie touched my cheek*
*with her fingernails, her movement squashing the little ball of sweat. I*
*reached to keep her near, but her body changed—thinner, smaller*
*breasted. A body I knew but couldn't recognize. I squinted, but no one*
*was there ...*

My eyes opened to the telephone racketing in my ear. In goaded self-defense I grabbed the receiver.

"Are you sure you're not on the fucking government tit? It's ten-thirty in the morning."

The hairs in my ear bristled at the sound of his voice. I pulled the phone into a position that enabled me to twist my body into human form. My neck felt like it had spent the entire night in a head-lock, and the lead keepsake in my leg ached its usual morning hello. I shook myself out of my jacket. "I don't remember leaving a wake-up call, Blackhead."

"You didn't, asshole, but it don't seem like you have too good a memory anyhow."

My mouth was dry and my body screamed for caffeine. I sat back on the couch, propped the receiver next to my head, and settled for a smoke. For a second I thought he had called to change his mind. A second later and I knew I had thought wrong.

"I told you to stay the fuck out of my business," he exploded. "Now I hear you're all over The End. Going to the damn school. What's the matter with you? Leave my shit alone!"

"Back off, Emil. My visit to The End had nothing to do with you."

"Right. And your visit with Melanie had nothing to do with Peter!" His voice was sarcastic-thick, but there was no mistaking the rage underneath. Or the tremble of fear.

"What's eating you? You're not the center of my universe." But I was starting to occupy a substantial portion of his. It set me wondering.

"I'll tell you what's eating me," Blackhead answered sharply. "You don't come around for twenty years, then you won't fucking go away!"

"I was curious about The End, that's all," I replied, annoyed. "You brought back memories and I wanted to see how people were doing."

"Isn't that sweet? The detective with a social work interior. The last thing this place needs is another fucking wet-nurse. Melanie's old man got a big enough udder ..."

"Boyfriend?" I interrupted.

"Are you for real? I'm talking about her fucking stepfather, Jonathan Walk-on-Water. I don't care if he stays in The End the rest of his life; fact is, he can always get out—the jerks that kiss his ass can't. I'm tired of visitors to the zoo. And that includes you."

"Since when were you appointed neighborhood guardian, Blackhead? Anyway, you invited me."

"I disinvited you, remember? I don't want you in my face, you understand? You in The End means you in my face. I'm warning you, stay away!"

When I hung up the telephone I wanted to wash the side of my face that had cradled the receiver. Instead, I went the whole nine yards and dragged myself into the shower. While the water soothed my knotted muscles, I thought about the call. Blackhead was probably nervous that I'd bust him for dealing. Still, his edge of hysteria intrigued me. Had he already cut a deal with his mystery letter writer? And what kind of deal? He'd never have hired me if he had a guilty connection to Peter Knight's death.

I stepped out of the shower and rubbed the steam off the medicine chest's mirror. My reflection was stained with tears. The image disturbed me, though I knew it was only due to my hasty swipe across the glass. I was curious about Blackhead's sudden change of mind, but digging into Peter's death would surely dredge up painful memories for Melanie. And for me. Peter's death had already triggered a chain reaction about my own shackled past.

I shook away the hesitations with my original suspicions. Even before Julius' suggestion, I'd believed Emil's story was an invite to some drug-related hustle. Perhaps a hassle between him and another dealer. If any deal had been cut, nickels to dime-bags it had to do with turf.

I pulled on the nearest pants and a denim jacket, assuring

myself no personal memories would quake from modern day dope-dealing. No one would be hurt if I nosed into Blackhead's business. I opened the door and let myself out to the alley. I knew the malls and Lou's potential visit had something to do with my driving curiosity, but it didn't matter. Warnings always held a fascination I found hard to resist.

# 10

PHIL PRETENDED ANGRY BUT IT DIDN'T WASH. "Twice in a couple of weeks. When it rains, it pours."

"Think of it as monsoon season."

"Let me guess—you're working."

"Eating your food is never work."

"The last time you ate here regular you were working. Then you wound up in the hospital." Phil rubbed his face and wiped his hand on his apron. "What do you want me to dig up now?"

Before Phil bought into Charley's, he'd been a cop. In the old days the restaurant was always packed with uniforms. Phil still had his connections, but I'd never learned why they'd stopped eating here.

"Musta been your fault," I joked. "I curse you out every time the bullet hollers."

He looked at me quizzically. "They left the bullet in?"

"Yeah. They said it was easier to leave it where it was."

He shook his head incredulously. "Fucking quacks. They just wanted the bed. Faster turnover, more money."

"Come on, Phil, not hospitals."

He started to bluster then noticed my smile. "Ahh, you're yanking my chain."

I nodded, but my mind was on his question. I hadn't intended to ask him to locate Peter's death report; but it wasn't a bad idea. I didn't think I could learn much, though if I kept it to myself, it wouldn't disturb Melanie. Maybe I'd get some background. Then I questioned whose background I wanted—Peter's, Melanie's, or my own. Before I could decide, Phil brought me back to the present. Hard.

"Your friend was in yesterday for breakfast."

"Say what?"

Red piped up, "Miss New York was here with her father."

My appetite fell with a thud. "Oh yeah," I said tentatively, caught in the intersection of their stares.

"Not her father, huh?" Red asked gently.

"Not her father."

Phil put my food down in front of me. "Ruined your breakfast, didn't I?"

"A little," I admitted. "How about some coffee? Black."

"I know how you like it." He glanced at me while he poured. "I wouldn't worry. He don't look like much."

I sipped at the steaming liquid. "Money don't have to look like much."

Phil walked to the booth and sat down next to Red. Every once in a while I felt their eyes on the back of my neck. To reduce everyone's discomfort I spun my stool around. "Listen, maybe you *could* help me out."

I told him what I wanted and he mulled over my request. "Twenty-year-old records, I don't know. Shit, cops ain't that anal. Anyhow, what the hell are you doing poking around The End? That place is a hellhole. Someone could put a bullet in a lot more critical location than where you got one now."

"'Anal'? Phil, you been closet-reading?" I tried to ignore the meat of his comment, especially since I already believed Blackhead's case involved the drug world. It was one thing to poke in people's lives, another to mess with fast-triggered AK47s.

"I was hoping they might put old records on microfilm or something. Like libraries."

He shook his head. "How come you always sound like you just woke up after a long sleep? If the file is anywhere it's on a computer, not microfilm. And I wouldn't bet on the computer. Where the hell have you been?"

I just shrugged. Phil walked past me and went to work cleaning his grill. I sat and wondered how this broad, bald, short-order cook had come to represent modernity. It made me anxious to think of myself as that much of an anachronism.

He looked back over his shoulder. "What about the Black Avenger?"

"Julie?"

A disgusted look crossed his face. "No, not Julius. Clifford. He could get what you want easier than me."

"Oh no. No thanks, I'll take a pass."

He walked back over and leaned across the counter. Before he spoke, he looked past my shoulder. I turned, but the place was still empty except for Red, who sat in her booth reading the paper and playing with a teaspoon.

He looked down at me. "I don't understand your reaction to Clifford. Word had it he thought you did a good job."

I shook my head. "Hard to trust a cop who beats the living shit out of you."

"So you want me to poke around and jostle cobwebs?"

"'Jostle cobwebs'?" I turned and called to Red, "Have you been reading to him, or has he been spending time with Julius?"

Red stood and stretched, her white waitress uniform pulling tight across her body. "You like that my honey is improving himself?"

She walked across the room and stood behind me. I felt a layer of heat between her chest and my back, and quelled a sudden impulse to rest my head on her shelf. Phil turned away, shaking his head. "Cut the crap, I've always read."

I popped off the stool and stood alongside his lipsticked lady friend. "Yeah, but never talked like you did."

Red looked at me and said with obvious pride, "Phil's never been a dummy and now he doesn't feel like he has to hide it."

I smiled my agreement. I never knew whether she was going to rip at his balls or inflate them. Red sauntered back to her booth knowing full well what the two of us were watching. Almost sadly Phil switched his attention back to me. "I don't think it's a good idea for you to be hanging around that cesspool, but I'll talk to a few friends. What do you think you're going to discover from a twenty-year-old police report, anyway?"

"Nothing, really. I'm actually more interested in what's up my ex-client's sleeve, but I gotta start somewhere."

"You mean I gotta start somewhere." He saw my face and added, "Don't look like that, it was a joke. Like I said the last time, just keep eating here."

Not surprisingly, it felt good to be out of the diner. The mention of Boots and Hal, then Clifford, submarined any desire to be out of the house. I like my humiliations private.

But privacy was rapidly becoming a premium. And would become more so, I discovered, when I found myself at home on the short end of a conversation with Lou.

"I thought I might visit over the holidays if that doesn't interfere with your plans," he said, already resentful, as if I could say no.

"Great," I lied, then grew momentarily confused. The Jewish New Year had long since passed. "What holidays?"

"Thanksgiving. The celebration with the turkey, Turkey."

It had been a long time since I'd celebrated anything, much less running Indians off their land. With a sinking stomach I lightened my voice and said, "It's a fine time, Lou. I don't have any plans."

"Maybe you could invite some people. Between me and Mrs. Sullivan, we might give your oven a trial run?"

I hadn't had a Thanksgiving party since Chana and Becky had died. The picture of Lou furiously slashing up a turkey, surrounded by Mrs. S and the rest of the building's misfits, tightened my throat. But this was Lou's first Thanksgiving without Martha. I swallowed. "You want people, Lou, I'll get people. You have tickets?"

"Not yet. It won't be a problem."

"That's good enough for me," I said, working to keep apprehension out of my voice.

I heard his laugh boom through the wire. "Don't bullshit me, boychik. Nothing is ever good enough for you."

I hung up the telephone, tried the television, but couldn't sit still. A Thanksgiving celebration in this apartment seemed like a cruel joke, if not an oxymoron. But, like a moronic ox, I did what I was supposed to.

I got high and went upstairs to chat about killing a bird. Mrs. S was delighted by the idea. She had planned to cook for Charles and Richard anyway, and she adored Lou. His visits were often the highlight of her year. I was glad someone was happy. Then she insisted on a formal guest list, and our only acknowledged disagreement centered around Gloria.

I knew Mrs. S wasn't thrilled about inviting Julius, so I gave in on Gloria. I didn't think my first client, aka my ex-shrink, had any more desire to boogie with me than I had with her. But Mrs. S would find that out for herself. I left when she started to talk about the menu and rejected my idea of pizzas: she didn't think I was serious.

Back inside my apartment I hit the couch. I needed a new one but didn't want to spend the time to break it in. The old one had the indentations of my body already memorized.

I'd have done the rest of the twenty-four in my personal version of fetal—on my back, eyes glued to the TV—but the telephone rang. Good doobie once begat good doobie twice. When I heard her voice I grew momentarily pleased, but the pleasure vanished as soon as I remembered her "father."

"Boots, how are you?" I kept the enthusiasm in my tone.

"I'm all right. What's the matter with your voice?"

"What do you mean?"

"You sound like you're underwater, and we haven't even begun to talk."

"'Oh ye of little faith.'"

"Right. Maybe I should call you Rabbi?"

"Wrong religion for the quote." I was running out of one-liners. Maybe I could just run out. I pictured Melanie on the other end of the wire but came back to reality in time to hear Boots' question.

"How about supper?"

"Me or you?" I regretted my rejoinder as soon as I made it.

"Both of us, but after we eat."

It sounded a lot better than it felt. What was the matter with me? The walls of my apartment were closing in, and I'd always welcomed her invitations before. What had happened to my desire to put our lousy breakfast behind us?

"I can't Boots, I'm sorry."

"I didn't realize you booked in advance." She kept her tone light, but there was no mistaking her displeasure.

"I'm sorry, hon, I'm working."

"Why don't you stop by after?"

"I don't know what time I'll be finished."

There was a pause at the other end. "What's the matter, Matt?" Boots asked. "Are you still angry about Hal?"

"Of course not, Boots. It's not part of the bargain."

There was another long pause and I steeled myself for a waspish onslaught. All I got was a very soft, "It would be nice to see you, Matt." Then I got a very dead telephone.

# 11

I SAT AT THE KITCHEN TABLE surrounded by my Fiesta Ware, wondering if there was any real reason to spit-shine my gun. Between swipes at the black barrel I smoked a joint and made little headway in understanding my hostility and sudden reluctance to spend time with Boots. Eventually, with everything but frustration exhausted, my mind skipped to The End.

I sketched Melanie's face and form in my head, returning to her look of anguish during our talk of Peter. A nagging voice wondered if I matched that same look whenever Chana's name came up: I hoped not. A mix of compassion and self-pity gripped me and I whacked at the second half of the equation. I already knew too much about feeling like a loser.

But I did want to know more about Melanie, to learn what had happened to her after I'd left The End. I had an urge to call Phil to see if he'd heard anything about Peter's accident, but knew it pointless.

He would need more time. My morbid curiosity would have to wait.

It wasn't only curiosity that made me impatient. Boots' telephone call had punched a hole through my couch daze and I wanted out of the house. My mind jumped to the director of Hope House, Jonathan, Melanie's stepfather. Maybe I had a shot at a two-for-one: some background about her, and information about Emil and his role in The End's drug network.

I was so pleased with my idea that I paid little attention to my misgivings. I could always quit; the only meter running was my own.

I stood, smudged the gleam on the gun with my fingers, and hung it in the holster on the back of the wooden kitchen chair. I often wondered what favor my grandfather had performed in return for chairs from Dutch Schultz's bar. But I'd never really felt comfortable asking. Mostly I saw my grandfather sitting at a small table in the back of his tavern, playing pinochle. He never seemed to be in a talking mood when money or cards whipped around a table.

I scurried to gather my things. If I stayed inside much longer I'd turn maudlin. Despite a moment's regret about leaving the cosy steam heat of my apartment, it was time to go.

I drove to The End, parked the car on a side street, and walked slowly to Hope House. The agency wasn't where I remembered, but I found it a few blocks north. I stood facing a four-story dark red brick house, a once elegant mansion that now proclaimed "institution." A small group of men in their late teens and early twenties were loitering on the steps, smoking. They did not look like institutional bureaucrats; they looked mean.

And meaner still when I crossed the street, angling toward the steps. I rammed my body against the stiff wind and tried to minimize eye contact. The guys on the stairs looked like they could get annoyed easy—real easy.

Eyed with sullen silence, I nodded and shuffled carefully around the two on the lower steps. I slowed, tense and watchful, as the top two reluctantly moved aside. I opened the large door and stepped away from the wordless confrontation into a large room alive with noise and activity.

The back half of the room was stacked with occupied metal bunk beds. About half a dozen people milled around a small Good-

will-furnished living room area. I walked to a long telephone reception station where four people sat behind a waist-high plywood
"wall" decorated with hand-drawn pictures depicting various forms
of urban blight. Behind the plywood cheer, right where a big orange
cartoon crane was shown snapping its jaws on a building bulging
with people, were two men talking on telephones. The other man and
woman huddled together in earnest conversation. All four seemed
oblivious to my presence.

I coughed, and the guy who wasn't on the phone looked up
smiling. "Sorry about the rudeness, but I just got off a heavy call and
needed to process."

"Yeah, making appointments puts a real load on." This kid
looked less formidable than the tackheads on the steps.

"Making appointments?"

I grew momentarily confused. "Isn't this Hope House?"

"Yes, but this side of the building is the Drop-in Center and
Helpline. You're looking for Administration, aren't you?"

I nodded and followed his hand with my eyes. If I hadn't been
so uptight about the Welcome Committee outside I'd have seen the
sign. I reminded myself I was here as a detective: rumor had it alert-
ness was part of the job.

I walked into a small room housing the real receptionist. There
were bulges in the midsection of her black spandex jumpsuit and she
had a beehive of tie-dyed hair. I liked the inter-decade look. Once she
hung up the phone she even seemed interested. "Can I help you?"

Interest didn't always mean originality. "I hope so. I'd like to see
Jonathan."

She pulled a large book from the side of her messy, oversized
desk, and put on a pair of speckled cat's-eye glasses. She looked in
the book, then up over her glasses. "Do you have an appointment?"

"No, I don't."

The black spandex rippled as she sat up straighter. "Would you
like to make one?"

"Only if it's for now."

She pushed her glasses up to just below the multi-color line.
"Are you for real? When you're talking Jonathan Barrie, we're talking
serious busy."

"I know what you mean. Good social workers are like rust; they never sleep."

"You can't just blow in here and expect to see Mr. Barrie," she said, the friendliness disappearing. "Even the pols call first."

For emphasis she popped two pieces of Dentyne into her mouth and chewed glumly in my direction. She looked tired, as if she'd already seen one too many crackpots.

For a moment I considered giving up, then had an idea. I glanced at the nameplate that perched precariously on the corner of her desk. "Well, Sally, I'm definitely not a politician."

She almost smiled. "I can tell."

I grinned. "Can we give it a try? Tell Mr. Barrie that Matthew Jacob would like to see him about Peter Knight."

She pushed her glasses back down. "Aren't you thinking of Melanie Knight?"

I shrugged off her doubt. "Please, just tell him Matthew Jacob is here about *Peter Knight*."

She shook her head, but picked up the telephone and punched a button. She cupped the mouthpiece with her hand and mumbled. After a moment she hung up and looked at me with surprised eyes. "Well Mr. Jacob, you might not be the Mayor, but you know something I don't. Jonathan says he'll be right down."

I nodded and walked over to a magazine rack. But before I could thumb through *S.I.*'s swimsuit issue, I heard my name and turned around.

"Matthew Jacobs?"

"Jacob. Without an 's.'"

"Sorry. I'm Jonathan Barrie. I'm very pleased to meet you."

He was about five-foot-ten, with thick, black, curly hair generously flecked with gray. It went well with the heavy, black, unbuttoned cardigan he wore over a maroon turtleneck. Dark green wide wales completed the ensemble. Jonathan Barrie might not be "just any social worker" but he sure as hell dressed the part. He reminded me of Judd Hirsch in *Ordinary People*. I walked over and stuck out my hand. "It's too early for you to be very pleased."

Barrie grabbed my hand, shook it firmly, then let it go. "Oh, I don't think so," he said, sounding like he knew something I didn't.

He turned toward Sally. "Can we use your office? I'd like to talk privately with Mr. Jacob."

He waited quietly while Sally left, then looked at me. "This is the only room in the building that has a door. I want our administrators to remember who they're working for." A small brisk smile covered his face. "I especially like to watch the looks on our funding sources when somebody from the crash area interrupts a meeting. It usually helps to speed our discussions."

I smiled as he waved me to the small couch. He sat the wrong way on a folding chair, crossing his arms along the top. A shadow crossed his face. "Sally said something about Peter Knight."

"That's right." I suddenly realized I hadn't planned beyond getting to him.

He leaned forward, no trace of amusement left on his face. "Why?"

I started groping for a lie, when there was a sudden hard rap on the door. Before Jonathan had a chance to respond, one of the men from behind the plywood graffiti helpline had the door open and was talking. "Jonathan, I have to see you for a minute."

Barrie stood and turned his wiry frame toward the boy. "Can it hold? I've got a visitor."

The kid pushed long sandy hair off his forehead. "I don't think so. We've been getting complaints all morning about Dennis and his friends hanging out on the steps."

Jonathan glanced toward the front door. "And no one wants to tell them to move?" he said without intending any insult.

The boy nodded and lifted his shoulders. "No one from here is going to tell Dennis what to do. We've been talking about calling the police."

Jonathan shook his head sharply. "No police without clearing it with me, remember? Let's see if I can help."

He moved calmly through the front door and I followed him out. One of the motorcycle jackets looked up and leered. "Leaving so soon, Jon-a-than? Too much do-goodin'?"

Barrie flashed a friendly grin in the jacket's direction, but spoke to the tall tough with a dirty-blond whiffle. "What am I supposed to do with you, Dennis? You know you can't hang out on the steps."

Dennis blinked, and drawled, "Don't do nothing, my man. Bad enough you threw our asses out in the cold."

Jonathan nodded his head. "You didn't give me much choice. The counselor said she didn't have an aspirin and you threatened to club her with your dick."

The guys on the steps had trouble keeping the grins off their faces. Dennis' lips curled downward in what passed for a smile. "She was afraid she'd faint if she saw my iron."

Everyone laughed and the tension eased except for the black guy at the bottom of the stairs, who muttered something indistinguishable. Jonathan tensed, looked at him intently. "What did you say Shakespeare?"

Shakespeare turned away, and gazed at the street. "Nuthin'. I didn't say nuthin', Jon-a-than," he mumbled with a lisp.

"Good, Speare. I'm glad you said nothing."

One of the other guys piped up. "Who's your bodyguard, Jon-a-than?"

Jonathan turned and pointed at me with his thumb. "A friend of mine, Matthew Jacob. He's a private detective."

Dennis looked like he had noticed me for the first time. "He hire you to shoot us if we don't move?" he asked.

At least I knew where I'd start my conversation with Barrie. I grinned at the Whiffle. "Only if he asks."

The situation threw me back to countless face-to-faces I'd had at the storefront years before. Conversations more pleasant to remember than they had been to have; especially since many of them were with Blackhead. Who knew, maybe twenty years from now I'd get a case from Dennis?

"Look, Den"—Barrie's voice was serious—"I had to give you the boot and, if you insist on staying here, I'm going to raise the stakes. Here's a better idea: go somewhere else for the week. Everyone will have time to forget about it."

"Jesus, Jon-a-than, I wasn't gonna do nothing to the broad."

Barrie cocked his eyes. "I know that and you know that. Unfortunately, the volunteers didn't. Let's face it, I can run this place without you, but not without them."

Dennis grumbled, but elbowed himself away from the railing. "Shit man, I thought you'd let us back in."

"I can't Dennis. Now, what will it be?"

"Keep it in your pants, dude. You got any smokes?"

Jonathan reached into his pocket and pulled out a pack of Kools. Suddenly there were hands everywhere. Jonathan glanced at the pack, then handed it to Dennis. "Enjoy. But I want that week."

Grabbing at the cigarettes, the group sauntered down the steps. Jonathan and I stood watching as they pushed and shoved their way down the block. Shakespeare was looking back over his shoulder, and yelled, "Fucking fag!"

Barrie smiled and showed me his palms. "The kid has trouble with his sexuality."

And I had trouble with Jonathan knowing my occupation. But before I could question him he looked at his Timex. "There went our time. I'd really like to talk with you but I have a meeting I can't miss. If you come back in a couple of hours we can talk."

He stared hard at my face. "Please try. I definitely would like to chat."

I started to protest but Jonathan was already inside the door. My two-for-one had become oh-for-two. I stood cold and suddenly lonely on the vacated steps. I cursed myself for having worn my denim jacket and wondered what to do. I considered calling on Boots, but walked down the steps and headed toward the storefront instead. No law said I had to go oh-for-three.

# 12

WHEN I GOT TO THE STOREFRONT I thought I'd added another zero. Although lights were on, the place was quiet and seemingly deserted. I was about to walk back to my car when, for the hell of it, I tried the door and found it unlocked. Almost immediately Melanie appeared from inside her cubicle.

"Matt. This is a surprise," she said neutrally, though her voice was accompanied by a strained look.

"A pleasant one?" It still felt like oh-for-three.

She showed a quick smile and raised eyebrow. "Of course, just unexpected."

"Predictability isn't one of my virtues."

"Isn't it?" she asked. "Not even a little?"

I flashed on my daily routines, my highway of habit that ran from morning to night. "Maybe more than I'd like to admit."

"Admit?" She shook her head. "I crave predictability. Working here, you never know what will happen next."

70

I didn't think I agreed with her. You might not know the beginning or middle, but you always knew The End. Somebody was going to lose. I shrugged and said, "The building seems quiet after the other night."

She smiled and pulled a cigarette from her sweater pocket. The tan cardigan hung open halfway down her khaki-jean-covered thighs. The sweater's sleeves were bunched just below her elbows, her white cotton shirt cuffs poking out from underneath. I felt a wave of comfortable familiarity.

"It's the calm before the storm," she said. "An hour from now, the school will be humming."

I walked to the big front desk, hauled my rump onto it, and lit a cigarette of my own. Melanie moved to one of the reception chairs and sat. This time I handed *her* the ashtray. "You really love it here," I said.

"This is my home," she said quietly.

"You said that the other night, but your home could be anywhere. That makes The End your choice."

"'Choice' is an interesting word." She inhaled on her cigarette and looked at me. "What about the things that are predestined?"

For an instant I hoped she meant us, then forced my mind to another direction: I'd had too many wrong turns to imagine the best now. "I'm not too religious," I said.

She laughed, stubbed out her cigarette, and handed me the ashtray. "That wasn't the predestination I had in mind."

I watched as she pulled her chair close to my leg. "I'm glad," I said.

Melanie's voice remained light, but she kept her eyes on my face. "I hope you really are glad and aren't just here because you're investigating something?"

I didn't want to admit my original return to the neighborhood had had to do with Peter's death. "I'm not working for anybody," I said. "I ran into somebody from The End a week ago. That's what got me curious in the first place."

"Who did you run into?" she asked. Though she didn't move, she suddenly seemed to have put a lot of space between us.

"Blackhead Porter. I knew him from the old days."

Melanie's glance went past my head, a small ironic smile on her face. "Blackhead?"

"I mean Emil Porter: I knew him as 'Blackhead.' I still think of him as that," I added.

She looked back at me. "So do I."

"You know him?"

She hesitated. "You really do have a lousy memory. My brother and I lived with him when we were kids." Melanie looked down at the floor, carefully picking her words. "That made it easier to accept Jonathan's offer. It was difficult for me when Peter died. Living alone with Emil ..."

"That's when Jonathan adopted you?" I asked.

"It was him or the State."

"You made a good choice."

"There's that word again." A sudden frown, then, "How do you know it was a good choice?"

I was caught short. "I don't, really. I met him this afternoon ..."

"You met Jonathan? How did you meet him?" A hint of suspicion glinted from her eyes.

I floundered toward an answer while she lit another cigarette. "Between running into Blackhead and meeting you, I wanted to reacquaint myself with the neighborhood. After what you said about Hope House, it seemed like a good place to begin."

Her face had a sudden tired, hang. As if she anticipated trouble. I appreciated the philosophy.

"And Jonathan met with you?"

"Not really. Something came up." Her questions put me on the defensive; I didn't feel comfortable telling her I'd been invited back. "He's a busy man," I said, wishing for a return to our conversation's brighter beginning.

"He is very busy. The End owes him a lot." She spoke with an air of finality, finishing the subject. I was relieved.

"We'll have to watch ourselves, you know?" Melanie spoke in a soft voice, the weariness gone from her face.

"About what?"

She smiled slightly. "About staying out of the past."

I had a brief, uncomfortable image of Chana skim across my

eyes. I watched it fragment as I shook my head in agreement. But before I could speak, Melanie glanced at her watch and got up.

"I should be busy too," she said tersely. "Pretty soon this will be a madhouse."

I reluctantly pushed myself off the desk. My foot had cramped and I gingerly pressed my toes against the floor.

"Are you all right?" she asked.

I looked at her and felt fine. "I'm more than all right. I hope you are too?"

She walked over to me and kissed my cheek. "Go now," she said quietly.

For the rest of the afternoon, I had a good time living my lie to Melanie. Although the streets were November-empty, I explored many of the old alleys, buildings, and spots. An occasional bout of paranoia kept me glancing over my shoulder, but I wrote it off to Megan's ghosts trying to jump me from behind. It was good to know I could outpace them.

But I couldn't outpace the increasing cold or the darkening sky. I cursed myself for wearing a thin jean jacket, and plotted a course to my car. No return to Hope House for me; I'd spent enough of the day in the past.

I walked to the end of the block and had just turned the corner when someone pushed hard against my shoulder. He was wearing a black biker's jacket with lots of metal. His brown hair had a streak of lime painted along one side.

"Can I help you?" I asked. He had a long cross dangling from his left ear; but I didn't think he wanted directions to the Cathedral.

He did a lewd raising of his eyebrows. I started to walk past. He grabbed my arm, and I let myself be pulled back. "You want something? A cigarette?"

He leered. "I figure you're the one wanting."

I stood still, wary and confused.

Looking at me, he spoke out of the side of his mouth. "Sixty for mouth, one-twenty-five for the tightest ass in The End."

Well, at least now I knew what was going on. I might feel like a resident, but I clearly wasn't mistaken for one. The hustler's age surprised me. By twenty, they were usually doing day labor or time.

"Thanks, but I'm not interested." I started to move away when three or four more punks stepped out of the shadows and blocked my path. I had a sudden urge to run, but I found myself surrounded.

"He's trying to drive down the price," a young-looking kid with bad teeth and spotty whiskers suggested to the biker.

No one seemed to be in any rush. "Look," I began, "it's fucking cold out here ..."

One of them laughed onto the side of my face. "He don't like that we're disturbin' him in the cold."

"I prefer the cold to your stinking breath. You want to give me a little room?"

Laugher grabbed my arm but I shook his hand off. The biker was staring at me with slits of eyes. "If you ain't jewing, what *are* you doing?"

Why didn't I look like a cop to them? Laugher grinned. "Maybe he ain't a fag, Sludge. A fag be crying by now."

"Don't you guys belong in school, or jail, or something?"

"We got ourselves an uptown comedian." Sludge gestured toward me and bowed. On his way up he slapped my face with the back of his hand. Hard.

The sting of the slap brought tears to my eyes, but I kept my head stock still. It bothered me that I hadn't noticed his fingerless gloves until one of them was on my face. I felt my own fingers curl, though I restrained myself from kicking him in the nuts. The odds weren't with me. Not until I had enough room to run. I noticed that the kid who stood by Sludge didn't look as comfortable as the rest. He kept peering down the street, worried about someone spoiling the fun.

Sludge rubbed his hands. "Well, shithead, if you ain't a fag then you must be lost. Do you need directions?"

I started to open my mouth but somebody from behind shoved me into Sludge.

"You clumsy bastard," Sludge said. He balled his fist and powered it into my stomach. "We don't like strangers in this part of town."

The air rushed out of my lungs, and I doubled over. I stayed bent until my breath returned, along with a hot rage. The odds were still lousy but now it didn't matter.

My leg came up hard, and caught Sludge just right. He started to crumple but I grabbed his jacket and smashed him on the side of his face. I let him drop, then turned my attention to the rest of the group. I was lucky; if one of them had had a gun I'd have been dead.

I wasn't quick enough, though, to dance around the knife Laugher shoved at me. I heard it rip through my jacket, then the sting as the cold blade slashed across the top of my arm.

My arm went numb; I saw my blood spurt. Someone grabbed my throat from behind, but I kicked back and caught him in the knee, loosening his hands. I grasped Laugher's knife arm and yanked it up belt-high. Behind me I sensed someone move, so I tore to the left and watched as a length of heavy metal pipe cracked into the knife arm I was holding.

Laugher didn't waste any time dropping the blade and I kicked it away from the fight. Unhappily, that gave the lead pipe time to catch me with a glancing blow on the back of my head.

On my way down, I prayed I'd kicked the knife far enough away and that none of them had another. As I kissed concrete I tried to roll, but a dark brown boot in my belly stopped me. I curled to cover my head and groin, then heard someone shout and saw the offending foot scuttle away. The party was over. I raised my head long enough for Sludge to warn me out of the neighborhood. At the moment, it seemed like pretty good advice.

I saw the reason for my friends' sudden departure in a group of people approaching from the opposite direction. The newcomers stayed across the street. As they got close, they avoided looking in my direction, but I wasn't insulted; if I looked as bad as I felt, I wouldn't want to see me either.

I thought about shouting my thanks, but it seemed smarter to use the energy to stand. It wasn't easy; I crawled to the lightpole and dragged myself up. I pulled at my jacket, then ripped off the rest of the sleeve to look at my arm. It was bleeding enough that I couldn't tell how deep the cut went. I bunched and pressed the torn sleeve against the wound; a little messy, but it would staunch the flow. When I felt the back of my head I was surprised to pull my hand away dry. Everyone had always told me I was a hardhead; this was real proof.

I took off the jacket, used it to clean myself as best I could, then walked slowly, very slowly, back to my car. I was scared silly of meeting anyone before I got to my parking spot. Although my attackers were long gone, I still felt like I was being watched.

But no one jumped me from any abandoned buildings, or from anywhere else. I kept the blood-soaked jacket sleeve pressed onto my arm and started the car. Sludge's advice rang inside my pounding head. I wanted to make good as fast as I could.

That I understood. What I didn't understand was why I wound up in Boots' hallway leaning against her bell.

**13**

"I DIDN'T THINK YOU WERE COMING," Boots said, her hand rubbing sleep from her face. "I ate and went right to bed."

I nodded and leaned my head against the doorframe. Her eyes widened as she noticed the bloody jacket. "What the hell is that?" she asked, anxious and afraid.

"Me." I held the denim away from my arm.

"My god, what happened to you?" She leaned forward, grabbed my hand, and pulled me into the room. She kept hold and started toward the bathroom but I yanked her to a stop. As I waited for the dizziness to subside, I looked at the spectacular view of the city pouring in through her living room's window wall. As usual, the glittering lights surrounding the ink of the river left me speechless. Nowhere else were the town's blemishes so well hidden.

"What happened to you?" Boots repeated, letting go of my hand and walking between me and the apartment's glass face. She wore a pair of men's black-on-black silk paisley pajamas, a couple of sizes too large. Framed by the magnificent wall, it was as if an advertisement from *Vogue* was superimposed over the city.

Most of the time I would have grown excited. Tonight, I saw myself in the picture, and felt like a bum who had slept through his train stop.

I started down the short hall to the bathroom without answering. Boots followed and leaned against the doorway while I cleaned and bandaged my arm. The wound was deep; I worked to keep the tears in check. Our silence gave me time to question why I'd come. Unfortunately, there wasn't going to be enough time to figure the answer.

I looked at Boots' reflection in the medicine chest above the sink. Her eyes were full of concern. I avoided them, staring instead at her lightly accented lips. I caught the faint fragrance of perfume, and realized she wore more makeup to sleep than Melanie wore during the day.

The comparision only added to my discomfort. I opened the chest and pulled out a container of Motrin. "Can I have something to drink?" I asked.

Boots pointed to the bathroom glass but I shook my head. "Stronger."

We walked back into the living room where I corkscrewed myself onto the floor next to her sleek, lacquered maroon Japanese table. She poured our drinks and carried them over; I was glad she brought the bottle. While she sat down behind the other side of the table I gulped the pills.

I lifted the bottle, added more alcohol to my glass, and teased, "Why don't you spring for a table with legs? You can afford it."

The worried look remained but she played along. "I can't bear to spoil the view. Don't you know what furniture looks like these days?"

"I don't buy retail."

"I know, I know." A brief smile flashed across her unhappy face. "If it doesn't come from the Forties, it doesn't exist."

I raised my good arm. "I'm no purist. I have lots of things from the Fifties."

"Sorry, my mistake. You're only forty years behind the times."

We'd run out of lines. I sat silent, sorry for myself. As well as for the hurt in my arm and the choreographed banter between us. I tamped down a sudden image of Melanie, and felt relieved when Boots broke the quiet.

"You didn't cut yourself shaving, did you?" she asked.

"I ran into a group of rednecks in The End."

"Did they rob you too?"

I shook my head. "No. I don't think it occurred to them. It was sport, trash a stranger. A game I remember from the old days." I wondered if I'd been on the ground long enough for one of them to grab at my wallet, but couldn't recall an accurate time sense.

Boots grimaced. "It's hard to imagine living there, much less returning."

Her remark reminded me of our breakfast at Charley's. Which reminded me of her breakfast there with Hal. "I told you I was working. It's not like I'm moving back." I couldn't keep the hostility out of my voice. "I'm sorry," I lied, "I'm still angry about the beating."

Her eyes combed my face. "Is that all?" she asked quietly.

The words were out of my mouth before I could muzzle up. "Why the fuck did you go to Charley's with Hal?"

Boots pushed herself back from the table and wrapped her arms around bended knees. "Okay," she said. "At least I know what's going on."

"Well, I'm glad someone does. But I really am angry about the beating," I insisted, embarrassed by my outburst.

She nodded at my last sentence then ignored it. "I planned to speak with you." Boots unwrapped her knees and curled her legs under her bottom. "Do you want to talk now?"

I nodded, but all I really felt was a mixture of dread, jealousy, and guilt.

"Hal wanted to meet. He wanted to ask me something."

I stood, walked to the expanse of glass, and looked down at the quiet river. A few months after I'd married Chana, we had visited Quebec for a long weekend. Our hotel overlooked the St. Lawrence Seaway, and we'd spent hours at the window holding hands, watching ships and barges work the water beneath us. The only boats you saw on the Charles were built for pleasure. But there was no pleasure on this river in November.

"You must have really liked Phil's cornflakes."

"I went to Phil's to keep my relationship with Hal in perspective."

I kept gazing out the window. She didn't have to tell me Hal's question. Off in the distance I thought I saw Melanie invite me to come back. I turned toward Boots. "I don't see how cornflakes could do that. Even Phil's."

"Look, I want you to understand," she said.

I glanced away. "There's nothing to understand. It's a free country. You can eat where you want, marry who you want."

She waved her hand. "Look at me, will you? I took Hal to Charley's to turn him down." Boots stood, giving a characteristic shake of her thick black hair. She took two cigarettes from a bowl on the island between the living room and her tiny walk-through kitchen, lit, and brought them, and a gleaming crystal ashtray, to my side. I took the offer and inhaled gratefully.

Her voice had a brittleness that surprised me. "I can't really imagine myself married," she continued. "You see, I'm more like you than you realize."

"I still don't understand what Charley's has to do with anything."

She ignored me. "But I'm tempted by security and, the fact is, marriage to Hal would be as secure as it gets. If he left his wife after thirty-five years, I wouldn't have much to worry about."

"Sounds like a good deal."

She looked directly into my eyes. "Fuck you, I said tempted. Whatever it's taken, I've lived this long without that kind of 'deal.' I took Hal to Charley's to reinforce our differences. It's exactly the kind of place I love and he hates. I wanted him to understand why I could never feel at home with him—or he with me."

"Are you sure it wasn't just to protect yourself from entangling alliances?" I *wanted* to push her away.

"You still can't see past my makeup, can you?" she snapped. "If I went there to protect *myself* from anything, it was from giving you up."

Giving me up. I felt a rush of panic cleave my gut. I didn't know what was happening between us, but I didn't want her to give me up. I walked back to the bathroom and fished around in my jacket. Miraculously, the joint was still intact, and I lit it off the cigarette. I returned to the table and sat awkwardly on the floor.

"I thought you were getting your jacket to leave."

I still wouldn't meet her eyes. "I don't want to go."

"Good. I don't want you to go either." She reached across the table and took the joint from my hand, inhaled, and placed it in the ashtray. "We have more to talk about."

"Yeah," I agreed halfheartedly. "But not tonight."

I thought she would protest, but she nodded and looked relieved. "Will you tell me about your case? I don't want to sit here in silence."

And we weren't yet ready for sex. I filled her in while we both calmed down. I thought she looked at me strangely when I gave her an abbreviated version of my meetings with Mel, though I couldn't be sure. But I was relieved when she asked, "Could Blackhead have arranged your beating? He said he wanted you out."

"Nah, I don't see him willing to go to the trouble, nor able to pull it off." But something inside me still wondered, and I mentally added the question to the others I had. I smiled grimly: I wasn't done with The End yet.

"What's so funny?" Boots was calm. Probably as pleased as I to be back on the right side of our line.

But we weren't on the right side and I knew it the moment we sprawled across her damask sheets. When I closed my eyes and touched her breasts, I felt Melanie's. I pushed the head of my cock into Boots, but felt Melanie open and bathe me with her wet. I grew more excited as Melanie's mouth ate mine, and her hands held me in. It was Melanie's softness, not Boots' muscle, I felt, until someone's cry pierced my shudder. I opened my eyes, startled to see Boots' face. We shifted positions and I felt the ache in my wounded arm as my movements took their toll and the Motrin its leave.

Boots' head was on my belly, her hand stroking my thigh. "Something was different," she said.

"The beating, our fight," I lied to the back of her head.

"No, something else." She kept her head where it was, but her fingers stopped moving on my leg.

"Only thing left is Lou," I lied again.

"Lou?" She turned her body and propped herself up with her elbow.

"Yeah, he's coming to visit."

"You don't want him to?" She sounded surprised.

This was one time when "out of the fire, into the frying pan" really was upwardly mobile. I could tell the truth about this problem. I sat up, lit two cigarettes, and handed her one. "You don't know how he's been lately," I said. "It's like there's no air left for me to breathe when we talk. I'm afraid I'll suffocate when he comes to town."

"He's needy, Matt. Martha ..."

I was immediately defensive. "Believe me, Boots, I understand about Martha. And I don't mind trying to help. But I have trouble with someone grabbing at me."

"I know."

"What's that supposed to mean? Damn, woman, how many times do I have to apologize for my reaction to Hal?"

"I wasn't talking about you and Hal, *man*. I was thinking about how it feels the same for me."

I felt like a fool. The back of my head throbbed where it had been hit and I wanted to disappear. From her, from Lou, from my head.

"He's coming for Thanksgiving," I said. "There's going to be a party. Of course, you're invited." I stubbed the cigarette out in the ashtray and passed it to her.

Boots took the ashtray, put out her smoke, but kept her eyes averted. "I won't be able to come."

I started remembering where I'd dropped my clothes. "I'm going on a trip with Hal." She paused, then said gently, "I didn't know about Lou's visit. Holidays never mean anything to you."

I stood up and hunted for my pants. I didn't think Boots would object: Hal gets his consolation prize, I get to go home. "Holidays don't mean anything," I agreed. "It'll go all right."

"If everything is so okay why are you running out of here?" she asked.

"I'm going to work tomorrow."

"You're leaving because of the malls?"

"The End."

That sat her up. "Why?" She jumped off the bed and pulled on her pajamas. "Why?" she repeated. "You don't have a case. He fired you."

"I got a new client. Me." I finished dressing, hoping to leave while the ensuing argument still obscured the real conflicts between us. It even brought us closer.

"You'll freeze if you don't wear your jacket."

I looked at the bloody ball of denim in my hand. "I don't want to wear it." For a moment I was tempted to tell her to call when she returned from her trip, but I bit my tongue. I leaned down and kissed her lips. "I'll be fine," I said, pulling out of her grasp, then out of her house.

But I wasn't fine. I walked to my car, threw the damp jacket on the back seat, and took off, hardly giving the engine a chance to warm. I drove straight for home. Hard. Too hard, and too fast to decide whether I felt lost or free.

# 14

DR. RUTH MIGHT SAY IT'S ALL RIGHT to think about one person while you make love to another, but my night-to-morning was a long painful do. Face after face kicked me awake, and, by daybreak, I was more uneasy than I'd been the previous night. I understood the dreams about Boots and Melanie; it was Megan's continued appearance that threw me. I almost surrendered to the living room sofa. But years of Fritos and commercials asking whether I was the type of guy who liked to work with my hands but hated having dirty fingernails made me leery of couching it before noon.

I dressed and thought about checking with Phil for the police report but didn't want to push him. Hell, I was in no rush myself. Countless shopping malls stretched before me when I finished with The End, and I needed stronger ammunition in my struggle to remain vertical.

As the morning minutes dripped away, upright rapidly became

more difficult. I thought about visiting Blackhead, but my arm was pretty sore, making me reluctant to add to the pain. And there would be additional hurt if I caught the slightest hint of his involvement with my beating. Truth was, I didn't trust myself; it'd be too tempting to beat on him without any hint at all.

The soreness in my arm finally spurred my feet. Revenge wasn't my favorite motivational tool, but this morning it kept me off the couch. If Blackhead was behind the mugging, there was a chance Jonathan Barrie might be of help.

During the drive to The End I noted my change of focus: I was a lot less interested in Peter Knight than in Emil Porter. I remembered thinking, before my breakfast with Boots, how the past infects the present. Today it was evident how easily the unpleasant present supplants the unpleasant past.

The thought of Boots disturbed me till I shook her out of my mind. Unfortunately, the vacuum gave Melanie room to appear. After a little while, I longed for the days when my emotional problems came one at a time though, I reminded myself, during my days with Megan they *had*.

The sky halfheartedly threatened snow by the time I parked across the street from the social agency. The same group who'd been on the steps were there again. And no less reluctant to let me by. But now I knew the coin of the realm; it cost me close to half a pack, but my price included taking a good hard look at their faces. I finally got to the door, disappointed. I couldn't tie any of them in with yesterday's beating.

The room was louder and busier than the other afternoon. It looked like Hope House would have no trouble calling for that *minyan*. I quickly ducked into the receptionist's office and closed the door. I wanted to avoid the neighborhood people. I didn't know if my guilt reflected a sell-out or embarrassment as to the nature of my concerns. Maybe they were the same thing.

Sally stood alongside the desk, fist on ample hip, glaring. "Why'd you close the door?"

I smiled. "I didn't want anybody to die of shock when Jonathan breaks up a busy day twice in a row."

She shifted slightly and rolled the day's version of spandex against the side of the desk. "Ain't you a funny customer. You want me to call him, don't you?"

I nodded. Sally shook her head but made the call.

This time I made it through *S.I.*'s bikinis twice, plus the first of a three-parter on the Merchant Marines. Changing locales all the time like the M.M. didn't read like fun; you took your head wherever you went.

Barrie didn't sound very apologetic when he hurried through the door. "Sorry you had to wait," he said. "I keep a tight schedule that's difficult to juggle." He stopped talking and a frown appeared. "Why was the door closed?" he asked.

I pushed myself off the fake leather couch. "My fault, Mr. Barrie. I got agoraphobia." Before he took me seriously I added, "I'm joking. I just closed it automatically." I wondered if Sally would tumble to my wisecrack but she remained silent.

"Just Jonathan." He glanced at his wristwatch. "I expected you last night," he said grumpily.

"Sorry, I didn't think to call. I was busy getting knifed and beaten." I saw Sally draw back and lift her hand toward her mouth.

Jonathan looked at me closely. "In The End?"

I nodded. I saw his lips tighten and he turned toward the secretary. "Can you excuse us for a while?" She nodded and left the room, carefully leaving the door open after her. Barrie walked over and closed it.

"You really have a thing about the doors, don't you?" I asked.

"Not exactly," he said. "When I first came to Hope House the people who worked here were extraordinarily distant from the community, and that's putting it politely. Arrogant and elitist is probably closer to the truth. I should have fired the lot of them, but it was my first job in a new career and I didn't have the nerve."

"So you took the doors off instead," I grinned.

"I took the doors off," he said, still pleased with his strategy. "They fired themselves; it just took a little longer." He smiled at me. "But not much longer. Sometimes it's a pain in the ass, but it still works."

Jonathan walked to the chair behind the desk, rolled it out, and sat. I went back to my seat on the couch.

"You didn't come here to talk about doors, did you?" he asked.

"No. I'm hoping you'll help me find out about last night." I told him what had happened, and described the gang as best I could. I thought I saw a flicker of recognition when I painted Sludge's picture, but I couldn't be sure.

"I don't understand what you plan to do with them," he said pointedly. "Unless you plan to turn them in?"

"I want to know if it really was random."

"You think it wasn't?"

"It probably was. But I want to be sure." I thought for a moment then added, "I'm pissed about it."

"Of course," Jonathan nodded, then, abruptly, "Why were you in yesterday asking about Peter Knight?"

He tried to keep his tone conversational, and for the most part did. For the most part. "Today is one beating later," I said. "Today I'm not really interested in Peter Knight."

"You've visited with Melanie." He said it easily, without a demand for an answer.

"Let me guess. You knew I was a detective because you had spoken with her about me."

"Don't flatter yourself," he answered without malice. "We speak all the time, about most everything. Your name came up."

I grinned and stood. "Yes, I'm interested in Melanie, but that's not why I'm here. Can you help me?"

It took him a moment or two to get started but, when he did, he tore into it. We went to his office upstairs where he sat down behind a modern bank of Ma Bell equipment. I listened to short staccato conversations with people whose numbers were dialed automatically. No one asked for his last name.

Despite Barrie's activity, we were as if in the eye of a storm. The din from downstairs surrounded us; every few minutes, someone charged into the office, usually holding a form. They'd look at Jonathan on the telephone, grumble, and leave. It wasn't long before I realized that, had I worked at Hope House when Jonathan came on board, I'd have been among those who fired themselves.

At one point I thought he called Melanie; though he never used her name his tone softened and swelled. Finally he rose and shrugged. "I don't have anyone else to call. One guy was out but he'll say the same thing as the rest."

"Which was?"

"No surprises."

Before I could react, Barrie looked at his watch and caught me off-guard. "Why don't you buy me a drink?"

I owed him. "Sure, where?"

Sully's had a different vibe than the Wagon Wheel. Butcher-block tables, hanging plants, and the reproduction old-fashioned mahogany bar gave the impression that we'd stepped out of The End. Despite place warp, I knew the stack of expensive bottles contained as much cheap as fancy. A bar is a bar is a bar.

We tucked into a corner booth and gave our order to a thin, blond, bowtied waiter. I looked around the room at the other customers, felt my homophobia stir, and thought of Shakespeare's cat-call. Then I felt disgusted by my three-legged connection to the family of man.

The waiter's return took me out of my silent self-reproach, and I celebrated with a long pull of my German dark. Jonathan toyed with his Poland Springs and, for another moment, we sat staring at each other.

"Everyone heard the same thing," he said. "Stranger hostility. Nobody likes it, but it won't go away. Some of those kids have probably never been out of The End. They're too afraid. Mugging strangers supports their denial." He raised his eyebrows. "Sorry if that wasn't what you were looking for."

"It's what I expected."

"What *were* you looking for?"

"Does it matter?" I lit a cigarette and swallowed more beer. I liked Barrie, but he had something personal working.

He reached into a pocket, brought out a pack of Gaulois, and lit one.

"I thought you smoked Kools?"

He smiled. "Nah, I buy them for the kids. They hate these."

"Don't you think calling that gang 'kids' is a reach?"

He settled back in his seat behind a smelly cloud of smoke. "At my age they *all* seem like kids. Look, I don't want to appear pushy, but I'm concerned about your interest in Peter. Frankly, I'm protective of Melanie."

I frowned. "Why?"

"I know the two of you go back before my time. I also know you haven't been to The End in a very long while. Suddenly you turn up, a detective, asking about Peter. If you hadn't returned to Hope House, I would have rung you up."

Jonathan took another long sip of his mineral water, then went back to his smoke. "I might have called even if you hadn't mentioned Peter. I don't want anything to blindside her."

He punched out his cigarette, then immediately lit another. "No one has spoken about Peter in years. What is it you're after, Matthew?"

"His accident came up in one of my cases. I'm not working on it anymore."

His eyes weren't friendly as they searched my face. "Yesterday the case was active, and today it's not?"

His suspicion stubborned me up. "I can't get into the details. That falls under the ..."

"Rubric of client confidentiality?"

"Rubric?" I asked. "Isn't that some sort of game?"

"Isn't this?"

His tone was sharp; I decided to see his raise, and call. "All I originally wanted was some details about a twenty-year-old death. Instead, I get a dose of suspicion. You tell me what the game is."

He stubbed out his cigarette and compulsively lit another. He offered, but I stayed with the one I had. Barrie considered my words. When he spoke, most of the hostility was gone from his voice. "I'm not playing at anything. I told you, I'm protective of Melanie."

I shook my head impatiently. "You keep telling me that, but you don't say why."

He sipped his water, then shrugged. "Mel has come a tremendous distance since you last knew her. She went from a life straight out of hell and turned it into something pretty good. When you worked in The End she was a depressed dropout. Well, she didn't get that way accidentally. Her mother was a prostitute, her father a convict. When Peter died, what little support she had was shattered. It's been a long road back."

"Where do you fit in?"

He puffed on his cigarette, and exhaled with a sigh. "I moved into the neighborhood shortly after Peter's death. I'd taken the job at Hope House where I had gotten to know Melanie. Even then you could see her potential. Giving her an opportunity to reach that potential became important to me."

He paused, grimaced, and added, "Some of it started as a test of my social service commitment. Only it didn't stop there."

I was disarmed by his story, his loyalty, his twenty years in The End. "How old were you?"

"About 35."

I was surprised. "Jesus, you don't look your age."

He chuckled. "Thanks. I work at it."

"How did you start to help her?"

"At first in just little ways. Money, time, shoulder to lean on. Eventually, the state initiated foster care proceedings, and then I intervened. A somewhat unofficial adoption."

"Isn't that a little unusual? A single man with a teenage girl?"

"Isn't everything here a little unusual? Let's face it, when it comes to The End, out of sight is out of mind. The less outsiders have to do with this community, the better they feel. I had a couple of contacts downtown who worked it out. It helped eliminate a statistic."

Jonathan's voice had dropped while he spoke about the past. He looked as if he didn't see me but some distant figure or memory. I decided to keep him there.

"So you never knew Peter?"

Barrie stared over my shoulder. "I knew him. I'd done volunteer work before I decided to make a career of it."

"You were around, then, when he died."

"I was around, but hadn't moved in."

I detected an odd catch in his voice and asked, "What really happened?"

His earlier suspicion flared up. "I thought you weren't interested in this?"

"For myself, that's all."

He hesitated, then continued, "Peter's group of friends were at a party. Apparently, Peter wanted to go swimming and left ahead of everyone else. Early the next morning, someone found his body in Quarry's End. He'd banged his head diving and drowned. A bright, wonderful kid had his life snuffed out by a freak accident. That's what happened."

He sounded like a wire service sob story. "Where was the party?"

He shrugged, "I haven't a clue. Peter's death left a gaping hole in Melanie's life. He had been her rock throughout their childhood. Suddenly he was gone." He fixed his look directly on me. "From what Melanie says, you had been one of her few close friends."

I was surprised by the characterization. "Not really. I knew her, but not that well."

He looked at me carefully. "Mel doesn't usually exaggerate."

I didn't remember any friendship between Melanie and me. I flashed on the electricity between us now, my dream fragment, and wondered what I might be repressing. I shook my head. "It's been a long time."

Jonathan didn't seem to hear. "She fell apart when Peter died, and I helped her pull it together." A note of pride had entered his voice. "She's more intact now than she's ever been. That's why I'm concerned about your reappearance. I don't want anything to hurt her."

"I have no intention of hurting Melanie."

He shook his head. "You can't snoop into Peter's death without hurting her."

"I have no intention of snooping into anything."

He sighed, shaking his head again. "I want to believe you're not on an active case. Let me be simple and direct; do anything you want in The End but leave Peter's death alone. You may not have felt particularly close to Melanie, but I'm sure you know how difficult it is to escape quicksand. Reopening old wounds never keeps you afloat."

Before I could react—much less sort through his veiled warning—we were interrupted by a broad-shouldered, shaggy-haired young man lugging a guitar case on his back. Jonathan looked star-tled. "Darryl, what are you doing home? I didn't expect you for another week."

"Couldn't stay away," Darryl drawled, winking at Jonathan conspiratorially.

His surprise appearance obviously left Barrie at a loss for words. He peered around the room, then sneaked a sideways glance toward me before he spoke. "Why did you come here for me?" He stared at the table, and added, "Why didn't you call to let me know you were coming home?" Jonathan's voice carried a truculent accusa-tion.

Darryl rolled his eyes. "You're wanted back at the ranch. Some-thing to do with Dennis and the police." He looked at me but direct-ed his words toward Barrie. "It's lucky I know where to find you."

Jonathan jumped to his feet, stuffing his cigarettes into his pock-et. "Matt, please take care of the bill and meet me at the Center. I'll repay you there."

Before I could respond, Barrie rushed out the door. Darryl stood over me as I got ready to leave. "I don't know if you caught my name." His tone was less polite than the words. "I'm Darryl Hart."

I stood, stuck out my arm, and grasped a dry, firm hand. "I caught it."

"You gonna return the favor?"

"I'm Matt Jacob."

He nodded but remained silent until we were walking toward Hope House.

"You always carry a gun?" he asked, his lips twitching with a small smile.

"Only when I feel sorry for myself. Don't fret, I'm a legal PI."

He glanced at me, the smile twisting into a frown. "Private cop, huh? What are you doing in The End?"

"Nothing important."

"Jonathan wouldn't leave the Center for something that wasn't important."

"His idea of important might be different from mine. You'll have to ask him."

This time Darryl showed a row of gleaming white teeth. "I plan to, PI. And when I do he'll tell."

I was relieved to be near the agency. Darryl's smug grin made me uncomfortable. Darryl made me uncomfortable.

I quickened my pace as I made out the scene at the top of the steps. I wanted to see how Jonathan handled the two Blues standing just inside the door.

# 15

I SQUEEZED PAST JONATHAN AND THE POLICE, with Darryl trailing behind. I walked a couple of steps more and stopped, but Darryl kept going until he was behind the painted plywood. I looked out the front window, noticed Dennis in the rear of the patrol car, then turned back to the conference.

One of the uniforms had a puzzled look on his face. "I don't get it. The snot blames you for his break-in, and you want to help his ass out. Christ, what are you, one of those liberals who need to be punished?"

Barrie didn't blink. "Look, Officer, I understand he was caught inside a building, but the building was abandoned."

The other cop, gray-haired with a florid face, interjected, "Private property is private property."

Jonathan looked at him. "Cold is cold, and it's freezing outside." His voice grew harsh. "Now look, you didn't bring the kid here to

94

gloat. Either you fucked up the bust, or you don't want to do the paperwork. Leave the kid with me and let me deal with him, or haul his ass to the station."

The older cop stepped forward, jaw thrust out, but the younger guy restrained him. "Let it be, Ralph." He turned to Jonathan. "How you gonna keep him out of the empties? He says he got nowhere to go."

Jonathan grimaced. "I'll let him stay here."

The young cop smiled. "That's what we wanted to hear, isn't it?" Ralph didn't say anything, and the younger cop glared. "Isn't it?"

"I guess."

The young one turned back to Jonathan. "We'll send him right up."

As they left Jonathan looked at me and shrugged. "Dennis will tell us what happened." Dennis limped up the steps as the squad car squealed away. Jonathan shook his head. "I don't think he fell and hurt himself, do you?"

No, I didn't. Barrie opened the glass door to Sally's office and shoo'd her out. As Dennis entered, Jonathan pointed, then followed him into the reception area. I followed the two of them, and surprisingly, Jonathan didn't seem to mind.

"A tough way to get back inside the building," he joked to Dennis. "What happened?"

"Nothing."

Barrie groaned. "Don't be an asshole, Dennis. Why'd they let you off with a beating?"

"I don't know what you're asking." He sounded petulant and surly.

"Cut the crap, kid. If you want me to help you, you will, *will*, tell me the truth. Otherwise get the fuck out of here and go play with the bulls."

"I don't want to talk with anyone else here." Dennis jerked his head in my direction.

Jonathan looked at me for a long moment as I prepared to leave, then raised his hand. "Stay put, Matthew." He turned his eyes on Dennis. "I told you he was a friend of mine. Now talk or fuck off! I have enough to do without nursing you."

"They took my dope." Dennis' voice was a whisper. "They told me if I said anything to anybody they'd take care of me. They knew how to use those sticks, man."

"What kind of dope?" Jonathan sounded disgusted.

"Grass."

"How much?"

"A few lids, maybe a quarter."

"Where did you get the money for a quarter-pound?"

"I thought you wanted to know about the cops, Jonathan."

"I'll tell you what I want to know. Who fronted you?"

Dennis' voice was almost inaudible. "Emil."

I felt my stomach lurch, but Jonathan seem unruffled. "And the cops just took the stuff?"

"Yeah, I made the pickup and went to the building to break it down when they busted in."

Jonathan started to say something, then thought better of it. Finally he asked, "Where'd they hit you?"

"My legs mostly."

"Okay, go up to the fourth floor and stay there. Use the bed."

"Jonathan."

"What?"

"What about Emil? I'm in deep shit for losing the dope. He'll kill me if he finds out I talked to you."

"He won't find out. Now get upstairs."

Dennis walked gingerly out the door while Barrie took a seat behind Sally's desk. I leaned against the far wall and asked, "Would this Emil really hurt him?"

"Emil? At worst he would cut him off for a while." He rubbed his eyes and said, "This shit tires me out."

"You don't seem surprised by any of it."

He raised his shoulders. "This is The End."

"What are you going to do?"

"Probably tell Emil to organize his dope before he pushes it. Gives the cops less opportunity to steal."

"You don't have much of a 'Just Say No' attitude?"

A spark of anger ran through his eyes though his voice remained placid. "You're not really a stranger to The End, Matt.

There aren't many ways people earn a buck in this neighborhood; most of them, except day labor, are illegal. And day labor should be. When the city provides real opportunities, I'll change my attitude about selling marijuana." He looked wearily in my direction. "Given your reputation, I'm surprised by the question."

"Reputation?"

"You weren't considered a button-down. People felt they could relate to you. Believe it or not, your name still comes up."

"I don't believe it."

"Well you should. Melanie wasn't the only reason I came out of my office. I wanted to meet you. Twenty years ago there weren't many people organizing in this neighborhood. Everybody thought the only way to do things was one case at a time. Damn, there was one story about you working the street during a gang war, forcing a truce."

I felt embarrassed. "Don't make too much of it. I was young and a lot of stupid behavior seemed exciting."

"That's bullshit. You see, I got to The End right after you left. Although there were more social workers than Carter has liver pills, no one had the reputation you had. You were a part of this community." He smiled. "That much was clear by the anger people felt when you left. Folks around here are usually happy to see outsiders go."

"I don't recall having a fan club."

"Then your memory is faulty." He met my eyes. "Look, that was then, this is now. Twenty years gives someone plenty of time to change. Now I can't assume you're back here riding a white horse, especially when you could hurt Melanie."

"You seem awfully damn protective of her. She looks grown to me."

"She's grown all right, but that doesn't mean she doesn't need a little protection."

"You don't make it sound like just a little. Anyway, how'd we get back to Melanie?"

He put his hands on the desk and pushed himself toward the door. "The stuff with Dennis, Matt, that's routine. You're not."

Outside, the weather had grown worse. Colder, windier, grayer. So had I. Jonathan's decision to keep me in the room during his conversation with Dennis disturbed me enough not to press him about Emil.

It was time to press Emil myself.

I drove to the address Blackhead had scrawled at the Wagon Wheel, and lockpicked through the heavy front door of his building. I wasn't surprised when the numbers led me down, not up; his cellar living seemed as fitting as my residence in the alley. By the time I got to his apartment, the parallel disturbed me.

I rapped loudly, waiting in the gloomy basement hall until he finished his "eye over chain" routine. The apartment was cleaner than I'd expected. I carefully removed a pile of clothes from a faded purple mohair chair, placed them on the floor, and sat down. Blackhead slouched on a dull yellow corduroy-covered couch and peered at me with reddened eyes. "They weren't going to bite, you know."

"I didn't know."

"What is it you want now, shamus? I thought I told you to stay away from me."

"Shamus?"

He looked at me distrustfully. "Why are you being polite?"

"Emil, you don't seem happy to see me."

"I'm not," he replied warily. "How'd you get through the fucking front door?"

"Somebody left it open," I lied. No need giving away building managers' secrets.

"So you're here. Now what?"

"Did you chase me out of The End because I might not like you selling drugs to kids?"

"I didn't chase you anywhere. I asked you to leave, that's all." He waved his hand dismissively. "What's with this kid shit? There ain't no kids in The End."

I started to answer, but he pulled his stringbean body upright on the couch. "I don't need a conscience; I still remember which side of the fence I'm on," he said scornfully.

"Blackhead, the only side of the fence you're on is your own. You begged me to help you with what sounded like bullshit, then warned me off. Next thing I know, a group of punks add meat to the warning." I waited to see his reaction.

He hunched his skinny shoulders, scratched at his beard, and said in an insulting tone, "I heard about the other night. You're trying to pin that shit on me?"

"Just coincidence?"

"Not coincidence, asshole. Just nothing to do with me. You're a stranger and people here don't like strangers." He smiled meanly, showing his ugly teeth. "You stop to think that maybe I warned you off for your own good? I was doing you a favor."

I checked my irritation with a humorless grin. I started to rise and he shrank back in his seat.

"Hey, there's no reason to hurt me. I didn't have nothing to do with the other night."

I took a deep breath. Except for the instant when I would feel the crunch of his body against my fist, hitting him would not relieve my mounting tension. Coming here had been a mistake. It was only adding to the blind, jailed feeling pounding inside me. For the first time in hours I felt the gash in my arm ache. "You sure found out about it quick."

"It's a small world, isn't it?"

"Maybe small enough to have something to do with your dealing."

"Man, what do drugs have to do with anything?"

"I think you pulled me into The End as some sort of bait. Then you cut a deal and needed to get rid of me. Was someone supposed to see us together at the Wagon Wheel?"

He shook his head. "Jesus, man, you are crazy."

"Smarter people than you have said the same thing."

"Well, you ought to fucking listen. Drugs, drugs, drugs. How'd they let a paranoid get a license?"

I wasn't about to tell him my homeboy Simon had bought it for me.

"Jesus," Blackhead shook his head. "I suggested we meet at your house, asshole. I'll tell you again—I wanted you to help me with that letter, then I changed my mind. That's all. Christ, why don't you go the fuck away!"

I could. And I should. But I didn't. "Show me the letter."

"I don't have the goddamn letter. I threw it away." He saw my look and added, "I didn't start out to hire anyone." His voice trailed off into a whine. "Why the fuck would I keep it? I don't need stuff like that around my house. I worry enough about what I got to keep here."

I bit the inside of my cheek in frustration. My head was banging and his nasal lamentations squeezed the breath out of me. Short of pummeling him half to death, I wasn't going to learn the truth. The afternoon's darkness had crept into the apartment and I had to get out of there. I had to breathe.

My alley's gravel was still on my shoes when the telephone rang. I draped it with a dark blue towel, hoping the damn thing would fall asleep. I wandered to the couch and looked for something on TV. One quick scan and I knew I'd have better luck high.

Sort of. Donahue jerked his body around the audience in response to a panel extolling the virtues of open marriage. The show raised memories of my marriage to Megan, but hers had been the open half. Maybe that's why I couldn't really relate to its virtues.

The discussion didn't help my mood. I turned off the tube, and flicked the radio on to the local call-in show. Here people complained bitterly about welfare recipients: there was no escaping The End.

Before I could sift through the day's events and information, the phone blanket defected.

"Boychik, is that you?"

I pitched the towel onto the chair. "Lou, how are you?"

"I'm fine, but what's the matter with you? You sound like you're just waking up." There was a mixture of concern and disapproval in his voice.

"I'm not depressed, if that's what you're asking. I've been up all day working," I said, unable to control my defensiveness.

Lou chuckled. "Doesn't sound like malls."

"You're right, it's been mall-less in Gaza. A case."

"You want to talk about it?"

It was my turn to laugh. "Nah, it's not going to amount to much."

"That's what you said the last time, and you were dead wrong."

"Not dead, wounded."

"Sorry, boychik, bad choice of words. How is the leg, anyway?"

"Lets me know when it's going to rain."

"But you haven't been going to the malls?"

"What's with malls? You looking to buy at cost? Are you okay?"

"You'll see for yourself. I get in on Saturday."

It didn't take an accountant to figure he'd be here for at least a week. I mustered an enthusiastic, "Terrific. You want me to get you at the airport?"

"Don't bother. I'll cab over." His voice dropped an octave. "You don't sound like you're expecting a good time?"

"Don't be silly," I lied through my guilt. "I'm looking forward to it."

There was a strained silence on the other end; I could hear his familiar wheeze. "Okay, Matt. We'll talk when I get there. Have you spoken to Mrs. Sullivan about a holiday meal?"

"She likes the idea."

"Great. You take care and I'll see you Saturday."

I put the phone down and lit another joint. I hated this. I was used to feeling alienated, but being on the outs with both Lou and Boots was a new riff on an old song.

And now Jonathan Barrie had me walking on mental eggshells about Melanie. My jaunt into the past had given me nothing but bad dreams and a sore right arm. And my future had me staring at shopping malls and an overcrowded apartment.

# 16

MORNING BROUGHT ME A DAY CLOSER to Lou's arrival, but that didn't explain the cement mixer disguised as my head. A glance at the steamer beside the bed did. I was in the grip of a next-day hash hurt. And barely enough hash left for another high.

I lit a cigarette and morning-coughed to the kitchen for coffee and a medicinal roach. I ducked into the alley for the newspaper, then sat at the table staring blankly at the sports pages. Lou was coming, Boots was going, and I was in a bad mood. Best to ignore it all with chemicals. But any more drugs would tear my head off.

I was dragged from my neurotic gridlock by the ringing of the telephone. I hesitated, worried it might be Lou, but answered it anyway.

"Is this Matthew Jacob?"

I felt my body warm at her husky voice. "This is Melanie, isn't it?"

"You have a better memory than you led me to believe. Am I disturbing you?"

Disturb? Try resuscitate. "Of course not. What can I do you for?"

"It's been a shock to see you and we haven't had much chance to visit." Melanie paused, then her voice grew shy. "I wondered if we might get together." She stopped again, then the words began to stream, "This is a little hard for me to do and ..."

"Whoa, slow down." I felt untied from my earlier immobilization. "I think it's a fine idea. Where and when?"

"You don't waste words, do you?"

"I'm not a telephone freak."

"Are you free this evening?"

"Sure. Supper?"

"Why don't you come to my place after dinner and we'll have drinks?"

From the outhouse to the penthouse, and all I needed was to survive the day. "Sounds good. Where do you live?"

She told me and we rang off. As soon as I put the phone down I killed a rush of guilt. I hadn't given Boots any trouble about her vacation with Hal, I sure wasn't going to give myself trouble about going to The End to be with Melanie.

There was a difference in Boots' feelings toward Hal and mine toward Mel; but I spent the rest of the day convincing myself I didn't know what it was.

I did know it was a hell of a long rest of the day.

Anticipation rapidly faded to second thoughts when I pointed my body into the harsh and increasingly damp wind. I reached the car, twisted into the front seat, and looked at the plastic stick-on dashboard clock. I had plenty of time before I was due at Melanie's.

Time enough to change my mind. I conjured up Melanie's teenage image, but it wasn't enough to send me back into the wind. She'd been a kid twenty years ago; now she was a woman.

I considered calling with an excuse: I didn't need more complication in my life. But I talked myself out of it with a mental promise to keep things light. To catch up on old times.

As I walked through her door Melanie's eyes followed, but she didn't speak until we were in her living room. "A drink?" she asked.

"Bourbon, straight, no ice."

She made a face, but walked to an old-fashioned Hoosier and lifted the louvered door. I moved to a pale blue plastic recliner, circa '63, surprised to notice three bulging moving cartons pushed haphazardly against an unadorned wall. Melanie poured two neat, left the bottle on the slate pull-out, and handed me mine on her way to the couch. "Going somewhere?" I asked.

She looked puzzled until I pointed toward the wall. "Oh no," she said shaking her head. "I haven't finished unpacking."

I nodded, suddenly feeling like I'd dropped another ashtray. Mercifully, Mel came to the rescue, asking about the beating. By the time I got to the brown boot, a hot anger coursed through my body.

She commented, "At least it was something you're familiar with."

I felt my face stretch. "To tell the truth, you never get used to eating strange shoe polish."

"I didn't mean that. I meant why," she said.

"Sorry, I don't follow."

"You're an outsider. You know what people in The End think of that." She sounded almost bored. Maybe she was. Just a routine incident in a day seething with ugly. I didn't have the same clinical distance.

It was nicotine time, but my cigarettes were in my jacket pocket. Melanie read my mind, flipped me her pack of Camels.

I worked the plastic lighter from the coffee table, lit two, handed her one. "I didn't expect a Welcome Wagon when I came to The End, if that's what you mean. But I didn't expect a trashing either."

"Jake."

Given the reproach in her voice, it might be easier to keep it to old times than I'd thought.

"Matt," I corrected.

"Matt." Melanie stood up, and went for refills. She brought the bottle to me, leaned forward, and poured. She wore a pale gray skirt and an open-necked white blouse. I was surprised by the emerald camisole under the blouse. My undershirt stuck to my chest as my breath quickened with her nearness. I was kidding myself about the trip down Memory Lane.

Melanie returned the bottle to the Hoosier and went back to the couch. "It's no different now. You know what people in The End think of strangers. Especially the teenagers," she said flatly.

I felt my anger dislodge the tension. "These weren't hostile four-teen-year-olds!" I wanted Melanie to curse, not defend them. She shrugged slightly. "You're lucky they didn't know you were a private detective."

"They were lucky this damn detective wasn't carrying his .38."

Her full lips opened slightly. I anticipated a shocked retort, but grew confused as the atmosphere went electric. It was almost a relief when she finally admonished, "What has happened to you? You're talking about shooting children. I don't remember you this way."

"What way? These goons don't qualify as children." I caught my breath, the heat between us melting my anger. "I wouldn't shoot them; that's just my temper talking."

I thought she looked disappointed but she quickly slam-dunked that fantasy. "You have to remember the context of these people's lives. Violence occupies every inch of their world. It is their world. When you add violence to 'us against them' it makes for difficult sit-uations."

"Difficult? Spare me, Melanie, please. I recently donated blood to the cause and it still hurts."

Mel leaned deeper into the couch and crossed her bare legs. She removed her glasses, took a long sip of her drink. When she finally looked up, her eyes were friendly. "I sound like a lifelong social worker." She shrugged, then smiled to take off the sting. "I am a life-long social worker. If I'm not careful I'll end up a Jonathan clone."

I welcomed the change of topic. "I doubt it. He's a nice guy, though. He asked around about the beating for me." I wondered whether he'd mentioned my curiosity about Peter, but didn't ask. The heat in the apartment was turned up high and I wanted to unbutton my shirt, but I didn't do that either.

"I know." She motioned for the cigarettes and I caught another flash of green as I passed them to her. She lit one and returned the pack.

"He's very important to me." Her eyes scanned the room. "Almost everything I have is due to him." She took a long drag, and exhaled. "He saved my life."

"I'll bet you had something to do with it."

She brought her eyes down to my face. "After my brother's death I was lost and alone. I was headed for an institution, maybe even jail. I was gaining ten pounds at a clip and just didn't give a damn. Jonathan taught me to care. To believe in myself and my abilities."

Despite her words of appreciation, I thought there was an incongruous undertone of resentment. It made me uncomfortable. I pushed to my feet, and walked to the liquor cabinet. Melanie joined me, leaning her body into mine as she held out her glass.

"There haven't been too many people important to me." All the hardness was gone from her voice.

I felt a wave of excitement as I refilled her glass. I poured myself a double. My platonic intentions were heading south, or in this case north, as the distance closed between us. I placed my glass on the slate and lifted her chin until her lips were in reach. I kissed them gently. "You underestimate. Five minutes ago you were defending punks. Lots of people matter."

She walked back to the couch. I didn't know whether I was relieved or disappointed. I picked up my glass, settled back into the chair, chagrined to see her staring stony-faced.

"You kissed me like I was your sister."

"I never had a sister."

"Don't be flip."

"Melanie, I'm not trying to wise-guy you, I'm confused. It's been a really long time since I knew you and back then you were a kid." I felt my face grow hot, reached for my glass, and took a long swallow.

She kicked off her flats, leaned forward, and challenged, "What exactly are you doing here?"

"You invited me," I said stupidly.

She shifted her body. "I mean with me. There's something special between us that you pretend not to notice. You keep trying to place us, me, back in the past ..."

I shrugged helplessly and stayed quiet. I didn't want to drag us backward. Maybe Jonathan *had* spoken to her about my interest in Peter. I suddenly regretted not having any grass.

"Why did it take you twenty years to return?" she asked carefully.

I answered honestly. "I don't know, Mel. The End was a complicated place for me. The parts of my life that included Megan became shit. It was easier to stay away."

"You never remarried?"

Her voice had grown quieter, her eyes curious. I was too far along to stop.

"Yeah, I did," I said tensely. "We had a kid, but they both died in an accident."

She murmured something I didn't hear, but I nodded anyway. I didn't trust my voice and kept my eyes on the bulging cartons. Melanie got up, walked over to the wall, and turned down the rheostat. When she faced me again, the subdued light tinted her skin ivory. A rush of desire lashed itself to my anguish. I unbuttoned my shirt. She had refilled my glass, but now she took it from my hand and placed it on the table. She settled herself on my lap.

A picture of what she looked like twenty years earlier floated into my already crowded head; I blocked it and everything else from my mind, relaxing into the crook of her neck. She draped an arm around my shoulders, careful not to touch the bandage.

"Was I complicated for you too?" Her voice was a whisper in my ear. I felt her shift slightly on my legs. My pelvis rose to meet her body.

"You're complicated for me now." My voice sounded like gravel.

Her mouth was on mine, lips soft but insistent. I felt her move off my lap, and opened my eyes. She was unbuttoning her blouse. Her lush body smoothed out any possible wrinkle in the camisole. I could see the emerald matching underpants before I closed my eyes. Her tongue licked both our lips and I heard a moan deep in her throat. She was tugging at my undershirt, so I leaned forward and pulled both shirts off my body. Before I could take a close look at her she pitched forward and pressed her upper body into mine. I felt the softness of her breasts and the points of her nipples under the green satin.

As her hips twisted in my lap, I thought my shorts were going to strangle my cock. I broke our kiss; despite the dull ache in my arm I lifted her off. I stood, wrestled myself out of my clothes, and sat back down. She was standing directly before me and I stared as she slowly stripped the satin off her skin. An interior voice stabbed at my desire and my decision, but it was much too late for me to listen.

Her dark, almost purple, aureoles virtually covered the front of each full breast, their color contrasting dramatically with her golden complexion. Insanely, Megan's face danced in my mind. Then the instant was gone, any transgressions ignored, and I pulled Melanie toward me. When her breasts were close I leaned forward and took one in my mouth. I could feel the nipple expand and, still seated, I put my hands on the smooth cheeks of her ass and pulled her closer.

I opened my eyes to her hand squeezing her other breast, massaging its nipple between thumb and forefinger. I moved to rise, her breast still in my mouth. But she pressed me back, signaling me to stay where I was. She pulled her breast out of my mouth and lifted herself up and on my straining cock.

I looked at where our bodies met and saw her thin blonde hair glisten in the dim light. My erection, harder, was rubbing against tight, wet walls. I reached out, cupped her breast, and was rewarded with a contraction and a moan. Slowly, she slid up and down. I watched her thigh muscles tighten with her movements, caught glimpses of her wet lower lips as the base of my dick appeared, then slipped back up inside.

We stayed coupled for tense, fiery moments: she drinking my erection, my eyes feasting on her stunning body. Maybe it was hours. I circled her back with my arms, pressing my hands on her buttocks. I closed my eyes, afraid I'd come if I kept them open.

Leaning my face into her breast, I inhaled its softness. I recaptured her breast in my mouth and, at every suck, felt her vagina ripple. I squeezed the lower part of her ass, forcing her cunt tighter; she gasped, little sobs quickly following. I pushed my face heavily into her breasts, savoring them against my closed eyelids, my nose, my open mouth. She thrust wildly on my lap, both of us pushing toward orgasm. When she started to cry I groaned, exploded, then felt myself showered by my sperm and her wet.

As I began to soften I could feel the walls of her vagina shudder. She put her arms around my head and buried her face, crying, in my chest. I lowered my head to kiss her neck.

But something inside me shook when I heard her call for Peter. My trembling passed as my own tears for Chana loosened and fell.

# 17

MEL WOUND UP BACK ON THE COUCH, smaller, somehow, in her naked-ness. "You feel disappointed with me, don't you?" Her eyes a mask.

The only thing I felt was stuck to the blue plastic. I half slid, half pulled myself upright and began to gather my clothes. By the time I finished putting on my underwear and pants, Melanie was in her skirt and blouse, sitting on the couch, staring at her curled toes. She had left her emerald outfit on the floor. I felt our leftover heat on the recliner when I sat back down. But our interlocking, my sense of bonding, was splintering. Something inside tried to hang on; it wasn't often I felt whole, felt met.

"Aren't you going to say something?" Melanie demanded tightly.

I felt the space between us widen. "I'm not sure I have anything to say." I couldn't understand how she could be angry with me now. It left me uncertain of what was to follow.

"You heard me call for Peter, didn't you?" This time she spoke in a harsh whisper.

"Yes, but ..."

"You're disgusted with me." Louder now, louder and flat; it wasn't a question.

"Of course not." A last hope of clinging to our mosaic urged me to continue. "We touch each other in ways that unlocks our past. When you called for Peter, I cried for Chana." I choked back the naked ache that suddenly reappeared in my throat.

Melanie pressed herself deeper into the couch. "You were married to Chana."

I searched her eyes for a place to meet while she sat very still, the only movement the curling and uncurling of her toes. With a heavy heart I finally realized I was back inside myself. "I don't see the difference."

"For you it was pain that was unlocked, for me it wasn't so pure."

I successfully fought the desire to block my face with my hands, but had no control over the tension in my chest and belly. Mel hesitated, and I grabbed for the cigarettes on the table. Let there be one familiar reminder of after-sex.

She motioned and I tossed her the pack. She lit a cigarette and said softly, "I need to talk."

I rued her need, but I nodded.

A couple of long inhales later she said, "I once saw this film where a bunch of scientists fooled a baby goose into thinking a garbage can was its mother. The goose grew up with that can as its love object. When I grew up, my love object was Peter. Most of my life I've had fantasies about him."

Melanie's jaw moved, as if to better loosen her words. "No one had to fool or manipulate me. I had no choice. My mother was too busy with her damn men."

She spat the last words, but her eyes had dulled; her voice immediately softened. "I can't remember before Peter. He was all that was mine. He cared about me, took care of me my whole childhood. He was the only hope that life didn't have to be as ugly as everyone made it." She frowned, expecting an argument.

There was no fight in me. Just the desire to flee.

Melanie turned her head sideways. "I've always associated my sexuality with Peter. It never occurred to me that it was wrong. I loved him."

"Melanie," I protested, "you don't have to tell me any of this."

She turned back to me, and stared.

"This is a hell of a first date," I said weakly.

A smile eased her mouth. We both laughed away some of the rawness. She stubbed her cigarette into the ashtray then lit another. "I'm used to Gaulois," she said, almost matter-of-factly. "I started with these when I moved out."

She made it sound like yesterday. Despite the cardboard cartons I'd imagined her having left Jonathan some time ago.

Mel continued to explain with words less terse, eyes less guarded. "Jonathan taught me to reach, but it was Peter who taught me to survive. When I was little I could hardly speak. Peter was very popular, and I got attention because of him. Eventually, I improved. When you knew me I was still very shy, but not completely withdrawn."

Melanie paused. "We had our talk, didn't we?" The tension was back in her tone.

I thought she meant we'd finished, but she was referring to something in the past. Her eyes were cold, but a small smile brushed her lips. "I didn't think you remembered. I had an intense crush on you. I knew nothing would come of it, but I forced myself to talk with you about it." She grinned without humor. "It was extremely difficult for me to do."

"Melanie, I'm sorry." I wasn't sure whether I was apologizing for her crush, my not remembering, or even tonight, but I desperately meant it.

She looked over my shoulder but spoke evenly. "There's no apology due. You were very kind. You took me seriously, talked about your relationship with Megan, your difficulty mixing work with personal relationships." She smiled tightly. "When we finished the conversation, you kissed me. It was comforting to feel your concern and passion."

I remembered the couple of times attractions had developed between me and community people in The End. But the conversation and kiss with Melanie were a blank. "Melanie ..."

"There's no need to explain, Matt," she said sharply. "It's reassuring to know that tonight wasn't just the conclusion of some unfinished business."

She couldn't know I was sick of that phrase. It reminded me of Megan at Charley's, it reminded me of Megan now. But the thought of Megan helped me recognize my need to withdraw. I felt around on the floor for the bourbon, held the bottle to my lips and drank.

Melanie reached, took the bottle, and followed suit. We exchanged small smiles and I said, "Tonight has nothing to do with history. It has its own set of complications."

She eyed me carefully. "You said that earlier."

"You have a good memory."

"I remember everything." Her voice was quiet fire.

I felt a chill meld with a rush of desire, and, instead, reached for the Camels.

"Are you in a relationship?" she asked bluntly.

A momentary picture of Boots and Hal lounging on some sun-drenched island filled my head. "There's someone I spend time with, but neither of us wants to be locked in." The phrase "locked in" recalled my earlier emotions about Chana. Suddenly I felt overwhelmed by all my relationships, overwhelmed and unprotected. I needed distance.

"Tell me the truth, Matt." Her eyes searched my face. "If you are disgusted by me, say it."

"No, Melanie, not at all."

The next was a choice between truth or distance—the outcome unfortunate but guaranteed.

I thought for a moment, then chose my lie. "The complications are similar to the old days. The case has a couple of loose ends. So right now it feels like the work and personal thing mixing again," I added glumly, embarrassed by the untruth.

"I thought you had no case. That you had quit." Her voice steady, though strained.

"I just want to satisfy my curiosity," I waffled. "Sometimes it's why I do this work."

"The Work," she intoned sarcastically. "'The more things change the more they stay the same.'" She finished being nasty with a small, mean smile.

Having quoted the same phrase to Blackhead, I tried to tease us onto more comfortable ground. "How can you say that after what happened tonight? We did more than kiss."

I reached down for my shirt, slipped it on, and spent time on the buttons. I didn't want to meet her eyes. She walked over, leaned down, and kissed me. The blue of her irises looked like freshly polished glass. I rose to my feet.

"Will I have to wait another twenty years?"

Her tacit understanding of my desire for distance reawakened my attraction. I held her face between my hands and met her lips.

Echoes of Chana, Megan, and Boots began to surface. I pulled away.

Melanie stared directly into my eyes. "You weren't simple back then, and you aren't now."

A part of me felt "pardoned." Another part of me felt a pang of regret as she moved toward the door. I quietly finished dressing, looked around for forgettables, and reluctantly trailed after her. At the door I straightened my clothes and waited.

Mel stood on her toes and we kissed again. "I won't spend much time on those loose ends," I said, unhappy with my lie.

"We'll see," she answered, then kissed me goodbye.

Alone in bed, neither Valium nor a joint the size of a torpedo kept my anxiety, shame, and raggedness at bay. Melanie had triggered memories from every period of my life. There wasn't an emotional nerve ending that didn't feel undressed. After a while my safety valve blew and I simply went numb.

I ate another pill, slow-motioned into the living room, and sucked on bourbon. By the time I made it to the couch, I was dizzy, but didn't know whether to blame it on the pills, the liquor, or an anxiety attack.

I stayed on the couch and forced myself to watch television. Bouts of panic occasionally cracked my drunken, stoned stupor, but I trampled them until the numbness returned. A movie and a half later I prayed that sleep would win the race with sobriety. When the movie ended with my eyes still open, I fixed the result.

**18**

FRIDAY STARTED AS FAMILIARLY AS A WELL-WORN SUIT—hangover, drug-over, body aches, and depression. Not pretty, but right then an ally to help quell leftover ripples of vulnerability.

I peered at the clock. It was too late for breakfast, too early for supper, and I rarely ate lunch. Home sweet home. I rubbed the sleep from my face. The bitterness was familiar too.

I crawled off the couch, found my stash, and rolled a j. Familiar or not, the bitterness was hard to figure. The guilt I understood. I *should* feel compassionate toward Lou. Perhaps I *should* have waited to work through my differences with Boots before making love with Melanie. The guilt I understood.

But bitterness, hostility? I no longer thought of Boots without Hal, or Lou without loss of breath. My attitude felt crass and ugly. The kind of ugly I'd felt when I lived with Megan.

I finished the dope and spent the rest of the day moving from

couch to bed and back. From sinkhole to sinkhole, picking up around
the house in between. Whatever my mood, Lou was due tomorrow.

Late that night, in drunken practice for the next day's delivery, I
answered the telephone and caught a reprieve. Lou wasn't coming
until Tuesday. Despite another round of shame at my relief, the
upcoming pocket of isolation enticed me like a sauna in a house with
busted radiators. I yanked the phone and turned the lights low or off.
I didn't need full power; it had been a long time since I'd read anything other than a magazine or newspaper. I used to gulp mystery
novels. Now when I read them the enjoyment was replaced by com-
petitiveness and envy. Lew Archer never worked a mall.

During the next few days I had little life for anything other than
television and drugs—seasoned with stampeding guilt, discomfort,
and numbness. After a while, though, my depression wore thin, and I
began to get angry. But that didn't help much either.

Despite my attempts to slow its arrival, Tuesday managed to
arrive. Before I left my apartment, I silently thanked Gloria; I owed
the ability to function at all to my many years in therapy. However,
along with my ability to function came a two-hour wait at the airport.

"Boychik." Lou's voice boomed across the terminal, shaking me
from a glazed patience. I had no trouble locating the source. Always
large and overweight, he had really blimped up since the funeral.

"Looks like you enjoy your own cooking?"

He stared at me with hangdog eyes. "Nice to see you too. I tried
calling a few times in the last couple of days. Depressed again?"

"Okay Boss, truce. You have any luggage?"

"No. I travel light."

I tried to take the oversized overnight bag from his hand and
wound up in a tug of war. I knew immediately my worst fears about
the visit would be true. Still, as he pulled the bag, I felt another kind
of familiar sneak up inside. A warm one. "Let me take that."

He shook his head. "Boychik, the day I let you carry my bag, my
fat body will be in it."

I dropped the handle. "You're calling *me* depressed?"

He ignored me and lurched toward the exit. "What are you
waiting for?" he called over his shoulder.

I caught up and managed to open the door for him without

inciting a riot. I led us to the parking spot where I saw the violation on my windshield. Once I'd gone into terminal wait, I had completely forgotten to stuff the meter. As I grabbed the ticket off the window, Lou said, "Don't tear it up, Matty. If you can't get it fixed, pay it. Otherwise it'll just cost you more."

I nodded and stuck it in my pocket. I'd add it to the rest of my collection.

"What about Simon?" Lou asked. "Can't he take care of it?"

"I wouldn't bother him for something like this," I replied, neglecting to add that I hadn't bothered him for anything in over a year. Lou had already guessed something was wrong, though; at least that's how I understood his look and grunt. But knowing something and knowing what isn't the same.

"Do you want to stop somewhere to eat?" I asked.

He shook his head. "Ate on the plane. I told them beforehand I wanted a seafood plate."

"You mean kosher, right?"

"What's the matter with you? Kosher can taste just as bad as their regular *chazerai*. If you ask for a seafood plate they give you a meal from first class. It's a little trick I picked up."

The idea amused me. Now, if I could just fly somewhere. Anywhere.

We drove into the tunnel on reasonably good terms. I enjoyed his cheating the airlines; he seemed pleased by my approval. We were out of the tunnel and on the Expressway when I glanced in his direction. "So, *nu*, how are you doing?"

"*Nu* nothing," he growled. "Watch the traffic, will you?" Lou looked at me wisely out of the corner of his eye. "You think I'll tell you something different if you sound like a Jew?"

My attention turned to driving as my back stiffened against the car seat. The visit was going to become the flip side of yesterday's isolation. Detoxed from bourbon, hooked on Manischewitz in one round-trip to the airport.

After a couple more minutes of silence Lou shifted in his seat and asked, "And everyone here?"

"I haven't spent much time with anyone recently. But last I looked everyone was okay."

"What about the girl?"

"Girl?" I could feel a band around my head tighten.

"Shoes. Are you still seeing her?"

I couldn't tell if he was teasing me. "Boots, not Shoes. Yeah, once in a while. She's away so she can't come to the Thanksgiving dinner."

The dinner perked him up. "So who is coming?"

"I'm not sure. Mrs. Sullivan. Probably Charles and Richard. I haven't checked."

"Why not?" He sounded indignant.

My lips stretched against my teeth. "Mrs. S was taking care of it. I haven't seen anyone," I muttered.

"Or answering the telephone."

I grunted and concentrated on the road. Finally we entered my home turf. I slowed the car and watched the passersby. It was a cold, clear day, and the sidewalks were checkered with black and white. The usual assortment of music students toted their misshapen cases, and a few same-sex couples held hands. At least some people weren't allergic to romance.

I caught Lou holding his breath. His daughter used to have the same habit. "What are you pissed about?" I asked. "We'll have people over for the holiday."

He shook his head angrily. "It's not the damn dinner. I can't understand your attitude. It's not just toward the buildings, it's toward me, and it seems, toward everyone else. 'I see her once in a while.' What's that supposed to mean?"

I nearly rammed the ass of a silver Taurus. "Maybe it means once in a while."

"I wish you were as simple as your words." His voice was harsh. "I can't ask you to do a single thing. You won't even lift a finger to get a lousy dinner organized."

"I told Mrs. S!"

"Listen to yourself. 'I told Mrs. S.' No one matters to you, boychik."

I pulled the car into the alley and parked behind my apartment.

"You won't even drive in front of the buildings so I can look."

"Jesus, Lou, you're paranoid. I planned to walk you through the damn place. You want to see it from the car, then we'll see it from the car!"

I shoved the stick into second, popped the clutch, and peeled out on the alley's gravel, back wheels spewing stones in all directions. I whipped around the corner without bothering to pause, tore up the block to the front of the six-flats, then jerked to a stop.

Lou sat next to me breathing heavily. "Enough already," he said. "Fighting like this will get us killed. You were right; better to walk through the buildings."

I spun the car, wheeled back into the alley, and parked with a skid. Although the machine had done the work, I was exhausted. I turned my head and looked at Lou. He wore a small smile, but his eyes were grim. "I don't know what you were trying to prove; I already know you are crazy."

"You don't seem to think about much else." I was still irritated.

"Why don't we talk inside?" he asked mildly.

"If we make it there."

He chuckled and twisted his bulk to unfasten the door while I gathered the strength to walk from car to house. It was close, but we both got our respective tasks accomplished.

"Coffee?" I asked, once we were inside.

He nodded and walked around the remodeled apartment. I heard him call from the office. "You want me to park the body in here? The couch opens up?"

"There or in the bedroom. Your choice."

He returned to the kitchen without his suitcase and looked around. "The quality of work is the same throughout both buildings?"

I lit a cigarette and turned toward him. "Yeah. It looks pretty good, I think."

He grinned. "It looks terrific. Richard monitored the construction and decorating?"

"Construction, mostly. Charles actually did the finish work." He opened his mouth, and I leaped, "Please, no gay jokes."

"Pour the coffee, will you?" He shook his head sadly. "And stop acting like a *shmuck*. I was going to ask whether you let him work on your place. You have strong opinions about your home."

As soon as I could finish pulling my foot from my mouth I apologized. "I'm sorry, Lou, sit." I readied the mugs, then retrieved my stash from the living room.

He eyed the silver container as I rolled a joint, but all he said was, "Good coffee."

"Thanks. Lately I've had a lot on my mind." I wanted to convince both of us that he'd been wrong when he said no one mattered.

He nodded and watched as I lit the dope and inhaled. He leaned over, reached into the ashtray, and stubbed out my smoldering cigarette. "You don't need both of them going at once, do you?"

I smiled as the grass found its way home. "They're not the same, you know."

"Believe me, Matty, I know. What the hell is bothering you?"

I pulled a problem off the bottom shelf, something I knew he could understand. "I got work from a guy I knew twenty years ago. I've used up the malls. But I don't trust him, I have the feeling he was using me for something other than his case."

"Like what?" Lou was all ears, our fight pushed aside. He'd spent half a century with the Daley machine: duplicity grabbed his attention.

"Maybe drugs," I said.

He shook his head. "I don't understand."

"He claims someone threatened to link him with a twenty-year-old death. The police had it as an accident, but he wanted me to find the person anyway." I shrugged helplessly. "He deals dope and I felt he was using me as a stalking horse."

Lou seemed almost pensive as he recapped. "He hires a private detective, lets that information out, then looks to see who it worries or who responds?" Lou paused. "You're sure this old accident was really an accident?" he asked.

"Mostly, but it happened to a kid the cops wouldn't belch over." I dragged deeply on the joint and began to relax. The conversation off-loaded a lot of the tension between us. "On top of everything, I got mugged."

Lou's forehead furrowed, and he looked at me anxiously. "Are you all right? Did you get hurt?"

"Just a scratch. But it reminded me how much I hate getting hit."

"This happened here?" Lou waved toward the alley.

"No, The End. Where I was working."

"If the case bothers you and it's unsafe, why not drop it?"

I laughed. "That doesn't sound like my Lou. You're always pushing me into things."

Both of us had the same thought at the same time, but I spoke first. "I'm not talking about the buildings."

It was his turn to smile. "Good. So why not drop the case?"

I shrugged and fetched more coffee. "I pretty much have. I was entranced with the old neighborhood, but it's starting to lose its charm." My mind flashed to a picture of Mel; I missed what Lou said next. I grimaced. "Sorry, could you repeat that?"

"You really hate the malls, don't you?"

I thought about the mugging, the smell of the Wagon Wheel, and the interior of Blackhead's apartment. I drank from my mug, then said, "I don't hate them enough to continue with this shit. I just wanted to discover whether the mugging was connected to Black-head."

"Blackhead?"

"The guy that hired me."

"No wonder you can't trust him. It's a nickname, no?"

I laughed again as more weight lifted from my back. I looked at the last part of the joint, but lit a cigarette instead. "Yeah. His real name is Emil."

Lou raised his thick brows. "That's supposed to be better?"

WE SPENT THE REST OF THE DAY rediscovering how much we liked each other. Lou avoided any talk about Martha, and I didn't ask. We toured the buildings, his impressions from my apartment reinforced. He especially loved the skylighted, postage-stamp indoor garden Richard had crafted between the buildings. So much so, that he began to excitedly outline plans for the expansion of our empire. I didn't think he really meant it so I let myself enjoy his enthusiasm. If I had believed him it would have ruined my day.

We had dinner at a fish place on the pier. With luck, our crustaceans had managed to creep through last summer's red tide unscathed. It didn't bother Lou that he'd eaten seafood on the plane. Whenever he visited, he felt compelled to bottom fish.

After dinner I spoke to Mrs. S about the Thanksgiving plans and reported back to him. I tried inviting Julie, but he wasn't home. I'd try again the next day.

My misgivings began to center on my ability to tolerate a holiday scene. Despite the pleasant day, I still felt a strong undertow toward my privacy. Nonetheless, for the first time in what seemed like a long while, I went to sleep without a pill. Apparently, anxiety had taken time out. At least until tomorrow when the three of us—Mrs. S, Lou, and myself—would meet to cook. That is, three would meet, two would cook.

Lou slipped out early the next morning, and returned with enough food for a sitdown with an army of ants. He must have strapped the enormous bird on his back to get it home. He stood, partially hidden by the bags on the kitchen table, breathing heavily. "You know, for all the times I've been here, I've never walked around the neighborhood. I always told myself I'd rather spend the time inside, or with Mrs. Sullivan. I didn't want to admit I was intimidated."

I thought he referred to the drunks who, despite the city's intermittent roundups, thought my neighborhood home. But then he added, "I always believed I could deal with different kinds of people, but I've never felt comfortable with what they call 'New Age.'"

The expression "New Age" seemed incongruous coming from this Damon Runyon character. "New Age?"

"You know, artist types," he grumbled.

I didn't understand. "Your daughter was an artist type."

He stopped rummaging in the food. "I know. That's why I was happy she married you. I had someone to talk to."

I didn't want to continue this conversation, but heard myself protest, "Come on, Lou. You never had trouble talking with Chana."

"I did okay, but you helped. She was different from me. I had to fight for everything, and I swore she wouldn't have to."

"She loved and appreciated you."

He sat down in a chair behind the bags while I leaned up against the sink. "It wasn't a question of appreciation. Certainly not love," he said thoughtfully. "Just different experiences. My world was stuffed with minefields waiting to explode. Trust was something built with power. In the beginning you cracked a few skulls, later, you jerked around jobs. For Chana, trust was built right in."

What he said was true. Chana saw people's meanness as a shield for their frailty, a cry for affection, for love.

Lou broke into my thoughts. "With you, it was different. Even though you were much younger than me, and could understand Chana's point of view, you were a *lantzman*. You saw things with one eye like her, the other like me."

I felt my molars grind against the bittersweet ache of loss. "You underestimate your ability to appreciate things that aren't familiar," I deflected. Protected ...

He peered out from behind one of the bags. "What do you mean?"

"Take Charles ..."

Both his arms shot up in the air. "You take Charles."

"That's exactly what I mean." I paused for a moment and found him looking at me intently. "You have an attitude about gays. But you like Charles. You especially like Richard. The idea of gay disturbs you. Charles and Richard don't bother you at all."

His fingers pulled at his thick eyebrows as he blurted, "That's exactly what I was going to say about the neighborhood. Before I left this morning, I thought I'd hate walking around here. But the sun was out, I wasn't too cold, and I actually liked it."

He stood up, began to pull the food from the bag. It felt as if he had more to say but, after a lengthy silence, I moved to the table and helped him sort the groceries. "You better like the neighborhood, you have an investment in it."

He chuckled, relieved to have the quiet broken. "Believe me, boychik, I've invested in plenty of things I couldn't stomach. That's something Chana wouldn't have understood."

The groceries were finished. For a few seconds we were silent, dragged out of ourselves by the sensibility of someone no longer present. Lou finally broke the hush. "So where is Mrs. Sullivan? I thought we were supposed to cook today!"

And cook they did. My fears about a lack of oxygen had been greatly exaggerated. Everybody was on their best behavior, having fun. I grew momentarily anxious when Charles dropped by wearing a flamboyant green and gold scarf wrapped gypsy-style around his head. But conversation focused on the dinner and the decorating. At least it did after the round of Joan Crawford jokes.

Lou laughed along with everyone else, and so did I. The apartment filled with smells and sounds that it, and I, found unfamiliar. It had been a long time since there were more than two people in my kitchen. And when there were two, it usually meant trouble. Or drugs.

When the telephone rang I left the noise to answer in the office. In the quiet moment before picking up, I had a shot of missing Boots. She belonged, somehow, with the odd clutch of people in the other room. But when I picked up the receiver it wasn't Boots.

"We have to talk." The voice was low and husky, but I could hear the iron.

I sat down, opened the desk drawer, and fiddled with the roach box. The other night must have left her feeling overexposed. Hell, it had driven me underground. "Sure. Look, if it's about the other night ..."

"This is not just about the other night."

It was impossible to miss the current of rage. I understood: my medicine had been depression. "You sound chilly, even for November."

"Chilly or not, I want to see you soon."

I flipped open the lid and stared into the box as I spoke into the phone. "Listen, Mel, I know I've disappeared for the past few days. The other night affected me too."

"I'm sure it did but I prefer to talk in person."

It dawned on me that I hadn't gotten high all day. I felt a wave of tension, took the box out of the drawer and said, "Name a time."

"Aren't we solicitous?" she said harshly.

Jonathan had told her I was nosing around Peter's accident, and she probably thought I still was. I was a dunce not to have realized it sooner. Somehow, I'd imagined that, once I took myself off the case, the subject wouldn't come up.

"When do you want to meet, Mel?"

"Tonight."

I listened to the noise from the other room and shook my head. It wasn't often I was reluctant to leave home because of fun. Then I thought of the other night—Melanie, naked on my lap, taking me somewhere I'd thought dead and buried. "Tonight's fine, Mel. Where and when?"

"The storefront closes at ten-thirty. Why don't you meet me there at eleven?"

"The storefront?" Hers hadn't been a question; mine was.

She chuckled sarcastically. "This isn't going to *be* like the other night, Matt."

"I could only hope." Hope to ease some anger, that is. I didn't want to fight with her.

"You're lying to me."

It hadn't worked. "Listen, we'll do this in person."

"Count on it," she snapped. "Tonight, not twenty years from tonight."

"I'm not usually that late. See you at eleven."

I heard laughter from the kitchen, but the voices sounded a long way off. My fun afternoon had become something I had to survive. I opened the hand-painted wooden box and extracted a long roach. I lit up, and felt the comfortably familiar sense of withdrawal.

I heard another peal of laughter, and felt myself lose air. I smoked the roach down to my fingers, lifted the telephone off the hook, then slammed it back down. I must really be crazy; what the hell did I have to say to Boots?

# 20

I SMOKED ANOTHER ROACH before I forced myself back to the kitchen. As the afternoon dragged into dinnertime and dinnertime into night, I moved farther toward the group's periphery, distanced by my inability to check a growing apprehension.

Lou's arrival had artificially removed me from the swamp generated by my night with Melanie. Her telephone call threatened another immersion. Frequent retreats to the office and bedroom helped stave off overt public hostility, but it couldn't shut down an intense desire to be on the couch.

On the couch, but not alone. Despite my reluctance about admitting to my lies, and the fear of ricocheting memories, I wanted to see her. My body tingled when I thought of her. Mel shook me in a way I hadn't thought possible. And if that shake contained difficult, painful moments, they were, at least, honest moments. Moments reflecting the best and worst of my life.

Eventually, The Great Chefs of the Six-flat filtered home. It was a relief when Lou walked Mrs. S back to her apartment, and I was finally alone. Unfortunately, the relief was short-lived.

Lou wheezed his way to the couch, beer in hand. I stood next to the television and asked, "Can I get you anything?" There was time before my appointment, but I didn't want to hang around the house. With only Lou present, the nearness of alone would become overpowering.

Lou rotated on the couch and looked at me. "What's going on?" he asked somberly.

"What do you mean?"

"Matty, you weren't the same after the telephone call."

"It was that apparent?"

He swallowed his beer and shook his head. "I don't know what anyone else sees."

I parroted my lie to Melanie in order to smooth my way out the door. "It's nothing, really. Something related to the case. I'm going to meet with someone to tie up those loose ends."

Lou grunted and shifted his bulk around on the couch. "I thought you were finished with your case?"

"It's just a chance to know for certain."

He looked at me watchfully. "You have to go now? I was hoping we could iron out some things tonight … find a way to work together on our buildings, for me to be more involved. But we can't take care of business unless we talk."

I heard the condemnation and felt my stomach sink when "more involved" hit the air. "I wish you had said something earlier, Lou. I didn't know you wanted to talk tonight."

His mouth curled downward, his fingers feeling for his eyebrows. "You think everything can just take care of itself, don't you?" He didn't bother to hide his annoyance.

My rule was no more than one confrontation a night; so I tried to placate him. "Not everything, just as much as possible."

His cheeks started to puff. "Always with the jokes. That attitude is the reason you work in malls."

"Christ, Lou, I made an appointment, that's all. I don't work nine-to-five. We'll have plenty of time to talk. What's wrong with you?"

His eyes bulged, then retreated. "There's nothing wrong with

me. Every time I try to become involved with the buildings, you disappear. Call after call. Each time you have another excuse to change
the subject, or hang up. Now it's this."

"This is no excuse. You heard the phone."

"You can't postpone? This Pimple character and his case are
more important than taking care of our business?"

"To tell you the truth, I'd rather fight with him than you."

He waved disgustedly then said, "You're worse than a brick
wall." He looked like he was going to throw the beer can at me.

I started to respond but he angrily shook me off. "Just bring me
the remote, will you? My feet are killing me. I'll spend the night with
the television, since you have so many important things to do." He
turned away and stared at the blank screen.

I wanted to grab him and tell him he was too heavy to hitch
onto the back of a life I could barely pull myself. But I didn't. I wanted to scream that he was choking me, but I didn't do that either. I just
found the remote and dropped it gently onto the couch.

When I got to my bedroom I pushed away fat fingers of depression with a nip bottle from the collection under the bed. I felt my
shoulder twinge gently when I reached for my leather, thought about
taking the gun, then thought better. I was on my way to eat crow, not
kill it. I no longer cared about Sludge and his boys. Or even Emil.
Like the knife slash itself, the beating seemed distant, irrelevant
rather than important. When I passed the living room on my way to
the alley I waved goodbye. Lou, apparently lost in a "Lucy" rerun,
didn't return the gesture.

I drove directly to The End. I didn't pass-go or collect-two-hun-
dred-dollars. I couldn't even manage a what-to-do or where-to-stop.
The storefront seemed like a rotten idea, and I wasn't going to pay
Blackhead a social call.

I parked the car deep in the bowels of The End, and decided to
walk. At first I was hesitant, but got pissed at being scared off the
streets. I regretted leaving the .38 and reached under the seat for the
small lead pipe. Keeping an equalizer was a habit since high school,
though since high school, one that hadn't been necessary.

The outdoors was a relief, though I knew it was only a matter of
time before I found it cold. I shoved the pipe into my pant pocket and

started back through time. The abandoned cars often rested on milk crates, windshields shattered, wheels stripped to the axles. In the old days the milk crates had been metal; now they were plastic. Back then, the storefronts were chain-linked, now they were sardine-canned against the same people their owners would greet early the next morning, smiles pasted to their faces, their palms up.

I kept moving, my memories a buffer against the wind. I saw—as I had twenty years before—people venting their psychic rage, each with his own signature; erroneously furious at his or her own body or mind for placing them in this unalterable circumstance.

The same sidewalks, the same feet. But now was a different lifetime. And later than I'd thought. I walked inside an empty tavern, downed a quick beer, debating whether to walk or drive to the storefront. By the time I left I decided to keep walking, aching feet and all.

As I approached the building I began to feel silly about the pipe in my pocket. I doubted Mel would hit me with a Mae West. Through the storefront's window, I could see her standing outside her office, speaking with her young friend Therin. Their heads were close together, the looks between them intimate and intense. I shivered, the fresh air finally freezing. But I waited outside until they finished their conversation, and Melanie had returned to her small cubicle.

Therin grabbed something off the front desk and stormed out the door. He saw me and stopped in his tracks. His face shone bright in the diffused light coming through the plate-glass window.

"Back where you started!" he snarled.

I didn't know what he was talking about. He reached out and grabbed my sore arm and I jerked it away.

"I'm not trying to hurt you, man," he said, his voice harsh and hostile.

"What are you trying to do, Therin?"

He looked surprised. "You remembered my name."

"It's an unusual name. What do you want?"

"I want to show you something. Come with me."

He started toward the side of the storefront, and I instantly grew wary. "What's this about?"

He glanced back at me. "I couldn't hurt you even if I tried." He sounded bitter and disappointed. "Just follow me, okay?"

I nodded and trailed behind. Therin walked along the side of the storefront toward the back. By now I had reached into my pocket and wrapped my fingers around the equalizer. You don't do rent with trust. "What's this about, Therin?"

He turned, held a finger to his lips. We got to a concrete alley behind the building where he stopped and pointed. There was no light, no moon, and I couldn't figure out what he wanted me to see. I shook my head, and his pointing grew more emphatic. I still would have missed it if I hadn't heard a groan from a dark pile of rags and newspapers. Therin pointed to another lump in the alley, and I saw what looked like smoke coming from the mound. It didn't take a weatherman to realize it was breath. Now that my eyes had adjusted, the landscape wasn't much different from warmer nights in my own backyard.

He pointed to another couple of sleeping piles, then signaled me to follow him out front. I was curious to hear what he had to say. I didn't think he was offering me a social-work job.

Back on the street he looked at me, his breath rapid and shallow. "Those are Indians. Native Americans. Indians." He made the words sound like spit.

"Okay, they're Indians. Where I live, the drunks in the alleys are white. Come over some time and I'll return the tour."

"This isn't funny."

"I don't know what it is, Therin. You've been leading the band."

He was agitated and began to pace back and forth in the small area between us. "Those people have been taught to be worthless drunks."

"We agree, Therin. White people suck."

"That's not my point."

"What is your point?" It was overcast and cold with no memories to keep me warm.

"Even though they are drunks and bums, they have more than me."

I wondered if *he'd* been drinking. "How's that?"

"Don't patronize me. I'm not stupid. Every morning the four or five of them meet, figure out what they will need in order to eat, get drunk, and prepare for the night. They sit in the back and divide up the work. Each of them is just part of the greater whole that is all of them. And all of them are just part of something larger." He stopped his pacing and stared hard at me, as if trying to drum the idea into my head with his eyes.

"They could do with better tasks, don't you think?"

He replied angrily, "They belong, you idiot! First to each other, then to something else. For almost all of my life, I've belonged to nothing. I've despised The End's Indians for being passive drunks. I've hated whites for doing it to them. Two years ago I found something to belong to."

He lifted his arm and made a fist in the air, shouting in a shrill voice, "I am not going to let you take it away from me. Do you understand? You are not going to take it away from me!"

Before I could answer, Therin turned on his heel and raced down the block. Before he disappeared around the corner he turned, shook his fist at me, and yelled again, "No one is!"

I hadn't gotten through the door, and I was already beat. I felt bad for the kid though I didn't understand what was going through his mind. I wanted to retreat to my car and home to my stash. Instead, I pushed through the storefront's door, hoping Melanie kept a full jar of aspirin. It would be too much to hope for codeine.

# 21

MY REQUEST FOR ASPIRIN WAS MET with a sarcastic grimace. "Did somebody bother you again?" Melanie asked, as we stood by the big front desk.

I shook my head, though it felt like a couple of Kennedy halfs rattling in an empty tin cup. I stopped moving and protested, "The other night was a little more than a bother."

"Was it?"

Melanie turned her back to my open mouth so I shut it. She walked to the back room, then returned with a paper cup of water and two pills. I'd wanted half a dozen.

I gulped the aspirin and said, "Your young friend just threatened me about something. Does that count?"

"My friend?" Melanie looked at me. "Who are you talking about?"

"Therin."

"Oh." A frown stayed on her face while I followed her to the back of the storefront. She sat down at a cheap folding card table. I took a seat across. Melanie reached into the pocket of her tan cardigan, pulling out an open pack of Camels.

"Still trying?" I asked, still hoping to tease away some of her anger.

"What are you talking about?"

"The cigarettes. Trying to like Camels?"

She dismissed my peace offering. "I don't know what I'm trying. Do you want one?"

"No, thanks." I reached for the Kools and started to puddle in my discomfort.

"What did he say to you?"

It took me a second to realize whom she meant. "He showed me a small tribe in the alley, then warned me about ruining things for him. Apparently I pose a threat."

She looked past me toward the back wall. "He's a lonely boy."

It wasn't much of an explanation, but we weren't there to explain Therin. Melanie took my silence for an invitation. "Why are you investigating Peter's death?"

"I'm not."

"Don't lie to me," she snapped. "Jonathan told me you were." Her voice was strained; the hand holding her cigarette trembled. "You traded on my attraction to you to get information about my brother."

She pulled her mouth into a bitter smile that looked like my arm's slash. "You got your information, didn't you? More than you bargained for, I bet?" She sat still, breathing angrily, her eyes flecked with worry.

"Melanie, I didn't question you about Peter."

"You didn't need to, did you? All you had to do was sit there!"

"I didn't visit because of the case," I objected. "I came because there was, is, something between us."

"Apparently what's between us is Peter's death," she snapped. "Something you neglected to mention when we were talking about your work." She reached up with her hand and plucked at her hair. "I shouldn't feel surprised," she said. "You didn't volunteer that you were a detective when you first came to the storefront, either. Was that due to something between us?"

Beneath the hostility lay a tremor of panic. A reflection of vulnerability, I thought, a variation of what I'd been going through.

"Mel, when I first came to the storefront I hadn't decided to take the case. By the time I arrived at your house I had quit. I visited for the pleasure of your company, not for business. When I said I still had things to finish up, I was grabbing at the easiest way to withdraw."

"Withdraw from what?" she demanded.

"From you." Boots' breakfast litany rang in my ear and I tried to rid myself of it in a rush of words. "Not really you, Mel. Ghosts. My own. I brought up Peter's death with Jonathan because I wanted to learn more about you."

Her breathing slowed. "What are you trying to say?"

I shook my head. "I'm saying that the other night scared the hell out of me. I'm not on any case. Even my curiosity about the beating is gone."

"You were never in The End on a job?"

"Emil wanted me to look into something, but I didn't want to." And I didn't want to tell her that Peter's death had been Blackhead's Trojan horse.

Equal parts of relief and anxiety showed on her face. "Why didn't you want to investigate?" She cocked her head, trying to be certain she understood my next words.

"When I don't trust the client, I don't do the job. I'm not just a hired gun."

She looked away, but I could see the side of her jaw work. She turned back and asked, "And you didn't trust Emil?"

"He's hard to trust."

Even with her hand over her mouth she couldn't contain her laughter. It reeked of tension and relief. "You didn't trust your client," she squeezed out, followed by another round of giggles. Eventually she caught her breath.

"I don't get the joke."

Melanie took her time to answer, staring past me as if I'd disappeared. When she finally spoke someone, or some force, had taken an oversized mallet to her anger. "There is no joke," she said calmly, removing her wire-rim glasses and placing them in her sweater pocket. "I'm relieved, that's all. You're not the only one visited by ghosts. I can't bear to have you actively involved around Peter's death, whatever the reason. You drag up enough memories as it is."

"I never intended to thrash around anything, Mel. I'm sorry."

Her head gave a little jerk and her eyes strafed my face. Finally, in an odd tone of voice, she conceded, "No, Matt, you have nothing to be sorry for. None of us can help our past."

She looked away then. "Some of us can't even do anything about the future."

I was thankful for the following minutes of silence. Her strange tone and rapid emotional swing had unsettled me. My mind wandered to Boots: her ability to jump start different moods. As far as women were concerned, I danced on shifting sands.

Melanie's face was still turned away as she exhaled her smoke. "What about me? What did you decide about me?"

"I didn't know there was a decision to be made."

She kept her face averted. "Even without choices there are always decisions to be made." As if to prove her point, she stood and turned back toward me. "I hope you didn't get angry at Therin," she said. "He thinks of me as his only friend. And he knows there is," she paused, "a great deal of intensity between you and me. It frightens him."

I slowly got to my feet. "Look, I'm sorry I've caused everyone this much turmoil."

"I told you, Matt, there are no apologies due." Melanie led us toward the front of the building, but stopped halfway and turned to me. "If I thought you were doing something to intentionally hurt me I'd be very upset."

She resumed her progress to the front where we stood by the plate-glass window and looked at each other. A smile crossed her face as she reached out and grasped the equalizer in my pant pocket. "Is that a pickle in your pocket, or are you glad to see me?" she asked slyly.

So much for a second career as a soothsayer. "I like seeing you."

She nodded, leaned over, and kissed me on the cheek. "Then we'll have to see each other again."

I smiled as the remaining fissures between us closed.

*    *    *

On my way to the car, leftover images of the night streamed into my head: Lou's snub, Melanie's rage, Therin's Indian friends. But I felt good when I left the storefront, finished with the lies. Melanie complicated my life, but she was a problem of riches, not poverty. The street itself glistened with the sheen of the season's first real snow, snow that hadn't yet had a chance to turn a gritty urban gray-and-yellow. As much as I hated the cold, the city seemed quiet and peaceful.

A peace interrupted by the sudden sound of a powerful engine springing to life. I looked up and was blinded by a bright spotlight from the 4×4's roof. Expecting the light to move, I lifted my arm to shield my eyes, but the harsh gleam just bored in deeper. Even though I was on the sidewalk, the truck screamed directly at me. I was too surprised, frozen with fear to move. At the last second the truck tires swerved, and missed. I stood cursing the wet ground that, a moment before, I had admired.

The sound of the engine was still somewhere in range. I hoped his skid, and my near-death experience, had slowed the bastard to a more reasonable speed. I took a deep breath and slogged on, adding yet another reason to hate winter.

I had walked another block before the truck came at me again. This time I was crossing the street when it gunned out of an adjoining alley. Same thunder, same blinding light. I started to run back to the sidewalk, but didn't have the time. I turned and dashed in the opposite direction. As I ran by, a figure in the driver's seat wearing a dark hooded sweatshirt pulled low over his face had his fist raised and waving.

I raced down the street, still hearing the engine. It grew louder, and I turned my head to see the 4×4 slide out of a U-turn and pick up speed. I knew I should get to a secure location; but I panicked, and just kept running. I heard the engine's roar reach a crescendo, and felt its lights heat the back of my head. Suddenly the engine whined, and, at the same time, my feet slipped out from under me. I sprawled face-down on the wet concrete. In that instant I thought my life was over.

The hooded fucker must have stood on the brakes because the truck stopped inches from my back. The smell of gasoline, oil, and grease filled my nostrils and I threw up on the street. Before I could collect myself, the truck backed away, and disappeared.

Once again all was quiet except for the fading hum of the truck. I might have believed it was all a terrible acid flashback, but the stenches of gasoline and vomit were still there, along with tire tracks. I picked myself up and limped the rest of the way to my car—frozen, frightened, stinking, but alive.

Back home, before I climbed into bed I dropped to my knees and dragged out the gun box. I put two months of unread *Americanas* on the floor and placed the box on the night table. I pulled out the holster and .38 and strapped it on. I looked ridiculous sitting on the edge of my bed in a pair of boxers and undershirt wearing a gun, but I didn't care. It helped calm my nerves. Lying on my back, I pulled my gun from the holster and rubbed the barrel across my sweaty forehead. Another bout with the shakes was coming, and I tried to short-circuit it with more grass. The night's final images tugged for what seemed like an eternity, but sleep finally approached. I put the gun back in its holster, but kept the holster strapped to my chest.

Right before sleep I saw the mental picture of my mess on the street. There is no way to keep an urban snow clean.

# 22

I WAS PUSHED DEEPER INTO THE BED as my panic hit. Eyes closed, I twisted away from the hands, remembered the gun strapped on my body, and lunged. Before I got to it something clubbed my chest and knocked me back onto the mattress. I opened my eyes and stared into two liquid red pools, my nose filled with the smell of whiskey. It took another second before I realized it was Julius' arm that felt like a fallen redwood across my chest. As I regained my breath, he relaxed his grip. I saw Lou fill the doorway to my bedroom, a look of horror on his face.

I nodded to indicate I knew where I was. Julius lifted his arm and took a step back. He turned toward Lou, rumbling in his basso profundo, "Can you get him some coffee?" Lou nodded and backed out.

I felt my heart dislodge from my throat and descend to its normal place and beat as I sat up on the edge of the bed.

"You been screaming in your sleep, Matt."

"I'm sorry, man." My voice was thin and slurred. I tried to stand, but my legs wouldn't obey.

"Wait for the jo," Julius ordered.

I sank back down accidentally knocking the gun box to the floor. The crash and rattle squeezed the back of my head. Lou walked in with a steaming mug, looking anxiously to Julius.

"It's all right Lou. He be fine. It was just the box that fell." Julie paused, then said, "Something smells good out there. Maybe it needs tending—don't want to scorch nothing?"

Lou looked relieved and, with a sideways glance, said quietly, "Call if you need anything."

I sipped the hot black coffee after Lou left.

Julius grunted.

"You expect an invasion, Slumlord? Only thing missing was a blade between your teeth. Got us some serious nocturnal artillery here."

I tried to grin but my face wasn't ready. I buried my nose in the cup. But the smell that filled my nostrils was grease and gasoline. I felt a hot murderous flash race through my body, and I put the cup down on the table.

"I thought I was going to buy it last night." The rage lent body to my voice.

"What drug you overdose?" He sounded fatigued.

I shook my head. "No drugs. Hit-and-run."

Julius' eyes flickered as he pulled over a chair from the corner, dumped a pile of clothes, and sat. His action reminded me of Blackhead's clothes-strewn mohair chair; I swore silently to clean my room.

"Your case?"

"I think so."

"That close?"

"Closer." He sat quietly while I gathered my thoughts. I reached for the coffee, and felt the belt of the holster chafe my chest, and removed it.

"Tear on your arm don't look like last night."

I sipped at the coffee. "That was a few days ago."

"You been keeping funny company."

"The cut's nothing. Punks from The End playing Whack-a-Stranger. Last night was hardball—this truck ran my ass ragged."

Another bolt of fury shot through me. "Like that joke about the farmer who sold someone a horse that needed medicine. The new owner couldn't get the horse to take the fucking pills, and brought it back to the farmer. The farmer grabbed a 2×4 and walloped the horse upside the head saying, 'First you got to get its attention.' Well, my man, somebody sure got mine."

"What part in that story be yours?"

"The fucking horse. I was finished with the damn case, finished poking around the neighborhood. Now someone tries to drive me away."

"Literally, it appears."

"I don't think so. He could have, and didn't. Just a little game to run me off. Not over."

"You ain't making sense. Why would someone bother to run you off if you were leaving anyway?"

"Whoever it was hadn't got the news." I drank more coffee and steamed along with it. Julie sat on the chair, waiting. After a while I said, "My ex-client is one possibility." Whoever Blackhead had cut his deal with was another.

"I told you that place was worth avoiding," Julius interjected.

I heard something clatter in the kitchen and lowered my voice. "Lou says I take everything personal, but I never really took the case that way. This rundown changes things."

Julie placed his hands on the knees of his baggy pants and leaned forward. "Not going to be any stopping you now?"

"Don't try."

Julie showed palms. "No use trying to talk you out of anything. You usually do that for yourself." He twisted in the chair and looked out the doorway. "You scared the shit out of your father-in-law."

I drained the last of the black and stood. My legs felt willing to carry the load. "I know. What time is it, anyway?"

"Noon."

"Shit. People are supposed to be here at three." I looked around the sloppy room; the first serious taste of stranger-anxiety crept into my system. The best of times made Thanksgiving difficult; now, it felt impossible.

Julie kicked the pile of clothes in my direction. "You looking for these?"

I made a face. "Not those. I puke whenever I have a near-death experience." I rummaged through the dresser, looking for something presentable. "You're invited to this thing, you know."

"I know. The Bwana made a point of it."

"You coming?"

"Smells better than Church's Fried."

I looked up into the mirror. "You're a little early."

He showed a flash of his gold-toothed smile. "I'd say right on time." He pulled a pack of Pall Malls from his pocket, lit two, and poked me in the back. "Why don't you stop looking for threads, man. You need a shower."

I turned, took the cigarette, and sat back down on the bed. "Since when do you smoke these?"

"Since a recent brokerage job."

Julie made markets on both sides of the law. Between both sides too. I inhaled and made a face. "Bad job."

He looked sleepy so I repeated my question. "What are you doing here? It's about two hours before your alarm clock starts working." There was some nasty in my tone.

Julie shook his head. "Came to see how ugly you were going to be. You've not been particularly social lately."

I jammed the cigarette into the ashtray, and ripped through the night table drawer for a leftover roach. "Fuck social."

"My concern does not appear unwarranted."

I couldn't believe it. Rod Serling must be hiding in the closet. I snort the Great Beyond, then walk into something worse: my dope dealer giving me shit about etiquette. "I didn't ask to have the party. If I could, I'd be out of here."

He showed more gold as he rose. "I can tell. I see you haven't resolved your relations."

I guess he saw a puzzled look on my face because he

cocked and nodded his head toward the kitchen. He meant Lou.

I raised my eyebrows and grimaced, then reached for my cigarettes and lit one.

Julius gently tapped the bedroom door shut. "Chill out, Slumlord. By and large we all been treated decently, and that includes you."

I couldn't keep a sardonic grin off my face. "Don't sweat it, my man. I won't let anything happen to the rent arrangement."

"I do like you, boy, but you have real difficulty separating friends from enemies when you're worked up."

Everywhere I turned, someone was in my face. I closed my eyes and exhaled through the constriction in my chest. "Well, you do have a 'worked up' slumlord here."

I opened my eyes. "And, frankly, I don't see it getting any better until I get my fucking hands on the owner of that 4×4."

Julius looked a little sore, but then his face settled into its normal repose. "Somebody almost stepped on deserves some allowances." He peered at me, his face set and serious. "Best let yourself settle down before you Rambo The End. Can't dance like a butterfly, sting like a bee when you're out of control."

He formed his hand into the shape of a gun, shot, and left.

I took his seat, tried to take his advice; but I felt pretty frustrated in the face of my own rage and suffocation. Twice Lou looked in to see if I needed anything or wanted to talk. Twice I felt trespassed upon, violated.

The smells from the kitchen just added to my distance. I was still a guest in my own home.

I took another hit off the roach. I finally had someplace to go, something to do, but I was stuck in a fucking goldfish bowl. I looked at my reflection in the dresser mirror, startled by its familiarity. This kind of living was supposed to change you.

I grabbed a towel and headed for the john. Lou looked out over the kitchen half-wall, so I forced, "Sorry about the wake-up hysteria. Bad dreams."

He shook his head. "You always sleep with a gun, Matty?"

"Only when I expect nightmares," I grunted. "You don't want to hear about it."

"You don't want to talk about it. Now, what do you want to eat?"

"Just more coffee. I'll pick at what's cooking."

"Chana used to do that. Drove Martha nuts."

This was the first time he'd mentioned Martha since he'd gotten here. Any faint hope that Thanksgiving might be free of death calls from loved ones wilted. I stiffened, waiting for more, but he had his jaw clenched and teeth working.

"That's who I picked it up from," I finally said.

He nodded and turned back toward the stove. I lifted the towel and retreated to the bathroom. It was going to be another *very* long day.

The world's daily dose of pleasant surprises wasn't finished until I opened the door to Mrs. Sullivan tucked under the protective arm of Gloria James. Gloria and I hadn't become complete strangers. We had become whatever you became when your ex-shrink had been your first client. One thing you definitely become is speechless when she shows up unexpectedly. I really hadn't imagined her accepting the invitation.

"Now don't you say anything with that smart tongue of yours!" Mrs. Sullivan commanded. "Glory and I were talking and …"

I gritted my teeth and bowed. "Mrs. Sullivan. It's a pleasure to have two lovely ladies grace my apartment at the same time."

Mrs. S beamed. Gloria rolled her eyes. I took Gloria's coat and placed it on my freshly made bed. I dug for the hash, stuck it in a pipe, and quickly inhaled. It was the only way I knew to flatten my anger. I started to put the pipe away, then snuck another little hit.

By the time I returned, everyone coming was already there. Since they were all from the building and didn't wear coats, there was no easy excuse for more excursions into the bedroom.

The crowd gathered around the kitchen doorway and half-wall. Richard had his tweed look working, Charles looking like a cross between Cyndi Lauper and Black Sabbath. I pictured Lou greeting him at the door, and wondered when I'd hear the first remark about Charles' black eyeliner. People were chatting and drinking and I motioned to Julius for a beer. The hash was working, melting my rage into a soggy dreariness. For a dope-engendered instant I wished for Boots. But Boots was with Hal, and I was against the wall, looking like I belonged but feeling the truth.

Gloria, holding a glass of wine, walked over to me. "You seem out of it."

"Nah, I'm always a little awkward at parties."

"These are your friends, Matthew," she reminded.

Just what I needed, another head shot. "I'd be worse with strangers," I lied. "What are you doing among the alienated? I have you down for a family."

She looked at me and inclined her head. "You often 'have me down' wrong." She sounded wistful.

I suddenly felt uncomfortable. "Are you trying to tell me something?"

It was her turn to look awkward. "Not really. Some other time we can talk about me."

"Not today, huh?"

Gloria looked at me. "Do you object to my being here?"

"Of course not. I object to talking about it."

Gloria's demeanor switched to impatient resignation. "That's not a surprise, is it? Sometimes I wonder how we worked together, given your reluctance to talk."

I laughed. "You're wondering about it now? For me it was a much more pressing question on Thursday mornings."

A mischievous look darted across her face. "The Thursdays you made it or the ones you didn't?" It was plain she had decided to steer clear of complicated conversations.

Before I answered, Gloria leaned over and kissed me on the cheek. "Thanks for having me over. I'm glad you don't mind."

I watched as she turned to rejoin the crowd. She was wearing a short black skirt with a red satin blouse. The stylish hairdo, added since we'd last met, became her, and I felt a wave of lightheaded attraction. A feeling I could more easily stomp than savor.

Eventually the bird was hauled from the oven. I kept sucking beers and hunting for air. The party felt like a wholesale interruption of my real life; I was hungry, but not for food or talk. I wanted to go back to The End and grab people by the throat until I shook loose some answers.

The dinner droned on and on ... Julius and Richard debating the merits of postmodern architecture, Gloria and Charles chuckling close together, Lou pitching *woo* to Mrs. S. All the room needed was Charles on a chair singing torch songs. In between forkfuls, I drank and sneaked back to the bedroom.

They were an odd crew, but at least they left me alone. Occasionally, I'd look up and catch Gloria's eyes on my face. Once she threw me a quick smile, but I couldn't tell whether she was embarrassed for or about me.

The hash, food, drink, and conversations made me sleepy. I mentally tried to list excuses to get to the bedroom and must have dozed off in the chair. The next thing I knew, a hand was pushing my bad arm. I pulled it away and opened my eyes.

Everyone was staring, and Lou was breathing heavily. He struggled to keep his face pleasant as he stood, leaned down, and picked up his wine glass. "First, I want to thank everyone for coming today. I especially want to thank my host."

I knew it was a dig and felt my face flush.

Lou continued, "It was a relief when Matty invited me out for the holidays. He'd been so fuzzy over the phone about the buildings, I wondered whether they were still standing."

There were small chuckles from around the table but I didn't see the humor.

Lou turned toward me and raised his glass. "Not only are they standing, they're beautiful"—he turned back to the rest of the people—"why break up a winning combination?!"

I couldn't believe my ears as he launched into a variation of the other morning's land-grab fantasy. This time, though, he managed to include most of the people at the table. I thought everyone would laugh, but, instead, the table quieted as they bought Lou's program. Except for me. After listening to him prattle on about "sound investment strategy," I finally had enough: I'd be left holding the bag, the one explaining that Lou had gotten carried away by the occasion.

So I started to tune out, concentrating instead on The End and my hunt. Let them talk. All of them. Just as long as they left me alone. I was the stranger here.

But they wouldn't leave me alone. Somehow their discussion

had turned into gratitude for my stewardship of the buildings, and
they wanted my blessing on Lou's new ideas.

Charles raised his wineglass and chanted, "Host, host, host."

Everyone picked up on the beat, even Julius. I wondered what
drugs he'd taken. Gloria and Richard were smiling, while Mrs. S
drunkenly clapped her hands. I sat frozen, looking at their faces
through a Fellini camera angle.

Eventually I shook my head, trying desperately to keep my hostility in control. "I don't want to talk now, if that's okay?" I managed.

"I don't understand you sometimes," Lou broke in, before anyone else could comment. "I'm trying to talk about getting more
involved, getting something off the ground. And you don't want to
say anything."

He wagged his head as the words tumbled out. "You won't talk
when we're alone. You won't talk with your friends. I thought for
sure this would make it possible to communicate. Boychik, you have
a *stake* in all this."

I felt assaulted and naked, surrounded by prurient, prying eyes.
"Not steak, Lou, turkey. Good food and drink make me quiet."

"Bullshit, Matt! You just don't give a damn. That's what has
bothered me all along. You don't care about anything but yourself!"

His words landed smack in the center of my rage. First punks,
then trucks, now this. I had used up my quota of public humiliation.
"You are absolutely right, Lou," I said, getting to my feet. "I don't
give a shit about this." I glared down at him while the rest of them
kept their eyes averted.

Lou's mouth opened but no words emerged. When Richard
tried to intervene, I shook him off. "Don't say anything, Rich. The
dinner was fine but this 'one-for-all' crap isn't for me. I'm out of
here."

I had my back to the table when I heard Gloria ask, "Where can
you go? It's Thanksgiving."

I spun around and snapped, "I'm done with my thanks. You all
worry about your own."

## 23

THE FORCE OF MY OUTBURST carried me to my room. I stared into the mirror then shut off the light. "Say good night, Gracie," I said aloud to myself.

Only I wasn't tired, and it was barely night. I was just embarrassed by Lou's scolding, and ashamed of my own theatrical departure. Neither made for good company.

I sat on the edge of the bed listening to the murmurs from the other part of the house. I reminded myself that I hadn't been sent from the table, but the distinction suddenly seemed razor-thin. I rolled three joints, put them in my carrying case, and strapped the .38 onto my shoulder. I ached to get my hands on Blackhead, though Julius' warning slowed me down.

I grabbed my jacket, bit my lip, and walked past the party's line of sight. The dinner debris was still on the table; heads were bunched conversationally over coffee and cake. I stopped momentarily to eavesdrop, but sensed the strain my appearance had on the group, as their voices unconsciously dropped. I continued into the office to collect a fresh pack of smokes. I still didn't know where I was going, but I was in no damn rush to return.

I noticed activity outside the Wagon Wheel as I drove past, and was tempted to stop for a drink. But I felt angry, not suicidal. Instead, I pointed the car toward Melanie's. When I got there, though, only one small hall light shone. I ran out of the car to make sure, but she wasn't home.

When I spotted a parking space across the street from her house, I decided to wait. This time Mel would know what I intended to do in The End *before* I did it.

I spent a long time inspecting my bruises. Too long a time, because I nodded off as the weight of the last twenty-four hours gradually deflated my anger. When I awoke, early the next morning, I had slept through the night and was damn near frozen.

I uncorked and looked out my window to see the same single bulb holding down Melanie's fort. I crawled out of the car and began to loosen my back when someone slid up behind.

"What are you doing here?"

I whipped around, surprised I hadn't heard him approach. "You move quietly."

Therin shrugged. "An old Indian trick."

"I didn't think being an Indian thrilled you very much."

"It doesn't matter what I think. I'm an Indian and that settles it." He thrust his bony chin forward. "What are you doing in front of M's?"

I pushed his concern aside with a harsh voice. "I'll ask the questions. I want to know about the other night?"

"What about it?" Some confusion in his face.

"Where did you go after you left me?"

"I went home. Why?"

"Where is home?"

His round eyes were full of suspicion. "Why do you want to know?"

"Someone tried to kill me." A little exaggeration, but only after the fact.

He looked at me, suspicion replaced by disbelief. "Kill you? Why would anybody want to kill you?"

"I'd like to know that answer too." I kept hard eyes on him.

He seemed to draw into himself. "What does this have to do with me?"

"Just your little threat about an hour before I almost got run over."

He looked at me like I was crazy. "If I had the guts to kill someone, I'd have killed myself a long time ago."

I sighed. "Sad to say, Therin, I believe you."

A sudden look of fear crossed his face. "Is this why you're here? Is Melanie in some sort of danger?"

"She hasn't anything to do with this," I reassured him. "Doesn't even know it occurred. Therin, you say you'd rather be dead, but you obviously feel close to Melanie and she likes you a lot. Can't you take a hint?"

"What hint?" He looked at me like he had the night I'd first met him. As though he were expecting to be hit.

"Maybe you aren't as hateable as you think."

He grunted and averted his eyes. I opened the car door, then turned back around. "Do you know where Melanie is now, Therin?"

I didn't expect an answer, so I was surprised when he said, "She stayed at Jonathan Barrie's house. She spends holidays there."

I wondered whether he'd gone with her. "Where did you go?"

"I went to McDonald's. It doesn't have lines on the holidays."

# 24

I RUBBED THE CONDENSATION OFF THE WINDSHIELD and stared out at the bleak, silent neighborhood. Sleeping through a cold November night in a parked car was too similar to the alley mounds for comfort.

What had begun as an attempt to mine for bits of history had me lumbering like a stuck bull on the downside of a bullfight. Smart money said split. To return home, face Lou, and resume some semblance of ordinary. If junk food, drugs, television, and malls are ordinary.

Only it wasn't that easy. I took forever to get started, but once I did, I hated to let go. I wanted that truck driver. I just didn't have enough cheeks to keep turning. One slap needed answering.

I glanced into the rearview mirror, and knew I wasn't finished with The End. Megan's laughter pealed from inside my head, and I saw myself clinging to a mouth that bit me. I shook myself, and flushed the picture from my mind.

I also swore not to lose it with Blackhead. Either he had intentionally set me up, or the rundown had been an inadvertent offshoot of the hire. There was only one way to find out. It would test my new-found commitment to self-control.

I let myself into his building, went downstairs to the basement, and barged through Blackhead's unlocked door.

"Jesus Christ, man, you trying out for the Red Squad?" His tall, gangly body bent over, picking up his spilled breakfast of newspaper and pork rinds. He glared at me. "I oughta call the fucking cops. Watch them bust your ass." His hands full, he stood straight and faced me. "You're damn lucky I wasn't holding hot coffee or I *would* call the pigs."

Behind the hot words Emil's face was pale. Next time he'd remember to keep his door locked. "I should have knocked. But it's time for you to come up with the truth."

"The truth about what?"

"About the truck with its big fat tires kissing my ass." I lowered my voice, "Somebody has to answer for it, and I'm starting with you." The tire image sharpened my edge of anger.

He peered at me with a mixture of confusion and disgust. "What are you talking about? What the hell do I look like, anyway? Your personal punching bag?"

"You don't know what I'm talking about?" My voice was ice.

"Hell, no. I asked you for help, because twenty years ago you weren't a total asshole. Okay, I get it. Now you are." He put the pork rinds back down on the floor and stood shaking his head. "Damn, man, what call do you got busting in here? You're supposed to be history."

Any chance that Blackhead had been directly responsible for the 4×4 faded. He was scared, he was angry; but he wasn't guilty. And he was still running his mouth about his request for help.

Blackhead stared at me. "Are you high, man?"

I grinned, but couldn't get my teeth too far apart. "Two nights ago somebody tried to run me over."

"Whoever it was missed," he said glumly.

For a second my suspicion resurfaced, but the remark was just his pleasant personality. "Not by much, and only because he wanted to."

"Somebody tries to run you over, and you come here to fuck

with me?" Blackhead's eyes suddenly widened. "Oh no. Don't even think it."

I smiled into his concern. "Too late, Blackhead, I already have."

I'd tell him he was off the hook when the time was right. Maybe. He started to speak, but I cut him off with a wave of my hand. "If you don't want me to believe it was you, then you're going to help me discover who it was."

"Every time something happens to you you come after me." He sat back down in the chair and reached for the bag on the floor.

I kept silent, waiting him out.

"You didn't get a look at him, huh?" He fingered the rinds nervously, then put them down.

I wanted to hit him, but stayed very still. "A hooded sweatshirt chased me around in a 4×4. The truck had some sort of floodlight, either on the side or on top. It was dark, and I didn't get the plate. The tires came very close."

His mouth curled up in a tiny smile, and he asked, "What color was this truck?"

"Maybe silver and black, but I don't know. Everything happened fast. It was difficult to focus on the details."

He stood and turned his back. I walked up behind him, put my hand on his shoulder, and spun him around. He had a look of pure pleasure on his face. "Well, I didn't hear nothing, so I don't know what you want from me," he said.

"I want to know what's funny, Blackhead. Do you know who owns that truck?" I dug my fingers into his shoulder.

He yanked his shoulder out of my grasp. "Fuck no, man, I don't know who owns it. I was thinking what a lousy detective you are. You didn't even get the truck's color. You better not work on commission, like your fat friend."

He sat back down without his look of pleasure. "I want to know how a big, fat bleeding heart becomes a fucking fascist?"

"And I want to know about your drug business."

He was waggling his head "no" before I finished the sentence. "Why don't you get off my back? You're fucking obsessed. I'm starting to think you work for the Feds. Look around. Do I look rich? Jesus, you want to get high, ask."

I was tempted, but it wasn't the consumer side of the business that had my attention. Reluctantly, I backed away a couple of steps. "I'm not convinced you're clean, Emil."

"Look, asshole, I have no reason to mess with you. Except for doing the dope, I'm the law-abiding type. Why don't you leave? I want my breakfast, okay?"

"You can eat after you tell me about your dope business."

He groaned, "Here we go again ..."

I cut him off. "We don't go again, we go now."

"You act like you want to be the Drug Czar."

I moved a step closer, to tower over him. "We have a problem here. If it wasn't you, it was one of your business associates."

He shook his head again. "You're living in a fantasyland. I ain't important enough to have associates. Conspiracy theories went out with Squeaky Fromme. Hell, don't you think your so-called runover would worry me if you were right?"

"Look at me," I hissed, unmollified. "If you're so damn unimportant, you're going to tell me who is. I don't care if all you sell is powdered aspirin, I want to know who you buy it from."

He sensed the damage an impatient me might do. "You got to understand—I just deal fingers and quarters."

Selling joints for a living was barely curb-high from the gutter. "Who does your pieces?"

"Come on," he complained, "you're asking me to go out of business. I never did nothing to you, now I'm supposed to starve?"

I had a moment of irrational sympathy. "Okay, Emil, here's the deal. You give me the name and if you're clean, I won't give him yours."

My hard look silenced his protest. He rubbed his face, and said quickly, "Belchar, Tom Belchar. You happy?"

I walked around the room and found a pen and brown paper bag while Blackhead told me the address. I wrote down the information with Blackhead whining, "Please, man, don't mention my name, okay? I gotta make a living!"

I was already out the door, but I turned around and pointed to his sloppy crib. "You call this living?"

\*     \*     \*

I got to the car and stared at the brown bag. I had recognized the name. Tom Belchar had been one of the kids I'd known twenty years ago. From the same group as Peter, Emil, and Mel.

It wasn't hard to find his building. Getting to see him was. I was met by a five-year-old girl peeking up at me from under a latch chain when I knocked on Belchar's apartment door. She wore a ripped pair of pajamas crusted with grape jelly. I heard a television in the background, along with voices of other children.

"Is your daddy home?"

She put a finger to her lips, and said, "Shh, my Daddy is sleeping."

From the back of the apartment I heard a woman's loud whisper, "Grace, stop playing with the door, damnit."

"Is that your mother?" I asked.

Grace kept her finger on her lips and nodded silently.

"Could you ask her to come here?"

The little girl shut the door without a word. It was a welcome relief from the odor of grease frying in the over-hot, steamheated apartment. As I was set to knock again, the door rattled and swung a chain's width.

"It doesn't make a goddamn difference whether you people show up in the morning, or the middle of the night. We don't have any money neither time." Her eyes looked frightened and defiant at the same time, her sallow skin cemented to her bones.

"I'm not here to collect bills," I said.

Her look became guarded. "Who are you then? What do you want?"

Before I could answer, a kid's cry pierced the apartment. The woman turned quickly, calling in a hoarse whisper, "Shut up, damn you. How many times do I have to tell you not to raise your voice when your father is sleeping?"

She left me alone at the open door. I looked past the chain into the room. The place made Blackhead's apartment look kempt. Clothes and cheap plastic toys were strewn everywhere. I noticed a colorful metal top that reminded me of a Rebecca toy. I was grateful to have my memory interrupted by the woman's return.

"We're not buying anything," she said, squeezing the door against my foot.

"I'm not here to sell."

Her tone sharpened with annoyance. "Then why is your foot in my door?"

"I'd like to speak with Tom. I'm an old friend." It wasn't a total lie. When I worked The End Tom was everybody's friend. Talented, popular. If he had attended high school, and had come from a different neighborhood, he'd have been a candidate for "Most Likely To Succeed."

The woman shook her pinched face in a short vigorous burst. "Don't bullshit me. Tom don't have any old friends. Anyhow, friends don't stick their foot in the door."

"Well, 'friend' might be too strong a word. I knew him about twenty years ago."

She smiled bitterly. "You'd be better off with your memories."

"Can I speak with him?"

"Absolutely not. Are you a cop?"

"Absolutely not." I tried a smile but she wasn't having any. I paused, then asked again, "Why can't I speak to him?"

"Look, Mister, there's as much chance he'd belt me for waking him as there is of him talking to you. I ain't willing to take that chance." She suddenly looked down, and I followed her eyes. Holding on to her leg was a little boy. He only wore training pants. The woman shook him off her leg, and tapped his butt. "Get away from me. Go back and watch the TV. I'm busy."

She turned back to me and said, "I don't have time for this. The bastard works all night, sleeps all day, and I'm supposed to do everything around here myself. If you want to see Tom, do like everyone else and see him at the hotel." Her eyes clouded; she nervously picked at her cheek with red, chapped fingers. "He don't start work 'til eight but he likes it there better than here."

I didn't have the heart to keep trying. "Hotel?"

"The Leonard. In the Square."

I knew it. It's hard to miss a rundown, second-rate hotel in the middle of luxury. "What's he do?"

"I thought you knew him?" she said. "He plays the piano in the damn bar," she added miserably.

"What time will he get to the hotel?"

Her mouth twisted, and she laughed bitterly. "As soon as he can. He says he has to rehearse, but he means drink. No need to rehearse songs you've been playing five times a night for ten years, is there?"

I shrugged, thanked her, and turned. The door closed on my back and I left the building. Seeing Tom after all these years was not going to be fun. Standing on the stoop of a foul-smelling tenement, my dead daughter straining at the lid of the locked box of memories, wasn't too terrific either.

# 25

I WAS TIRED, BODY-SORE FROM SPENDING too many hours in the car, frustrated by my inability to speak with Belchar. Not yet ready to engage in another round of Slumlord versus the Bwana, I stopped at The Leonard.

Where I was the only person in the bar. The camphor-like smell of urinal disinfectant drifted from the restrooms. The plastic cover of a small pool table was pulled halfway off, exposing the table's dark green felt; I could see the cigarette burns from my seat. There was something comforting about the dark gloom of a tavern not yet filled with its patrons' anguish.

Eventually, a tall stocky man in a battered red waiter's jacket walked behind the oval formica. He nodded in my direction, and said, "We're not open." Then he winked, "What'll it be?"

You didn't have to tap kegs to know he was proposing an off-cash-register deal. Bartenders hate to put money in the box if they don't own the bar. I enjoyed his look of anticipation when I said, "Information."

"What kind of information?" He didn't bother to mask his greed.

"I want to know when Tom Belchar gets in."

"I got a bad memory."

I withdrew my wallet and handed him a five. "Throw in a bourbon. The answer is too easy for this."

He stuffed the five, yanked the short-waisted coat down over the top of his belly, and poured a shot. "He plays at eight, but he's usually here early."

"Why early?"

A sarcastic look and smile crossed his face. "He don't like kids."

I dug into my wallet again and came up with a couple more fives. I put one under my fingers. "Double if I like your answer."

Redcoat slid the bill out. "He meets with people." The man sounded envious.

"You just made a few extra bucks," I said, pushing him the five. "How does Belchar make his?"

The bartender's head bobbed from side to side. "Don't bother reaching for your wallet, buddy, I don't know. Ask him yourself."

I'd hit his limit. He wasn't going to tell me Belchar sold drugs, and I knew better than to press. I thought for a moment and came up sideways. "Is there anyone he regularly meets?"

"No one I want to see busted."

"I'm not asking about steadies. Someone who shows up once in a while, but doesn't hang around or stay for the show?"

I watched his dubious sense of loyalty battle with his greed. I yanked out two twenties. It was lucky I hadn't gone junking. Maybe I was doing it now.

He shrugged and said, "Some guy occasionally drops in. Drinks fucking Screwdrivers. Belchar calls him J.B."

I gave him the money, killed the shot, and felt the cheap alcohol set fire to my esophagus. "Are you sure?" I asked.

The bartender turned his back and walked away. Since he'd already pocketed the money, his loyalty was unexcelled. That was okay by me; I was done paying.

I sat at the bar for another few minutes trying to make sense of what I'd been told. The sense I made disturbed me enough to drive me through the door.

Outside the hotel, the day-after-Thanksgiving shoppers were out in force. I melded into the crowd, walking slowly toward the car. I felt a delicious moment of anonymity engulf me; then it slipped away as I approached my parking spot. Suddenly dizzy from morning whisky and lousy sleep, I hoisted myself on top of the fender. Once the dizziness passed, I slid down onto my feet and slipped another four quarters into the meter. Boots lived only a few blocks away. Right then I felt better about knocking on an empty apartment door than going home to company.

I dry-mouthed when I heard her voice respond to the buzzer. After an initial inclination to bolt, I managed to identify myself. On the elevator ride I cursed myself for not asking whether Hal was there. And, for imagining Boots wasn't.

She was, he wasn't. It was nice to catch a break. I walked in on her pouring two cups of coffee. She looked up and nodded, a grim smile across her face. "Have you been home yet?"

"What do you mean?" I was nonplussed; I didn't look much more wrinkled than usual.

"Your father-in-law is worried sick about you. He said you hadn't been home since yesterday. And you hadn't done too well the night before that."

I shrugged and drained my coffee cup. "I thought you were away. Do you mind if I take a shower?"

"Of course not. Why don't you call Lou and let him know you're all right." She walked toward the telephone adding, "I got back early."

I was already down the short hall to the bathroom. I turned around and looked out her wall-to-wall windows at the steady stream of cars cruising the Drive in front of the Esplanade.

"Did you hear me, Matt?" Boots asked, holding the phone in her outstretched hand. "Lou's worried."

"I heard you." I turned, stopped at the built-in hutch and grabbed a towel. "I'll be out in a second."

It took longer than that. As the hot water washed away the

grime and tension of the past few nights, I was filled with a physical weariness that occupied every molecular gap in my body: it was all I could do to lean against the wall of the shower and absorb the wet pelting onrush. I couldn't even think of a drug that might help.

Once again my spontaneity faced its cost; Boots was probably waiting to talk. I imagined her in the other room, saw myself hugging the shower wall, and couldn't guess what she was waiting for. There was nothing left.

The water turned cool before I finally pushed myself out. I dried off, and walked back into the living room dressed in my slacks and undershirt, the rest of my clothes in hand. Boots was sitting on the couch, the phone at her feet. "Reporting in?" I asked.

She ignored my crack and spoke quietly, without annoyance. "You could ask how he is."

I nodded in agreement. "Is there more coffee?"

She pointed to the sliver of walk-thru space that masqueraded as a kitchen. "Does that mean you want to know?"

I placed my clothes on a chair and poured the coffee from a silver container on the counter. "New?"

She smiled, though a troubled look flitted through her eyes. "Yes." Her smile disappeared but her voice remained soft. "I paid for it myself."

I kept my eyes on the cup. "I didn't ask that."

"Yes, you did. What's going on, Matt? You're fighting with everybody?"

I wasn't ready to admit the obvious. "Boots. I didn't bring up Hal, you did."

"I'm not just talking about us. Lou told me what happened yesterday. And he explained a little about what's been going on between the two of you."

I drank from my cup, and lit a cigarette. I reached for the ashtray. I always liked finding it clean. "It's not very complicated. I don't enjoy being squeezed. I especially don't like it when it happens in front of other people. People I have to live with. I ended up walking out on all of them."

Boots shook her head. "Not all of them, Matt. You're walking out on Lou."

I searched hard for some sound of reproach to justify my getting angry, but there was none. "What are you saying?"

"He's not doing well."

I felt my stomach lurch. "Is he sick? Do you know something I don't?"

"You don't want to know. He's not sick; he's lost."

"Lost?"

She moved across the room and stubbed her cigarette into the ashtray's gleaming surface. "He doesn't know what to do with his life now that Martha is dead. He probably wants to move here."

"Move here?" Boots had voiced the fear I'd been actively trying to obscure. Her words echoed inside me with an accuracy my double-clutched belly confirmed. Still, it was a truth I wanted to deny. "I don't believe that."

"Does it shock you? It shouldn't, really. You're all he has left for family."

I'd come here to avoid Lou, not to marry him. "Boots, you're being overdramatic. His whole life is in Chicago. The Democratic Party, everything."

"Matt, Richard Daley has been dead for a long time."

"But Boots ..." I protested without conviction.

"But Boots nothing." She walked back to her chair by the telephone. "Lou's glory days are gone, Matt. Gone since long before Martha's illness. She was his life in Chicago. Not politics, not friends, not even the track. Why wouldn't he want to move here?"

"Life hasn't exactly prepared me for family ties," I said weakly.

"Isn't that what you accuse me of?"

My existence had become a string of Hobson's choices. "How do you know all this?" I asked.

"Private detectives aren't the only people who can loosen tongues." She looked at me and grinned. "Lou kept calling me Shoe."

"He likes you."

Boots started to say something, stopped. "Why are you fighting with everybody, Matt?" she asked again.

I raised the coffee cup and put it back down, overcome by my earlier fatigue. I turned toward her, leaned against the counter, and shrugged helplessly. "I don't know. I'm tired, Boots, I'm just tired. I don't know what else to say. Nothing is right. We're not right. Lou and me aren't right, I'm not right." Then ran right out of words.

Boots rose, walked over to me, and took my hand. I followed her silently to the bedroom, where we lay down side by side. I shut my eyes but kept hold. She stayed next to me as I drifted into a depleted doze.

I sensed when she got up, and rolled over into a deeper sleep. When I opened my eyes, the daylight was gone and I was tucked under a puffy down comforter. The room was dark and it took me a moment to get my bearings. Once I realized where I was I took another moment to check my vital signs. I was alert, my body felt refreshed; I'd gotten a decent sleep.

The door to the bedroom opened and Boots waltzed through. "Sleeping Beauty awakens"—she hopped onto the bed—"before the kiss." She moved her head closer and I put my arms around her. I suddenly felt grateful for the comforter. My undershirt couldn't have kept out the cold.

Boots had switched from her baggy jeans, and now wore tight, tailored pants with a black silk blouse. I pulled her close; her tough, lean body felt good in my arms. "How come you changed?"

She laughed, pulled away, and sat on the bed. "Are you kidding? It's nighttime, Big Guy. What do you want to do for supper?"

"Supper? What time is it? I figured it was just another dreary afternoon."

"It's not afternoon, dear. We're talking seven here. We're talking famished."

I pulled the comforter over my head and toyed with the idea of moving. Tom Belchar came into my head. Tom Belchar could wait. "Baby, it's cold outside," I sang, my off-key growl muffled by the down-mixed-with-goose feathers.

"No one says we have to go out."

I poked my head out from under the cover. "You deliberately mistook my meaning," I accused.

"That's right." She smiled and jumped off the bed. "I'm telling you, boy, I'm hungry. When you only eat one meal a day, it becomes pretty damn important."

"Is that how you do it?"

"Do what?"

"Look so 'pretty damn' good?"

She gave me the finger and walked out the door. It took a moment or two to force myself out of bed, then I followed. "If it's this late, I can drink. Do you want anything?"

"Rum and something. Since when do your vices punch a clock?"

I fixed the drinks, and walked over to where she was busy at the pint-sized stove. "I can't understand how you survive in a kitchen that's skinnier than you."

She looked me in the eye as she took one of the glasses from my hand. "Are you making me an offer?"

I backed away.

She laughed. "Anyhow, you're a funny one to tout large kitchens. When's the last time you cooked anything?"

I felt relieved. "Hey, I cooked the other day."

"That's not what I heard."

"What did you hear?"

"I heard you ate, after watching everyone else cook. There's a difference."

I retreated into the living room and lit a cigarette. The ashtray contained more than a few lipsticked butts. Her afternoon hadn't been a garden stroll.

I looked out over the river lights and imagined I was looking at The End. It was impossible. The End was dark and squalid and on the other side of town. "I really made an ass of myself, didn't I?"

"Which time?"

"Let's not make these deliberate misunderstandings a way of life. What's for supper?"

She smiled at me, and turned her attention to the food. "Slices of roast beef, fried in olive oil with onions and peppers. If I'm only going to have one meal, it will be anything I want. Also, this dish is close enough to a steak sub for you to eat. Yes, you made an ass of yourself. But as usual, those who know you, worry about you. Just talk to them."

Dinner was good. Very good. We avoided mention of Hal, home, or any problem between us. The only uncomfortable moments came with her questions about my work in The End. I minimized my contact with Mel, and, blessedly, Boots didn't push.

"I noticed your arm when you had your shirt off."

"Turn you on?"

"Worry doesn't excite me. If you were leaving, and the truck-driver wants you gone, why don't you just stay left?"

"It's one thing if I make the decision ..."

She beat her chest theatrically with her fist. "Ain't gonna let no one drive me off my land, by golly," she drawled in a surprisingly good John Wayne. "Even if it ain't my land, and I do want to leave." She shook her head and said in her normal voice, "You are a stubborn fuck."

"Aren't you one foul-mouthed cowgirl? Listen, I'm in no rush to bust shoplifters."

"That I understand. Don't go back."

"What am I supposed to do? The building's not an option. Maybe I should drive a cab? I've done that before."

"Don't be an ass. Be a damn detective. At least when you're working the stubbornness is to good purpose."

"How am I supposed to get cases?"

"Talk to Simon."

"Forget it!"

"Sweetheart, if there's one thing you learn in Corporate America: you don't have to be friends to do business."

"You sound like Lou," I said and began to clear the table. I glanced at the clock on the kitchen radio and was surprised to read nine-thirty. "Speaking of business, I have to see somebody."

She was on her feet in a flash. "Oh no you don't. I don't care what we do"—she looked at my groin—"but we are doing it together."

Her eyes didn't put new ideas into my head, but they reminded me of what good ideas they were. But she was right about my stubbornness. I needed to talk with Belchar.

"Why don't you come with me? It won't take long and then we'll come back here." I had another thought. "Anyhow, I have to get my car."

"Where are you supposed to go?"

"I gotta talk with the piano player at the Leonard, and the car's right in front of there."

She was already looking for her shoes. "On one condition."

"What's that?"

"You dance a slow one with me."

WHEN BELCHAR'S WIFE TOLD ME he played the piano, I'd imagined an entire band. I'd imagined wrong. A small baby grand sat in the center of the tiny wooden dance floor. Tall stools were placed around the piano, ashtrays on its top.

The piano's stools competed with those at the bar for empty. Despite the few customers, the saloon was full of stale tear-stained smoke.

I looked around the room for someone resembling a musician but came up dry. We ordered our drinks, walked over to the piano, and sat. I hoped Belchar would get the message. It took about five minutes and a cigarette before he did. A tall, gaunt man, in a well-worn tuxedo, he wandered into the tavern from the restrooms' shadow. He looked at the bartender, who pointed in our direction. This wasn't the Tom Belchar I remembered.

The emaciated tux sauntered to the piano, and slid onto the

bench. He nodded toward an empty glass in front of his face. "Cash or trade buys you what you want to hear." He ran his hands lightly across the keyboard for emphasis, but he kept his face down.

If this was Belchar, he used as much as he sold. And I didn't mean marijuana. His cheeks were sunken; his hairline started at the top of his head. He reminded me of Pacino's partner in *Dog Day Afternoon*. Still, there was something familiar about him—maybe the light touch of his fingers on the piano keys. I remembered the hang-out nights in The End when we listened to Tom play. But now was a thousand piano playings later. And more than a few too many clubs, pubs, and taverns to be sure.

The waitress arrived with his drink and set it down. Without looking at either of us, he raised his eyebrows and said, "Thanks. What do you kind people wish to hear?"

"I want to hear whether you're Tom Belchar."

He looked up and stared at Boots. "What does the lady want to hear?"

Before I could respond Boots piped up, "'Don't Get Around Much Anymore.'"

His eyes went back to the ivory. "You don't look old enough to like Ellington, lady," he mumbled, as Duke's opening notes filled the room.

"I'm old enough," I said. "Are you Belchar?"

Without looking up he said, "Are you the guy who came to the house looking for me?" He seemed completely disinterested.

"Yes."

"You want more?" He glanced at us as Boots nodded, then segued into another melody. It brought a smile to Boots' face.

From the bar, a voice called out, "Christ, get into the twentieth century, fella."

Belchar grimaced and replied, "Paying customer here, Captain."

"I don't want to get you in trouble," Boots said.

"Lady, trouble is when I play 'Send in the Clowns' for the tenth time."

"You're really good," Boots said.

"Thank you, ma'am." He kept his eyes down, but nodded his head in my direction. "How come you look familiar?"

Before I could respond he began shifting back and forth between "I've Got a Crush on You" and "I'm Just a Lucky So and So." Gershwin and the Duke. Boots looked delighted.

"Jenny said you were an old friend. I don't have old friends. I figured you for another dun, but now I don't. Who are you and what do you want?" He suddenly brought the music to a close, and drained his drink. I signaled for another round.

"I'm Matt Jacob. We knew each other twenty years ago."

"Matt Jacobs, huh?"

"Jacob. Without the 's.' You knew me as 'Jake.' I was a community organizer in The End."

He screwed up his face. "Maybe I remember you, I don't know. It's five kids and one hellacious bitch later. That's a long time to remember anything."

"Well, you knew me." I had counted on his remembering.

"I believe you. Like I said, you look familiar. What other songs you like, lady?"

"Play anything you want. It all sounds good," Boots said.

He began to play a show tune. I'd have to tip Charles to the place. It had been a long time since Boots and I had fun together. Part of me wanted to leave the hunt alone, sit back, and enjoy the night. But, like the lady said, I was a stubborn fuck. "We're not really here for the music."

"I didn't think so, but I'm not in the market for an organizer."

I laughed. "That's okay. I'm out of the business."

"What business are you in now?" He raised his head and his eyes followed a group of people who had noisily entered the place. I hoped they would stay at the bar. It'd be even tougher to question him in a crowd.

"I want to know about drugs," I bludgeoned.

Boots leaned away from the question, and Tom stared at me, though his song didn't falter. "You don't look like a meth head."

Well, we knew his diet. "I'm not."

His eyes were back on the ivory. "You a cop?"

"No."

"Didn't think so." He slipped back into Ellington.

"I'm a private detective and I'm trying to find someone related to your side job. No Law involved, not even a client. It's personal business."

"A private cop, huh? I didn't think any kind of cop could catch a pretty girl." His hands swung into "A Pretty Girl Is Like a Melody."

I chuckled. "I'm not so sure I caught her."

"He's not so sure he wants to," Boots amended.

A woman from the party at the bar stumbled over. It was clear she had passed the midpoint of her night's festivities. She pushed her very soft, very uplifted pale white breasts close to Tom's face as she stuffed a rolled-up bill into the glass. "How 'bout 'Send in the Clowns'? Do you know that one?" she slurred.

Tom made his fingers work the song—his touch weighed heavier by automatic pilot. Unfortunately, the lady wasn't ready to let me go back to work. She turned to Boots and asked, "Can I dance with him, honey? He looks large enough for two." She rocked her hips at me, and I wanted to hide under my seat.

"He just looks big on the outside," Boots replied sarcastically. "You know what I mean, don't you?" She Groucho'd her eyebrows, and winked lewdly.

Tom's chuckle brought a wobbly glare from the woman. He quickly dipped his head and schmaltzed the song. The lady decided not to take offense.

Instead, she clasped her arms around her bosom and began swaying with herself on the dance floor. A man with a string tie and cowboy hat walked over and stuck another bill in Tom's glass. "Play that tune again, champ."

Tom nodded, waited until the cowboy locked steps with the woman's sway, and smiled toward Boots. "Are you a friend of his?" He nodded toward me. "Or are you a private cop too?"

"Friend. Why do you work here? You're a really good musician."

"Good ain't all it takes."

I found myself growing impatient, but stayed smart enough to keep still. The vibes between Boots and Tom were better than any I could produce.

Boots shook her head. "Look, I know the music business sucks, but you're talented."

Tom laughed bitterly. "Sometimes things don't work out the way you figure."

"That's for sure," Boots agreed.

I was about to demand what she meant when Tom continued, "I got married, had a couple of kids, then had some more. That Catholic thing can really screw up a career."

The dancers were done and Tom slipped back into the Forties. "You know how it is, gotta work to keep all them mouths fed." He looked at me, then back to Boots. "Your friend could probably tell you why I work here."

"He can sell a little dope on the side," I supplied.

"You got it," Tom said. "What do you want to know about? And who turned you on to me?"

"I'm looking for someone who tried to run me out of The End with a 4×4. I figure it was drug-related."

"Why do you figure that?" Belchar kept his eyes fixed on the ivory.

"My ex-client deals," I shrugged. "No other reason."

Tom stopped playing and looked at me. "Where I live nobody's got reason to run you out of anywhere. If someone really tried to scare you off, you're reaching higher than me. Us little shits just say, 'Thank you.'"

"The guy that started me on this is just a little shit."

A smile curled the corners of his thin lips. "The End, dope, a little shit, me." He shook his head. "What the hell were you doing working for Emil Porter?"

Before I could answer someone from the bar bellowed for music. Belchar began to tongue-in-cheek "Feelings." Boots was right, he really was good.

"What makes you think I'm talking about Emil?" I asked.

He glanced up at me. "The End is a small place. Those that collect on the bottom know each other."

I enjoyed his music though I wasn't ready to take him at his word. "Maybe the Leonard is getting too small for your part-time job."

He wagged his head, and grimaced. "It wouldn't matter." He sounded wistful. "I just make enough to use. Believe it or not, I like music better than drugs."

His head dipped again, and he murmured in a quiet voice, "But I like drugs better than everything else. Your information is lousy. I got no reason to run anyone out of anywhere. No matter what Emil told you."

"The bartender said you do time with someone named J.B. That lousy too?"

"That's right." Belchar's Adam's apple bobbed in his throat. "You gave the afternoon greedhead money, he had to tell you something."

It was his first lie. And he knew I knew it. I signaled for three for the road as Belchar mumbled something I couldn't hear. "What did you say?" I asked.

He kept his eyes closed, but talked louder. "What's this really about?"

"I told you. I want to know who doesn't like me—and why."

"Me too," he nodded. "What did Emil say that sent you this way?"

"You were his dealer."

He burst into muffled laughter; the music stopped midstream. The bar's customers reacted with scattered applause. Tom stopped laughing, looked at Boots, grimaced and shrugged.

"What's so funny?" I asked.

He went back to his playing. "I don't sell dope to Emil. He has you chasing your tail. You oughta ask him why."

I drained my drink and waved my hand for another. My mind drifted to my afternoon's match for the initials "J.B." I didn't like my hunch but, in its own way, it made for a perverse set of possibilities.

I drank while Boots and Tom talked about the great music of the Forties. They reviewed every composer and major musician of the decade. It was disconcerting and a little exciting not to have known about Boots' interest. The excitement urged me to take her home. All the while Tom's hands rippled over the keys, lilting and sweet; Belchar was having fun.

Before they started dissecting the Fifties, I rattled my keys. Boots reluctantly gathered her things. Tom suddenly stopped playing, but the noise in the bar had grown and nobody noticed. He stood and shrugged in Boots' direction. I began to thank him when he volunteered, "I wasn't kidding before. There really is no J.B. The afternoon man doesn't like me very much."

He stopped my response with a wave of his hand. "If you do get upstairs, try not to use my name, okay? I don't like stealing the old lady's food money for my drugs."

I almost told him I'd use any name I damn well wanted, but he'd taken the worry lines out of Boots' face. I closed my mouth and nodded. We left accompanied by the sounds of "The Party's Over," but I felt as if it had just begun. We walked to my car hand in hand while I wondered quietly about the "good" social worker and my opportunity to kick Blackhead's ass. I didn't even get angry about the parking tickets stuck on the car.

# 27

WE'D JUST LANDED IN BOOTS' APARTMENT when she said, "I don't understand the dance in your step."

"Oh shit, I completely forgot about the slow one. I'm sorry."

"I'm not talking about that. I've seen you get parking tickets before. You're usually insulted that you don't get a free ride, like the clergy."

The thought of standing in front of a congregation of well-dressed burghers amused me. "More like an Avenging Angel than a Priest." My eyes danced over the river and the lights below. "God, this room is wonderful," I added.

I could hear Boots move around the bedroom. "You seem awfully pleased about the conversation with Tom," she called.

"I am."

"Why?"

"I've finally caught Blackhead in an outright lie."

175

Boots appeared at my side wearing a midnight-blue satin night-gown. I felt a rush of desire flood through my body. I lit a cigarette and pulled the joint case from the wall-hatch where I had left it.

"Tom lied to you about not recognizing those initials." She stared at my face to see if the news would startle me.

"You caught it too?"

She smiled. "Honest men make lousy liars. I still don't understand why you're in such good humor. You walked out of there with no more facts than when you walked in?"

"A few more. Blackhead's lie, Belchar's cover for J.B. Not much, but a beginning. Mostly a confirmation that things aren't what they seem. Now I can pull at the edges until it takes shape."

Boots shook her head. "I'd think that would make you crazy?"

"Not when I have cards to play. I have an idea about those initials."

She raised her eyebrows and waited.

"Jonathan Barrie. Well placed, and has a young musician friend who travels. Remember, Barrie was the guy who took in the girl after her brother Peter was killed. Also, Blackhead hates him, and that might mean something."

"Isn't Barrie the community leader?"

"Yup."

"That doesn't slow you down?"

"Too cynical for you?" Before the sentence was finished, I felt a sudden sinking sensation in my gut. Melanie wasn't gonna be thrilled to have Jonathan in my crosshairs.

Boots climbed all over my decline. "What's the matter, Matt?"

"Nothing." I chose my next words carefully. "This Barrie seems like a decent guy, that's all. He took the girl in, and gave her a real shot."

"The girl?"

"Melanie Knight. Peter's sister. I've mentioned her."

"More than once."

"What's that supposed to mean?" I asked sharply.

Boots' tone was even. "You keep calling her a girl, but she's a woman now."

"Twenty years is a long time," I agreed blandly.

I sensed that Boots had more to say, but she deliberately stayed quiet, pointing to the dope. I quickly pulled a joint and fired up. When I handed it to her, she took it with a gentle smile. I ran my hand along her satined side. "No mistaking you for a girl ..."

"No more talk, please?" she asked.

I nodded. We kissed in front of what felt like the whole world. I took her hand and led us to the bedroom.

Afterward, while we lay in bed quietly smoking, I asked, "What am I supposed to do about Lou?"

Boots sat up and pulled the covers just over her nipples. I felt myself stir; she looked so damn French. "I think you are going to have to talk with him. Tell him about your problems with family. It won't surprise him."

Her words left me as unsettled as before. "I don't know what to do," I said glumly.

"You don't have to know. You just have to talk." Her eyes lit up. "Who knows? Once you're wired in, maybe you'll like it."

"Wired in, huh? Ma Bell talk?"

She whacked me on the top of my head as I burrowed under the comforter to nibble on her belly. "I have to practice wiring in," I said, between tiny bites.

This time our lovemaking was slow and languid. At one point I jumped out of bed, raised the thermostat level, and tossed the comforter to the floor. We sipped bourbon and toked dope between kisses and caresses. Sex became a lazy dream on a warm Caribbean beach ... her body warm and open, our actions tender and loving. When we finished I lay on my back, spacey, with Boots tucked into the crook of my arm. I dumped my cigarette, and shifted into spoons.

But the mood died in the morning when I awoke to Boots' talking on the telephone. She wasn't dressed for Saturday morning cartoons. I watched her gently place the receiver back in its cradle. When she turned in my direction she appeared startled to see me.

"I didn't hear you get up," she said. "There's coffee in the kitchen."

"Thanks, I'll be out in a second." I ducked back into the bedroom, and pulled on my clothes. If I didn't change them soon they'd walk home without me. I filled the tiny kitchen as I helped myself to caffeine. The atmosphere was tense.

"Hal, huh?" I glanced in Boots' direction, and she nodded. "No surprise," I said glumly.

A look of anger darted across her face. "There you go again."

I sipped at the coffee. There was something familiar about this scene. "I didn't hear myself give you any shit."

"It's in your voice, your attitude."

I raised my shoulders uncertainly. "What do you want my attitude to be?"

"A little more honest."

"What's that supposed to mean?" I said, suddenly defensive.

"I think you know. At first I thought it was only that ugly neighborhood, and your memories of Megan. Now I think it's all of that, and also the Knight woman."

A jolt of guilt ripped through me; I started to protest. Boots wouldn't let me. "Matt, please, I don't want you to say anything."

She walked over to a wooden chair, pulled it out from the wall, and sat down. I refilled my cup, spilled a little, and found a napkin. I waited while she found her words.

"Every time you talk about this case, your voice changes when you mention Melanie Knight. Your attitude about Hal has to do with you, not me." She blinked her eyes rapidly, then turned her face away. "I can handle things, if you'll just be honest. But not if you take your hypocrisy out on me."

Guilty defensiveness triggered my denial. "How come every time we get into a fight it's because of me? I didn't call you this morning, Hal did. I didn't expect you to get dressed up, Hal did. I expected us to hang out together. You interpret everything I say the way you want, then blame me for the hard times." I waved my hands. "Don't you think your theories are just a little too pat?"

I walked out of the kitchen and glowered at her as she stood and walked around the room gathering my stuff. The dismissal just annoyed me more. "What time does the Hal Show begin?"

There were tears in her eyes as she handed me my jacket. "I'm not trying to analyze you," she said quietly. "I'm trying to make sense of what's happening between us. I thought since we had a good night we could talk without the bullshit. But this morning you're still doing the same thing."

"You say 'us,' but just talk about me. You don't say a word about Hal."

Boots walked to the door and opened it. "What I'm talking about has nothing to do with Hal."

I didn't move. "It never does. That's what *I'm* talking about. You say you don't want to marry him, but you wear him like a damn shield." The speech diffused most of my anger, and I walked the rest of my guilt to the door.

There was a doubting look on Boots' face, but she took my hand once I was in reach. "I can't stand the same thing happening over and over. You're wrapped up with the case. Find the damned driver and finish with The End. That way we'll both have time to think."

She squeezed my hand and, when I lifted my eyes from the carpet, she was crying. I nodded awkwardly, caught in my own unhappiness. Boots finally let go of me, gently closed the door, and relieved us both of our immobilized misery.

I took a long slow boat to the car. She was right about one thing: I wanted to find that driver. The hunt had become a reprieve from making decisions.

Momentarily I thought I'd caught another reprieve when I got inside my apartment and found Lou gone. But relief was quickly replaced by the lure of action when I saw Jonathan Barrie's name and telephone number with the word "urgent" alongside the name, scrawled in Lou's sloppy handwriting.

The line was still busy on my third try when the door opened and Lou entered. I nodded but got busy dialing. Right then I had more to say to J.B. than to Lou.

He said, "I was worried, Matty."

"I heard, Boots told me. There was no reason, I was fine."

"She said you were working on the case."

I listened to the busy signal, replaced the receiver, and motioned toward the bedroom. Lou followed me in. "I thought you were quitting," he said.

"Things change. I'm up to my eyeballs." I sniffed. "I need a shower."

"You need to burn your clothes."

I grinned as I peeled them off my body. "A wash will probably do."

"Where are you going to bury them until you get around to a wash?"

"Lou, you're insulting my housekeeping."

"No, boychik, I'm insulting you." He said it with a smile, but he was upset. I stayed silent rummaging through the drawers for something to wear.

"I think we need to *shmooze*," he said quietly.

I kept pulling out clothes and stuffing them away. "Okay, okay, I'll do a wash."

"I don't mean about that."

I finally found usables, and threw them on the bed. "Look, I know I acted stupidly the other day. I'm sorry if I spoiled the party."

Lou lowered his bulk into the chair which creaked but held. "I don't give a damn about the party. I don't like the fighting between us."

"I don't like it either, Lou." I felt foolish standing there naked.

"That's why we need to sit and talk," he said.

He was right, but I wasn't ready. "This isn't a good time for me. Did Barrie say anything else?"

"No, but he sounded very upset." A look of annoyance crossed his face. "It's been difficult to find a good time for us, Matt."

"I know, I know," I conceded. "But now is really bad. I have to see this guy."

"I'm leaving in the morning, boychik."

I felt pulled when I wanted to push. The image of the truck's tires, and, oddly, Belchar's dirty kids, hit me and I rushed to placate him. "We'll talk tonight, I promise. Try to understand, two nights ago somebody tried to run me over. Now I have a lead to follow."

His face was set, his body stiff and uncomfortable in the chair. "You've been dodging me since I got here."

"Lou, didn't you hear me?"

"I heard you. Did you hear me?"

I started out of the room. "We're not getting anywhere now. Let me clean up at least, okay?" I continued to the bathroom and hoped he'd nodded yes.

When I came out, Lou was nowhere in the apartment. I pushed my misgiving into a corner of my head and dialed Jonathan's number. It was still busy so, after a couple of hits on my pipe, I quickly dressed. Halfway out the door I decided to wear the gun.

The hunt had generated an enthusiasm that left me engaged in something larger than my separation from Boots or my confusion about Lou. I still didn't know what I was engaged in, but I did know it felt terrific to work again as a living, breathing detective.

# 28

IT WAS DARRYL HART WHO HAD RUN OUT OF AIR.

Barrie met me at the door, his eyes red and puffy. He wore a pair of khaki twills and another wool cardigan, its elbow patches rubbed raw. He blurted out his message before I got to the top of the outside stairs. For a moment we just stood there. Jonathan worked to hold back tears while I, once I registered the name and digested the news, wondered why Barrie had called. But the November cold finally penetrated my jacket and I nodded my way through the door.

"What do you mean 'dead'?" I never let surprise spoil the quality of my questions. We stood in a long muted-pastel hallway as the "D" word hung heavy in the air.

Jonathan's mouth opened, but he was smart enough to ignore me. He motioned, then walked us through a misshapen doorway on the left-hand side of the hall. The opening led into a small dark room dominated by a modern free-standing, self-contained fireplace, its embers an empty threat to the chill.

Jonathan shrugged me toward the furniture, and I walked through stacks of magazines and books while he knelt beside the fireplace and rekindled the flame. His back gave me a few moments to look around the rest of the room.

Away from the fireplace's black enamel ugly, and the stack of New England logs, the odd tomblike room wasn't half bad. A couple of Pollock repros, naives, and an enormous number of books lined all available wall and floor. Their warmth softened the cavelike atmosphere, especially after the fire cast a warm glow over the comfortable second-hand furniture. I looked around and noticed there were no windows.

Barrie caught my wonder. "Strange about the windows, isn't it?" He turned back to check on the fire. "Don't know what this room was originally used for. I discovered it when I renovated. Much too big for a closet." He seemed relieved to make small talk.

I could wait. "Discovered it?"

He knelt and pushed at the fire with a long metal poker. "Yes. I stripped the hallway down to its bones and found this odd little doorway. Here we are, one serious urban archeology dig later."

He stood, turned toward me and planted his feet, his knuckles bloodless where he gripped the iron. "The police are calling it an accident."

I remained cautious. I had been used too many times recently to simply climb right in. "Calling what an accident?"

He took a deep breath, walked to the couch, and sank into its corner. The metal stick half thudded, half clanged as Jonathan dropped it onto the small Oriental throw and the floor. "Darryl was found drowned in Quarry's End."

I felt my stomach fall as if I'd been dropped into a hall of distorted mirrors. Barrie plunged forward while I forced my shocked bewilderment into the background.

"The police say it was an accident or suicide. Darryl had two ounces of cocaine in his pocket. According to them, if it had been a sour drug deal, the coke wouldn't have been there." He put his hands to his head. "When I tried to tell them about Peter's death they were polite but patronizing."

"Patronizing?" I trod softly, the twenty-year echo loud enough.

"They invited me downtown to see the numbers. A ton of people have died in that quarry in the last twenty years. They said it was coincidence." He opened both hands. "I'm sure plenty of people have died there, but this was no coincidence."

"Why not?"

He looked at me with a ravaged face. "The two people I planned to live with die in the same way in the same place?"

Planned to live with? The look between Barrie and Darryl in the butcher block bar flashed into my head. My nerves turned kinetic, though a calmer voice prevailed. "I didn't know you were going to live with Darryl?"

He reached into his sweater and came out with his blue-packaged cigarettes. I grabbed for my own. Jonathan leaned across the couch to an overloaded end table and found a deep amber ashtray. He placed it on the floor between us and sat back up. "We loved each other."

I couldn't stop my mouth. "Did you love Peter the same way?" A *New York Post* picture of a depraved Midwestern social worker showing police his burial sites steamed through my mind.

Jonathan stared at me open-mouthed. "You never found out about my relationship with Peter, did you?"

"Nothing more than what you told me. I guess you didn't tell me everything." I was surprised at my coolness. Despite the shock of Darryl's death and its similarity to Peter's, I wasn't ready to white-coat Barrie.

His expression didn't look any better, but a small ironic smile played at his lips. "I was certain you had discovered my relationship with Peter and could understand why I'm so upset." He reached forward, stubbed his cigarette into the ashtray, and at once lit another.

I finished mine and did likewise. "You thought wrong," I said. "But I'm here now." I left little doubt as I took my leather and placed it on the floor.

Jonathan stared at the gun but made no comment. When he met my eyes some of his strength had returned. "I lied to you when I said I'd moved into The End after Peter's death. I moved into the neighborhood because of Peter. I was a cruiser; he worked the street. He made his money selling his body to suburban men in big cars—like me."

I started to interrupt, but he waved me quiet. "Just wait. Before you start judging, you ought to know what you're condemning."

"I haven't condemned anything yet."

"Don't kid yourself. I've been down this path enough to know it's one-way." He sounded resigned. "Peter hustled since he'd been ten. He was fifteen when we met and no amount of smoothness could hide, at least from me, the desperation of his life." He bowed his head and said quietly, "It wasn't very different from my own.

"I grew up in the Forties and Fifties"—he raised his head and met my eyes—"when growing up gay was worse torture than now. A world of locked doors, fear, denial. By the time I was twenty, the hiding had become self-hate. By thirty, the hate played out in highway rest areas, public restrooms, and backseats of cars. Anonymous sex was the most someone like me could hope for."

He took a deep drag and flicked his ashes toward the bowl. "By the time I was thirty-five, cruising had nothing to do with pleasure. Sex was simply a way to forget about my life."

I couldn't keep my doubts, or my prejudice, quiet. "Look, Jonathan, I didn't come here to learn about your sex life. I came here because your name came up in a conversation about drug-dealing. You tell me two boys you fucked died the same way, one with coke in his pocket. Sounds like I'm at the right address."

His face turned red. "Whoever connected me with drugs is a damn liar! Whatever my sexuality, I am not about the business of destroying lives." His eyes scratched at my face. "You can think what you damn well like!"

"I think you've run drugs for twenty years. You used Peter until you were through with him, then did the same with Darryl."

He was on his feet instantly. "You filthy lunatic! You're disgusted by my relationships so you turn me into a sick, murdering queer! Someone like you might really make me kill. Just get the hell out of here!"

He stood over me, panting heavily, his eyes full of scorn. I let the moment ride and pushed the pieces around the board. "Sit down, Jonathan. I believe you."

He debated with himself, but returned to the couch.

"I'm not gay-bashing," I said. "It's you I'm having trouble with."

Jonathan met my angry stare. "Me and everything you ever heard about old gay men and young boys." He tossed his head and snorted. "I told you this was a one-way street. But I'll try it anyhow. You know what happens to pretty boys, don't you? Well, Peter was approaching a hustler's middle age. If anything, our relationship kept him out of jail. And, frankly, I don't know who was the benefactor to whom. My relationship with Peter taught me that when you care about someone and they appreciate you for it, you have less time to hate yourself." He looked away. "More time to learn to love."

Jonathan's face sagged as he stood up and walked to the fire. From my seat he appeared to be embraced by the flames.

His bone-marrow honesty was compelling, loosening my ties to the Moral Majority. I knew the score in The End, if not the play-by-play. I still didn't know what the hell I was involved in, but Jonathan no longer reminded me of someone from the newspapers. "Sometimes power gets confused with love," I said.

He stepped around a short stack of books and wearily sat back down. "Yes, it does. And I'm sure there was some of that between us. But don't discount the awareness and strength Peter brought to the relationship." He read the expression on my face. "Don't look so dubious. The street taught Peter plenty, despite his years.

"If our difference in age and stature had become destructive I would have done what was needed. You see, Matt, I could be honest and do right by Peter. He had been nothing but abused his entire life. I could give to him. To both of them. Three lives were going to be better off. How many relationships, of any sort, can you say that about?"

I tried hard to smell bullshit, but couldn't. Still, Jonathan had had plenty of time to twist his theories under the lights. I hadn't lost my skepticism, just its fire. "So say I buy it?"

He waved his hand. "There's been too much blood under the bridge for me to sell you anything."

"That's an interesting expression."

He looked as if he'd been slapped. Talking about Peter had given him relief from the present.

"Did Darryl deal drugs?" I asked.

He sat back in his seat, his anger seeping into confusion. "Not that I knew."

"You had suspicions?"

He shook his head. "Have, not had."

"Go on."

"I told you. The police found him with cocaine."

"You didn't know anything about him selling?"

He almost got angry again but checked himself. "I knew he sometimes had small quantities. That's all." His hand swiped at the air in front of his chest.

"But now you wonder? What did Darryl do for money?"

"He was a musician."

"Around here?"

"Here and Florida."

I shook my head and shrugged.

"It's easy to see today," he said, low, bitterness in his tone. "But I never had cause to question." He looked at me defiantly. "And even if he did deal, he deserves justice."

Justice. I wanted justice for my roll in the snow, Jonathan for Darryl's death, perhaps Peter's as well. I didn't hold out much hope for either of us. "How did the police get your name?"

He cocked his head. "A friend in the department who knows about my life. It was a courtesy."

"No one asked you to come down and identify the body?"

"No. Does that mean anything?"

"It means they probably found family."

He looked disconcerted and I watched him squirm unhappily in his seat.

I got up and looked over his shoulder at the fire. "You didn't know he had family?"

"He told me they were all dead."

I shrugged and walked to the fireplace. The flames had settled into a small, steady crackling, and I thought about throwing on another log, but it would probably put the damn thing out. "Sounds like there was a lot you didn't know."

I lit a cigarette. "You may not have known about his dealing, but you're too smart not to imagine Darryl doing it." I waited.

Jonathan read my mind because he joined me at the fire and picked up the tongs. "Last night I began to imagine a lot of things."

I walked away from him. I didn't think he dealt—or murdered. Darryl probably used Jonathan's initials for cover. It would be easy enough to find out whether J.B. translated into D.H. What wasn't easy was Barrie's relationships. "What did Darryl usually drink?"

"Drink? Screwdrivers, why?"

I ignored his question, walked over to a mini refrigerator, and opened the door. Six beers lined the back wall. I took one out and twisted the cap off. "You want?"

He looked over at me from the fireplace. "Thanks."

I opened another, walked back to the now blazing flames, and handed him his bottle. The fire licked the outside of the black enamel as we stood red in its light. "Why did you call me?" I asked, though I already knew the answer.

He looked thoughtfully at me, doubt in his eyes. He closed his eyes, then held the beer against his cheek. "I want you to find Darryl's killer."

# 29

I SHOOK MY HEAD, WATCHING HIS FACE TENSE. "Can't get beyond the sex, can you?" he asked bitterly.

"I don't know," I answered, running my hand through my hair. "Face to face is different than reading about it."

"More or less titillating?" He gave a sharp, humorless chuckle.

I hunched up my shoulders, and walked away from the heat of the fire. "The other night someone tried to scare me out of The End with a 4×4. I came here thinking it was you." I overrode his interrupt. "Whatever my feelings about this conversation, you're off the list."

"Then the only reason you have is my sexuality."

I shrugged again. "When you put a live person into a word like 'pederast' it loses an edge, but I don't know if it loses any of its meaning. Mostly it's none of my business."

I gathered my thoughts slowly. "You dropped off my list, but Darryl climbed on. I think he adopted your initials for his drug cover."

189

His eyes searched my face from across the room. "You agree with the police?"

I nodded. "Mostly."

"Mostly?"

"Either they really do believe it was an accident, or they think it's drug-related. Easier on them if it's an accident."

"Don't you think the similarity to Peter's death a little too coincidental?"

"We're not talking back-to-back here, Jonathan. There's twenty years between the deaths; and the major coincidence is you." That is, if I discounted Blackhead's story. Or understood it.

"I don't mean you had anything to do with their accidents. As unlikely as the coincidence seems to you, the cops are probably on the money."

He didn't want to believe it. "You don't think it was suicide?" I asked gently.

He met my stare. "No, I don't. I would have known if Darryl was that depressed. He wasn't." He shook his head. "Darryl didn't kill himself."

"You seem awfully certain about someone you've just discovered had a secret life?"

Barrie was more emphatic. "Maybe I didn't know everything about his life, but I'd have known if he was suicidal." Jonathan lifted the poker toward the fire, then smashed it hard on the rug. "There's no damn reason for him to be dead!"

"Is there ever, for anyone? Jonathan, it was probably an accident."

"You mean he was too high to save himself?" Jonathan said sarcastically. "What the hell was he doing there? Peter I could understand. It was summer and that's where they went to swim. But it's winter now, or damn close."

"Grams to dollars, Jonathan, he was there to sell dope. He might have fallen in before he made the sale. The water's near freezing, and if he hit his head ..."

Still grabbing the poker, he leaped to his feet. For an instant I thought he was going to attack me, but he turned, moved close to the fireplace, and whacked at the flames. "It's fucking cold in here," he muttered between hits.

I gave him a little time before I walked to his side and took the iron from his clenched fist. At first he resisted. "How many times do you have to watch your life fall apart?" he asked helplessly.

I shrugged; it was a familiar question. "As many times as it does." Zen Matt.

We stood quietly as the flame sucked at the dismembered carcass of the sacrificed tree. Occasionally a spark would fly up, and we'd flinch, but, other than the fire's crackling and the infrequent hiss of steam, all was silent.

"I don't understand why you won't at least look into the coincidence?" he finally said.

"I don't want to investigate Peter's death." I looked at him. "For reasons we've already discussed."

"That was before Darryl's death."

"Darryl's *accident* is twenty years later," I reminded.

He dropped the poker on the floor and walked, head down, back to the couch. "That's what Melanie kept saying."

"What exactly does Melanie know?" My voice bleated harshly.

Jonathan didn't bother with my tone. "She's always known that Darryl and I were lovers. I told her about his death and my problem accepting the police's version." He shook his head. "I couldn't push it with her. Quarry's End brings up enough as it is."

"Does she know about you and Peter?"

He seemed unruffled, though concerned by my sharpness. "To Melanie, Peter was a saint. She was shattered by his accident. He had somehow managed to keep his hustling from her, and I wasn't going to throw dirt on his life." He rubbed his face. "I didn't want to tell her."

"About you or him?" My hostility had reawakened; I was suddenly suspicious about Barrie's relationship with Mel.

He remained calm in the face of my attitude. "About either of us. Mostly I was concerned about her. Peter's drowning left a hole inside Melanie that she filled in destructive ways. I wanted to give her a chance to find herself. I had planned on living with both of them, you know, not just Peter."

He seemed to be looking inside himself. "It's impossible for people to understand that, despite the sex, my relationship with Peter was primarily paternal. My relationship with Melanie has only been paternal."

"'Paternal' is a hard word to swallow."

He smiled resignedly. "Then don't swallow. All I can tell you is what I know."

He ignored my visible discomfort. "Until Darryl, I simply avoided enduring relationships. For a long time I was afraid Melanie might interpret closeness with anyone else as abandonment." A frown passed across his face as he considered something in the past, but all he said was, "There were incidents which reinforced my fears."

He wandered into idle thought, then came back to the conversation. "Don't get me wrong, I've never viewed my years with Melanie as a sacrifice. Our relationship embodies what Peter had only promised. I love her more than I could have imagined loving anyone. She supplies a center to my life I hadn't thought possible. It hasn't been a sacrifice, it hasn't been altruism. It's been an honest, loving relationship."

"Was Darryl the reason she left home?"

"Not at all. I thought it important that Melanie be on her own. We both did. It's one thing for a middle-aged man to live a quiet, work-and-home sort of life, another for a woman in her prime.

"Like any father"—he glanced at me to see if I resisted his description—"I wanted her to have what I didn't. I wanted her to have an advanced degree. I wanted her to have a career." He smiled ruefully. "I wanted her to have a family."

He paused, a dark look passing across his features. "I had my own agenda as well. The brief time it took me to get involved with Darryl left little doubt of that."

I walked over to the small refrigerator and got two more beers. "Can you stoke that thing?" I pointed to the fire.

Jonathan threw another log onto the low-riding flames. "I forget how cold it gets when the fire dies."

His last sentence echoed in the windowless room. "In a way that says it all. For so long, Melanie was enough. Last year, after she moved into her apartment, I met Darryl. It was a surprise to realize I still wanted more from my life."

My mind flew to Melanie's unpacked crates. The move had been more difficult for her than he either realized or acknowledged.

Barrie returned to his seat. "It was a shock to discover I could still have romantic feelings for someone. When we decided to live together, I felt like hell about getting something out of life that Melanie didn't have. After a while the guilt faded, but the excitement remained. Until now." His voice trailed off as he stared at the fire.

Before I could speak, Jonathan added quietly, "All this comes as a shock, doesn't it? Is that why you don't want to get involved?"

I thought for a long moment, then shook my head. "I don't want to investigate because it's useless. And because I am involved. You don't want to push it with Melanie and neither do I. Doing what you ask would rub her face in something that will lead nowhere."

My words registered. "Is there something between the two of you?"

"Something." I frowned, then added, "I intend to find whoever it was that tried to run me out of The End. Darryl may have been a rung on a ladder I'll need to climb. If I turn up anything funny about his accident I'll let you know. But, Jonathan, I honestly don't expect to."

"What do you expect?"

"I think whoever tried to run me out of The End is drug-connected. I expect I'll discover more about Darryl's life, not his death."

"Will you tell me about that?"

I ran my hand across my eyes. "Melanie doesn't need you walking around wounded any longer than necessary." I leaned forward and picked up my jacket. "Let it rest, Jonathan. It's hard enough to deal with the death of someone you love without digging into the truth of their life—especially a hidden one."

I caught him eyeing me closely, but I'd run out of comfort. I stood up and pulled my jacket on.

He stayed seated and said in a wondering tone, "Did you ever feel that things couldn't be what they seem?" He didn't wait for an answer. "That's the quality of Darryl's death. I'm afraid it will drive me crazy not to know why he died. Maybe, why they both died."

The "they" bothered me too. Every time I came up for air, Black-head's story papered the wall. And I couldn't get the seams straight. But that was my problem, not Jonathan's.

"If something comes up, Jonathan, I'll tell you."

He nodded in silent agreement. The fire had damped down, and the chill crept into the room. Jonathan sat lost in his grief. I finished my beer and pulled my jacket tighter. It was time to leave.

# 30

I HAD ENTERED BARRIE'S HOUSE WITH A LIVE SUSPECT and left with a dead one. Now to discover whether Darryl had been behind the attempted runover and if someone had been behind Darryl. I also left Jonathan's with new questions about Emil's original story. I toyed with the possibility that Blackhead had tried to use me to smear Jonathan about his relationships with Peter and Darryl. But Emil didn't seem clever enough to concoct that idea. Or brave enough to pull it off.

I sat in the car, my mind limping up and down the block. What had happened to the Lew Archer in me? That desire to manipulate the pieces of an incomplete picture? Right now, the only pictures I wanted to manipulate were on television.

A surge of protectiveness for Melanie plowed through me. I fingered through the dashboard ashtray and found a fair-sized roach buried under the cigarette butts. I shook the dirt off my hand and lit up. When I finished I took off for the storefront. A decent roll-of-the-dice would put Mel there.

One of the Harrigan sisters, the bigger one, stared at me as I walked through the door. "Damn, a regular after-hours party. Melanie ought to ask me to cover on Saturdays more often. She said she'd be here, but didn't say anything about you."

"She didn't know."

"Well, I hope you can lighten her mood."

"Janice. Must you constantly gossip?" It wasn't a question. Margaret had stormed out from the back room to stand at her sister's side. "Why does Melanie's foul mood shock you? You've known her long enough."

Janice retorted, "Why does my talking shock *you?* You've known me your entire life!"

I broke into their argument. "You go back a long time, don't you?"

Margaret said, "Of course, we're sisters."

I smiled. "I meant the two of you and Melanie."

Janice nodded, glanced at Margaret and said, "All the way back."

"Was it as rough for you?" I asked.

Janice shook her head, eager to fill me in. "Not even close. We were the lucky ones in the neighborhood. We had a family—no money—but everybody lived together. Melanie was much worse off. Her home was so lousy she couldn't live there. She didn't have anything, except maybe her brother Peter."

"You knew her when she was little?"

Margaret piped up, "From a distance. We became closer after Peter died. Before that Melanie didn't have friends of her own."

"But you knew them," I prompted. "I guess you were shocked by Peter's death?"

Before anyone answered, Melanie's voice ripped through the hall like the crack of a whip. "Everyone was shocked, Matt. Why wouldn't they be?"

I turned around with a start. Mel had entered the storefront without a sound. She glared at Janice as if daring contradiction.

Janice shook her head. "Oh no. Don't look at me that way, Mel. I'm not the least bit interested in catching your shit. Just thank us for covering and we'll leave."

I noticed Therin slouched against the front door. I looked back at Mel, who wore a rigid smile. Her eyes glittered behind her round glasses, but all she said was, "Thank you, Janice. You too, Margaret."

Both women nodded and prepared to leave. I leaned against the wall while Melanie went inside her cubicle. Therin had a sarcastic smile on his face.

Margaret walked over and stuck out her hand. "I hope we meet again under more pleasant circumstances, Matthew." She said my name to let me know she had remembered. Janice strolled by, winked, and pumped her arm, Arsenio-style, as she walked out the door. Margaret shook my hand and followed. I felt foolish standing by myself in the hall so I was relieved, despite her sharp tone, to hear Mel call.

I'd barely closed the partition door when she snapped, "How dare you come here and question people about Peter's death? Don't you ever stop lying? Why won't you leave his accident alone?" Her jaw worked, and her fists opened and closed at her sides. She seemed a spit away from rage.

"Look, nothing's changed for me about Peter. I heard about Darryl and it's hard not to be curious."

She drew her head back and bit down on her lower lip. "How do you know about Darryl?"

I looked through the plywood wall toward the front desk. "Do you want to talk here?"

Melanie put her glasses on the desk and instructed, "Come with me."

I followed her down the corridor into the empty, unlit back room. She closed the door behind us, sat down at a table, and flicked her hand toward the seat next to her. I picked the one across. What passed for light shone through a pair of dirty windows set high on the side wall. The gray shadows added to her already frayed look.

"I think you owe me an explanation." There was more control, but no less anger.

"I had a long conversation with Jonathan today."

"Jonathan?" A note of surprise shared stage with her fury.

"He wanted me to look into Darryl's death."

A flash of worry crossed her face. "I don't understand."

I shrugged. "He's having trouble accepting the official explanation."

She shook her head impatiently. "I thought we had settled that."

"You seem annoyed at him?"

"I am."

I waited, but there was nothing more forthcoming. "I'm surprised," I finally added.

"Why?" Her bright eyes probed my face.

I felt confronted as if by police lights, but couldn't find anywhere to retreat. "His response to both of them dying in the quarry is understandable," I said carefully, steeling myself for a clubbing.

Melanie gave a brusque nod of her head. "You sound just like him. I'm not blind to the similarities either, Matt. Do you think I'm always this much on edge? But it only makes it worse to create something out of nothing. Something out of a stupid coincidence!" She flattened her palms on the top of the table, leaned forward and said, "There are three or four drownings a year in that damn quarry."

I nodded my agreement.

"I don't want anyone disturbing my past. Not Jonathan, not you, not me." She picked my hand off the table, held it close to her lips, and stared blankly at my knuckles. "First you, now this. It hurts me to have all these memories keep surfacing. I've spent a lifetime getting them under control."

"That's what I told Jonathan," I said. I felt bad for her. For all of us. I walked around to Melanie's side of the table and sat down. She turned her body slightly away, so I placed my hand on the top of her back. I felt her shudder as if she were crying. I couldn't see her face and she was silent, so I grasped her shoulders and pulled her into me. She laid the back of her head on my shoulder. She chose the sore arm, but I kept myself from flinching.

I looked down at her face; her eyes were squeezed shut. After a long moment she said softly, "I hope you convinced him."

"I don't know. At least, he didn't look like he was about to hit the street."

She pulled herself upright. Her eyes were clear and dry. "Are you going to 'hit the street' for him?"

I stood, pushed the chair closer to the table, and gripped the back. "No."

It had been a mistake to come. Confused relationships, especially mine with Melanie, simply highlighted the emptiness that had built up inside me. "No, I'm not going to work for him. I don't believe the deaths are connected. I don't really think Jonathan does either. But Darryl's death shook him and he's grasping at straws."

I took a deep breath and went on in a rush. "After I left you the other night somebody tried to run me down. Or at least frighten me, with a 4×4. I think it has something to do with Emil and drugs, but I'm not sure. I can't walk away without figuring it out. I told Jonathan that if I discover anything weird about Darryl's death I'll tell him. I also told him I had no intention of looking into Peter's accident." I listened to the fatigue in my voice.

"Why do you think you will learn anything about Darryl?"

She'd stood during my explanation and now moved close to me. I bent down and tried to wipe the look of defeat from her face with a light kiss. "I'll know how to answer that when I do a little more work."

Melanie closed her eyes again, and I silently debated another kiss. We were close enough to feel each other's breath. Hers was shallow and rapid, though I couldn't tell if it reflected excitement or anxiety. A part of me wanted to lose myself with her. To spend the day, the night, or however long it took to understand my attraction. To finally be able to understand this piece of my life.

But most of me felt distant, too tired to spend time with anyone.

The quiet was finally broken by the sound of Therin calling abruptly from the front, "It's time to leave, Melanie."

She looked at me with dulled eyes. "I promised to spend time with Therin. I hope you weren't ..."

I interrupted, "No, no, I just stopped by to see if you were okay."

She smiled sadly. "I'll be fine. I have to be. But it was sweet of you to worry."

She tilted her head; this time our lips met. I could feel her tongue search for mine. Despite my weariness I felt myself respond. I broke the kiss and held her at arm's length. A shine of tears glossed her eyes.

As we walked slowly toward the front she asked, "You have to continue, don't you?"

I nodded.

But she held my arm. "I'm afraid to let you go."

"I'm not in any danger."

We had arrived at the front to find Therin looking daggers, his feet up on the desk. I had a sudden impulse to lean down and slap his shoes. Instead I kissed Melanie on the cheek, and walked out the door.

I aimed the car out of The End, feeling a rush of fresh breathing air once the neighborhood's squalor sat squarely in the mirror. What had begun as a bridge to my past had somehow trapped me with Boots crying at her door, and Melanie crying in The End. About what? Her long-dead brother? Jonathan? Me? The past had become indistinguishable from the present, but the bridge had a two way toll. I only wished I knew the cost.

# 31

DRIVING THROUGH THE COLD, QUIET CITY, I almost looked forward to my talk with Lou. So much of my life seemed up in the air that a resolution of any kind might be a relief. I didn't think we could settle things, but we might get around to the real questions.

Which explained my disappointment when I walked into an empty apartment. Lou had departed a day early. He left a note explaining he could see I was too tied up in my work to deal with him. He asked that I give him a call when I finished the case. That he was fine and knew we just needed the opportunity to settle things between us. His lack of recrimination only fueled my guilt.

I threw the paper into the garbage and debated driving to the airport. I retrieved the note but he hadn't left departure details, so I threw it back into the pail and walked through to the office. The room was spotless, Lou's bed a sofa. I flopped down at the desk, remembered my stash was in the bedroom, got it, and rolled a fat one. As guilty as I felt, a part of me was relieved to have the television and couch to myself. I lit the joint and pulled the phone off the hook; it was going to be an ugly night and I preferred to do ugly alone.

I awoke the next morning with a strange burst of energy. I thought about smoking a little dope with my coffee, but decided against. If I took to the couch I'd be trapped into thinking about Mel, Boots, and Lou.

Instead, I spent the day thinking about Emil and The End. Up until now I'd been stumbling around with my hand out, waiting for information to drop in. Or, I'd been trying to bully my way to the truth. Maybe it was time to remember that *real* detective work had nothing in common with working a mall.

I transferred myself to the office, swung my feet onto the desk, and jotted down the things I needed. If I didn't know what to do about my personal life, I sometimes knew how to be a detective. Sometimes.

I wasn't sure why I waited until evening to begin the stakeout. Maybe I was a romantic. Or maybe I wanted to identify with the lumps behind the storefront. In any event, I had enough food, dope, cigarettes, and coffee with me to get through an uneventful night. Except for heat and television, it was just like home.

I knew Blackhead was too secretive to invite customers into his apartment, so I expected it to be a while until he led me to them. That was okay. I had nowhere else to be. But, as usual, what I didn't expect was what I got.

At five A.M., Emil left his apartment building and loped up the block. Oblivious to everything around him, he kept to the middle of the road until he came to a rusty old Chevy wagon. The lilt in Blackhead's step suggested an enjoyable journey: it would make him happy to turn a buck.

I was surprised he used a car for his business. At least I hoped it was business that had him up and out. After a few fruitless attempts he finally got moving, leaving behind belching trails of oily exhaust. I waited until he had turned the corner, then followed.

I was even more surprised when he pulled onto the Expressway and away from The End. The roads were deserted so I stayed a good distance back. The kick of adrenaline melted the stiffness from my uncomfortable night. It felt great to work.

Blackhead finally turned off the Expressway. I followed as the wagon hiccuped across town and pulled onto Route 9. The sky was still dark, hiding, I believed with all my heart, another overcast day. Occasional lights heading toward town flashed on the other side of the highway. If the drivers raced into center city, they could arrive in time to watch the hookers leave for their condos in the suburbs. These early morning commuters were the start of the day shift.

We continued up 9 until Blackhead turned into the parking lot of the mall where I'd been working when we met. My jaw dropped but I snapped it shut, killed the lights, and pulled in very slowly. I took the gun from my holster and put it on the seat next to me.

The Chevy kept driving though the huge almost deserted lot, still seemingly unaware of my presence. I hung further back and watched as he pulled around the massive concrete wall separating the shopping mall from the movie theater. There were empty parked cars dotted throughout the dark, quiet lot. I killed the engine, grabbed my gun, and used the wall and darkness to dodge from car to parked car until I was kneeling between a Volvo and the side fence. He couldn't see me; but I could see whether he'd keep going, stop, or set up an ambush.

I'd lucked into the best of all possible. Blackhead had parked his car in an open area, and was sitting on its heated hood, hands in jacket pockets, a cigarette dangling from the middle of his hairy face. He kept anxiously peering toward the far exit of the mall's lot. It didn't look like he was here to watch the sunrise.

I thought about slipping the gun back into its holster but decided not to. I twisted into a position between the car and fence that left me well hidden though uncomfortable. I watched him smoke and lusted for one of my own.

Either Blackhead was an early freak, or whoever he waited for was late. My body remembered how uncomfortably it had spent the night, and complained bitterly about the added insult. My knees ached and the ribbed wooden fence pressed indentations onto one side of my butt. And I thought it was good to work?

Just when my lungs and nerve endings were on their knees begging me to steal back to the car for a smoke, I heard an engine die. For a moment I tried to tell myself I'd imagined it: I really wanted that cigarette. But possibility quieted my complaints. I watched intently as Blackhead angled his face toward the small alley between the theater and the bank. Neither of us was disappointed.

A medium-built, thin-haired man with an expensive perm walked slowly into view. He wore a well-cut suit under his open London Fog. As he moved carefully out of the alley he looked thoroughly around the parking lot. When his eyes landed on Emil, he stopped dead in his tracks, gave a short angry wave of his hand signaling Blackhead off the car. Emil nodded, flipped his cigarette, and slid off the hood. When the Perm gave another angry wave, Blackhead opened his car door and got in. The man waited, then walked directly to the Chevy. There was no missing the disgust on his face as he climbed in the passenger door.

I prepared to scurry back to my car if they drove away, but Blackhead kept his engine shut off while he talked animatedly to the gray curls. I saw him throw another cigarette out his window, and wondered if there was any way to crawl over and pick it up. My body was numb and I seriously questioned my competence. I couldn't hear anything and could barely see. If I were a modern PI I'd be monitoring their conversation from my apartment. But I was the guy who wouldn't buy a fucking answering machine.

Finally the Perm opened his door. Blackhead acted like he still wanted to talk, but the guy wasn't buying. He walked to the front of the Chevy making shove-off motions with his hands. Blackhead stuck his head out the window. I couldn't see his face, but his tone was beseeching and I could hear him clearly. "Come on, man. I'm telling you I can do the job. I swear, I won't fuck it up."

The Perm's face turned ugly and he slapped the hood. "I told you to keep still!" His voice sounded like a mean Rod Steiger's. From my hidden position I could see the neat little hip holster that flashed when he banged the hood. "If I want to see you I'll get in touch."

Blackhead's nasal voice began to whine. "But how am I gonna get my regular stuff? He ..."

"Be quiet, Emil! And stay that way! It's time for you to go home."

"But ..."

The Perm moved up to the driver's window and slapped Blackhead's face. Emil turtled his head and quickly started the car. The man leaned closer and said something I couldn't hear. I saw Blackhead nod; as soon as the guy stepped away, the car began to move. The Perm shook his head disgustedly, carefully checking the lot to see if anything moved.

Satisfied, he started back into the alley. I stayed low and uncomfortable until I heard the sound of a motor, then ran to my car.

I almost flooded the engine, but it caught. I drove slowly around to the front of the mall where I saw the ass of a black 750il drive onto the highway. Since there were no other cars on the access road, the Bimmer was mine.

I allowed a couple of pre–rush hour cars to roll between us. Unless he pulled a *To Live and Die in L.A.* I wasn't going to lose him. I felt excited as I lit my long-awaited smoke. I'd gotten a better break than I thought possible. I had expected Blackhead to lead me to grunts.

We passed the Route 128 turnoff, finally exiting somewhere in Wellesley. Tailing now got trickier, since the roads were winding and curved, often looping back on themselves. For a while I thought he'd made me and was going through an elaborate shaking ritual. But before I got too nervous, he slowed his seventy grand and turned into a medium-length driveway alongside a spacious but nondescript suburban house. I noticed toys in the front yard. I intended to continue driving past but, as his garage door opened, I caught a glimpse of a 4×4.

Without thinking, I squealed into a U-turn and shot up his driveway. The Perm walked out of the garage with a puzzled look on his face. I screeched to a stop and jumped out of my car, but remained standing behind its open door.

His face had an angry scowl. "Excuse me, just what the hell are you doing?"

I took a stab. "Maybe I want a piece of Darryl's action too."

The scowl never left his face, but now there was a fresh wariness in his eyes. His hands also moved closer to the little hip holster I'd noticed in the parking lot. I looked back into my own car in time to see my .38 wink from the passenger's seat.

"I'm sorry, but you must be confused." But he made no move to leave.

"You got nice clothes, a fancy Newbury Street haircut, and clipped diction, but you're still just a dope-dealer to me." I heard my words and wondered if I wanted to get shot. I hoped the toys in the front yard meant he'd hesitate to use his weapon.

The Perm's molars worked overtime. I inched my way a little closer to my own gun, though I knew it was too far away to be of any use. By the time I finished soothing my raw nerves, he'd calmed his and, to my surprise, burst out laughing. "You got a pair of big ones, cowboy," he said without his diction.

I shrugged.

"Why are you so sure I won't use this?" He opened his jacket and let me see his gun.

"I figure your kids got better things to do than wash blood off a driveway."

His smile evaporated. "What do you know about my children?"

I nodded toward the toys. "Only what I see."

His eyes followed my glance. "I keep telling them to put their stuff away but they never listen. Never." He had a disgusted look on his face.

He turned his attention back to me. "Now what is it you're doing here?"

"I want to see your truck."

He turned around and looked into his garage. I leaned away from my car door and peered in behind him. I wasn't sure it was the same one. Trucks look like fucking trucks. Maybe I needed to put my face next to the tire treads.

He turned back to me. "It's not for sale."

"I don't want to buy it. I just want to see if it's the same one that tried to rub my head in the street a couple of nights ago."

Comprehension crossed his face. "I understand. You're Matt Jacobs."

"Jacob, without the 's.' I guess I don't have to look at the truck after all."

He grinned with no amusement, stirring his hand inside his belt, gun visible and accessible.

I held up one of my hands. "You don't have to worry. I don't intend to shoot you. All I want is information."

A suspicious look crossed his face. "Information? You want information?" He took his hand from his pocket and let his sport jacket close. "Enough with these threats. I have to take the kids to school." He slowly walked over, glanced inside my car, and shook his head when he saw my gun on the front seat. "Big ones, or you're stupid," he said.

"Stupid," I replied.

He clapped me on my bad shoulder. "I like a person who is honest about his limitations."

Wouldn't you know it? I had found me a funny dope-dealer.

**32**

WE BOTH HEARD THE DOOR. A second or two later, a neatly dressed little girl timidly wandered out of the garage's shadows. I immediately compared her pretty clothes with the dirt and rags worn by the Belchar kids. Still, it was hard to work up class indignation in front of pigtails.

"Hiya, honey." The man squatted next to the little girl and looked up at me with a warning in his eyes. "This is Cynthia. Say hello to Mr. Jacob, sugar."

Cynthia looked up out of the corner of her eyes and mumbled something unintelligible. I smiled and waved. An air of unreality began to filter into the scene. I was kissing distance from the guy who literally tried to run my ass out of The End, getting ready to play peek-a-boo with his kid.

I looked down at the top of the Perm's well-disguised bald spot. "We gotta talk," I muttered.

"Sure. Of course we'll talk." He patted the little girl on her bottom. "Run inside, sweetheart. Tell Mama I'll be there soon."

Cynthia ran into the garage without looking back. The man groaned his way to his feet. "Damn. One problem with having little ones at my age is moving around." He looked at me pointedly. "Of course, I have a lot more patience than I did the first time around."

"I didn't come here to talk about kids."

He looked at me with exasperation. "I'm not just talking about kids. So you're not stupid, you found me. But you don't come to a man's home to talk business."

"I didn't exactly look you up in the phone book. And I don't know the hours you keep in the parking lot."

A streak of understanding lit his face. "That fool."

"Yup."

"So you don't even know who I am?"

"Nope."

He grinned mirthlessly and shook his head. "I *am* getting old. I was too annoyed to pay any attention on the ride home."

"What were you angry about?"

He stared for a long moment, a thoughtful look on his face. Finally he said, "I'll talk to you in my office, tomorrow."

He made a sudden move with his hand and I immediately backed toward my car door, but all he did was look at the gold Rolex on his wrist. "Christ, I gotta go." He looked at me and shook his head. "Lighten up, will you? What the hell am I going to do to you here? Now watch. I'm going to reach for my wallet, to give you my card. Then you are going to leave."

"You seem awfully good-natured for a guy who wanted to run me over."

He looked bored. "Nobody wanted to run you over. I said we'll talk about it tomorrow. I don't work at home."

I took the card from his hand and slid it into my pocket.

"Aren't you going to look at it?"

"Right now I prefer to keep my eyes on you."

"You can rest your eyes. I don't plan to relocate just because you found me."

I hesitated, watching silently as he turned his back and disappeared into the shadows. After the garage door magically dropped, I climbed into my car, grabbed the gun off the seat, and jammed the fucker into my holster.

I pulled his card from my pocket and stared. The name seemed familiar, but I was too wired to know. I'd give my memory a better shot after I calmed down. And maybe after I drank one myself. I kept looking at his business card until the rest of the copper-embossed letters sank in. Then I started the car and pulled out of his driveway. My family-man, dope-dealing hard-guy was a banker.

I tried to retrace my path home, but got hopelessly lost. I found myself driving through towns snatched whole-clothed from New England postcards. I drove past pleasant white wood-steepled churches and rectangular village greens. The snow stayed white in suburbia. This was the "real" New England and its coiffed neatness made my skin crawl.

My short collision with Lonny Prezoil promised to explain the meat of my business. But I felt dissatisfied. His ease with our encounter, his willingness to meet, left little doubt he considered the attempted mayhem a minor matter, easily resolved. Prezoil's attitude was a letdown; the runover hadn't been minor to me.

I finally found the city's skyline brooding underneath the gray and white clouds fighting for its air space. I wasn't crazy about the town but, after my little trip into the hinterlands, I felt like an animal returning to its watering hole—anticipating danger, but danger on familiar turf.

I supposed I'd been a danger for Prezoil when I'd nosed around The End. For some reason he'd wanted me out. I tried to work up a mad, but all I felt was encroaching depression.

By the time I crossed the city limits I knew my sour mood had to do with the quick conclusion of the case. I'd wanted to know who instigated the attack, and now I knew. Tomorrow I'd learn why. I consoled myself with the possibility of uncovering something sinister about Darryl's death, but I wasn't going to give points.

I arrived in my alley about the same time the gray overhead drifted down, victorious. And the conversation, later, with Julius just added to the overcast.

*       *       *

He sat at my kitchen table toying with the card. "I know of the bank's department," Julie said.

"Since when do you do business with Merit Bank's philanthropic services? I don't figure you for big write-offs."

He placed the card face down and lit a cigarette. I pulled over another ashtray and lit one for myself.

"This is a city of mirrors," Julie said. "Same things happening all over town, only the images are separated thicker than that wall they pulled down." He stuck his thumb over his shoulder; I think he was pointing to Berlin. "Our friendly city is layered with generations of serious dislike ... the Irish, Blacks, Spanish, plaids."

"Plaids?"

"Protestants. But no matter how intense the divisions, the players know each other."

"And," I lifted the card, "Lonny, here, is a player."

"Works for 'em."

"The bank?"

"Takes money to do business. And Slumlord, you're dead on about the scare. They want to do you, they do you. A run-off is no big deal."

"To Prezoil, Julie. A bigger deal to me."

"I can understand that," he said. "Prezoil may have had a particular deal working and didn't want a stranger around. Might have been a general street clean. Maybe he'll tell you." What passed for a smile, a grimace for anyone else, lined his face.

"Why do I think I know this guy?"

"Maybe since you became a slumlord you been needing the write-offs."

"You're enjoying this, aren't you?"

"You are a piece of work, Matt. You say you got to know the who and why somebody showed you his tires. You know the who, and the dude says he's gonna tell you the why. I'd say you be one conversation from the couch. Why you sitting here frustrated instead of satisfied?"

"I don't know. Maybe it keeps me from thinking about the malls. Anyway, I don't feel finished with The End."

Julius shook his head. "With The End or some of the people?"

Julie left, but I stayed right where I was. Dissatisfied. Incomplete. I flashed on my conversation with Jonathan in his little secret room and remembered the look on his face when he spoke of his frustration. I didn't think I'd help either of us, but it gave me a measure of satisfaction to imagine Prezoil's smooth ruffled when I plucked at the strands of The End's underlife.

I might as well imagine, since I was exquisitely aware of the message behind Julie's words: Prezoil was connected—warning enough that I could forget any real payback. Imagination was as close as I'd get.

I sat nailed to Dutch's chair, disappointed and in a bad temper. Worse, the longer I sat thinking about my banker, the more certain I was that I knew him. But try as I might, I couldn't shake the memory loose. A couple cigarettes only added to my frustration.

My body started complaining about last night's indignities, and I faced the choice of bed or couch. It took a while, but I picked the bed. At least until a few semi-refreshed hours later.

I opened my eyes to early evening, trying to remember the day. I caught it on my third try. I needed coffee and nicotine. I showered, dressed, and grabbed a cup on my way into the office.

Where it eventually turned from dark to darker, the tip of my cigarette the room's only glow. My feet were on the desk between piles of bills. I was staring across the room at the collection of Bakelite radios. Twenty years ago the conclusion of one project always led to exciting possibilities of another. Twenty years later was a very different time.

When the phone rang I put my feet down and pulled the small desk lamp's chain, bathing the papers and telephone in shaded light. I reached into the small bright circle, and lifted the receiver.

"I've called to apologize," she said without a preamble.

Her voice did nothing to yank me free of the past. "Hello, Melanie."

"I feel horrible about my behavior."

"There's no need for any apology. I appreciate how easy it is to get driven into painful history. Anyhow, my contribution is almost finished."

"What do you mean?" she asked without the suspicion I associated with my work in The End.

"I found who I was looking for."

"Really?" There was a note of surprise in her voice. "So quickly?"

"Yeah. A lucky break. I haven't spoken to him yet, but I will."

She sighed, then asked, "Are you feeling different about me?"

"Of course not. Our last conversation is history."

There was a silence at her end of the line. I began to feel confused, but then she confused me more. "Why don't we get together tonight?" she asked, her tone as inviting as her words.

Despite a fleeting thought of Boots, the night loomed lonely with too much glum familiarity. "Sure."

Before I set a time she caught me short again. "Terrific. Tell me your address."

I WAS UNEASY ABOUT MELANIE COMING to my apartment. My picture of
her was framed by The End; other images were hard to imagine.
Also, I wasn't really used to women in my home. Hell, even Boots
and I rarely spent nights together here.

It annoyed me that I couldn't keep the two women separate.
While I picked up around the house I tried to convince myself that it
was Boots' fault. That her questions and requested downtime forced
me to link the two. I almost had it believed by the time I sat rolling a
couple of joints at the kitchen table. Almost.

I pushed my doubts aside at the rap from the office's alley
entrance. I shut the door as Melanie stepped inside, glanced around,
and rested her eyes on my face. She unbuttoned her coat and handed
it to me; I felt the intensity of her stare as I placed the coat on the
couch. When I turned she was still staring at me, her mouth slightly
open. She wore a short black dress that showed a lot of neck and

sheer gray stockinged legs. The shaped darkness of her clothes next to her soft ivory skin shattered the last of my reluctance to imagine her outside The End.

"I hadn't realized we were going out," I said. I felt my sexual anxiety recede as disappointment took its place.

She looked at me questioningly, then saw my eyes run quickly up and down her body. Melanie smoothed her hands along her hips. "You mean the clothes. I didn't plan on going anywhere. I just don't get out of The End very much." She stepped deeper into the room. "Especially for this."

Her look left little doubt what "this" meant. My disappointment faded and I invited her into the apartment.

The more contact I had with Melanie, the less I felt catapulted into the past. I'd worked my way past Megan; and tonight Chana seemed safely tucked away. If there was "unfinished business," it was with Melanie, and it concerned right now. Perhaps tomorrow The End might lose its nostalgic status and become just another savaged territory in a pockmarked landscape.

But while the night might not belong to the past, I was still me. And I wasn't ready for bed.

I led us into the living room where Mel sat on the couch while I picked a tape. Hartman and Coltrane seemed too romantic, so I eliminated Hartman and chose Coltrane's "Gentle Side." "Do you want some grass or a drink?"

"Whatever you're having will be fine. I brought cocaine, but it's in my coat pocket."

I hid a surprised smile. On my trot back to her coat, I questioned my surprise. The other night's passion had given more than a promise of tonight's sophistication. I shook my head as I picked a small bottle with an attached spoon from her coat pocket.

I stopped for the joints on my return to the living room. Melanie had her shoes off, legs curled under. I sat down next to her gray thighs, handed her the coke, and lit a cigarette. I wanted her, wanted her very much. But, in a flash of understanding, I knew my wanting was different from what Boots imagined. This was simpler; this was flat-out desire.

Boots' shadow faded under my doper's anticipation of the

cocaine. Melanie snorted from the little spoon and, after relinquishing my stranglehold on a cigarette, I did likewise. She nodded for me to repeat. While I hunched over my knees, Mel leaned forward and took the cigarette.

"It feels like stolen time, being here with you," she said.

"Out of The End," I suggested.

"No ..." She wore a twisted half-smile, then leaned to me and kissed me on my mouth; taking my lower lip between her teeth she gently bit. My mouth went electric. She let go, sat back, and took a long drag on the cigarette. "More like a forbidden dessert."

I reopened the bottle, snorted, and handed it back. I wondered what had happened to the brittle, angry lady in the storefront. But my desire wasn't interested in what had happened on previous afternoons. Or in any tomorrows. Tonight there would be no talk.

I stood up, watched her use the coke, then held out my arm. Coltrane was crying as we walked to the bedroom.

I could finally answer Boots' questions, though the answers did nothing to ease my situation. What drove me toward Melanie was my wish to drown in flesh. To lose myself in heat. To disappear.

We collided, naked, on my bed. Reaching across two separate lifetimes, demanding from each other a path to ourselves. Twisting into moments of combination, only to fall, come apart, then demand again. It was as if some compulsive lunatic repeatedly put a jigsaw puzzle together, then time and again ripped it apart, each time forcing the shapes to fit in different places. This wasn't the surrender of love, it was the attack of fragmented psyches looking for missing pieces.

Sometime during the night I awoke and stared at Melanie's full body. She breathed deeply, contented in her sleep. I wondered if this was everything I needed, or the best I could do. Before I grew too frightened, I blocked out the thought and fell back asleep.

I didn't need to open the shades to know it was morning. I reached onto the night table and lit a cigarette. Melanie immediately sat upright, as if she had been waiting for me to stir. "Are you cold?" I asked.

She shook her head and reached out her hand. I passed her the smoke and lit another. "Is something wrong?"

The pupils of her eyes dilated. She shook her head again. "No, nothing is wrong."

I pulled her down and kissed her. She twisted away with a crooked smile. "We're shadow people, Matt. We can't be together in the day."

Her harshness chilled me. Soul-stripping in daylight was something I, too, only did alone. But her voice recalled my middle-of-the-night fears.

I rolled out of bed and ran right into body hurt. As I stretched my back into working order, I watched her dress. She didn't bother with the gray hose.

"Would you like coffee, or something to eat?"

"Coffee would be fine," she said. "Also another cigarette."

I flipped the pack and lighter, then pulled on some clothes. Eventually we sat in the kitchen smoking quietly, waiting for the coffee. I looked at the clock, surprised to see it was still very early. Melanie followed my glance. "I work today," she said, smiling in a distant way. "I want to keep to my schedule."

The mention of schedule reminded me that Prezoil hadn't suggested a meeting time. I began to rise, but unless I wanted to see him at his house and engage in another round of dope-dealer domesticity, I had plenty of time to be anywhere. Besides, the coffee wasn't done.

Melanie watched me sit back down. "You look like you remembered something," she said.

"Yeah. My appointment."

"The grand conclusion of your case?"

"Yeah," I grinned. "Turns out the guy I want to talk to is a banker named Prezoil. But it's too early for anything but the money machines to be awake."

A small smile played at her lips. "I knew you weren't finished with us."

"With us?"

She hesitated before answering in a calm voice. "I mean with Peter."

"What does Lonny Prezoil have to do with Peter?" I asked. "Who the hell is he?"

She looked sharply into my face. "You don't remember? Lonny was a fundraiser for Hope House when you lived in The End. Everyone called him 'Pretzel.'" She paused, then added with contempt, "He was a real slick phony."

I thumped my forehead with my palm. "I thought he looked familiar but I couldn't place him." I kept knocking at my head. "We're all getting old. It's hard to recognize people once they pack a life."

Melanie sat quietly until the coffee perked. I played host and was back in my chair before I asked, "What did Lonny Prezoil have to do with Peter?"

Mel lit another cigarette, drank from her cup, then spoke deliberately. "There had been a party the night of Peter's death. At Lonny's place." She looked at me with raised eyebrows.

I leaned forward to ask for more, but she shook me off. "No, Matt. I'm not going to talk about this."

I nodded my okay, but she hadn't finished. "When you and I are together I feel very close to Peter. I won't have that disappear under a barrage of questions."

"There's no need to talk, Mel. By tonight I'll be finished with all of it," I reassured her.

"I already am."

I stood up and walked around to her side of the table. I leaned down, lifted her chin, and kissed her. She put her hands around the back of my head and pulled me tight. Her mouth felt alive, hungry.

I stepped back out of her grasp. "Shadow people or no, if we keep that up neither of us will get to work."

She stared at me for a long moment, then got up. "Where's my coat?" She sounded sad.

We finished our morning holding each other in the alley. Melanie buried her face in my neck. "I want you to remember last night. No further back than that." She pulled away from me, her eyes now bright and hard. "I'm finished with ancient history."

I nodded. "Be here now." Babba Ram Mel. I watched as she drove away.

I went back to the bedroom, picked the joint off the night table, and lay down. I could smell Melanie's body and last night's passion as I lit the dope and closed my eyes. Maybe I could sleep. I thought of Boots, and knew that while I too might be finished with the past, the present was unfinished and obscure.

# 34

I WOKE CURSING THE PITCH-BLACK BEDROOM. I thought I'd slept through the entire day. The clock radio read 2 P.M., but I didn't trust it and yanked the shades open. My city was locked in an ongoing audition for *Blade Runner 2*; the darkness just another gloomy day.

I worried about banker's hours, searching my wallet for the Perm's business card. I dialed the number and exhaled with relief when I heard his voice on the other end.

"Just checking," I said, working to squeeze the sleep out of my words. "I don't like vacant-signs."

"Where have you been, Jacob? I've been waiting for you all day."

It was clear he wasn't accustomed to cooling his heels. "It's nice to figure so prominently in your plans," I said.

"You have a loose mouth when you're on the telephone."

I laughed. "No, I just like to make a pleasant first impression."

"It's too late for that."

"Well, stay where you are and I'll try again." I pushed the button down before he could refuse. While I dressed I debated bringing the gun. Despite an ugly scab, my left arm felt almost normal, but my right shoulder was beginning to chafe under the stiff leather of the holster.

I stalled the decision by walking into the bathroom. I brushed my teeth with cold water, staring into tired eyes. I spat the water into the sink and threw the toothbrush in after. It wasn't difficult to understand my ambivalence. The finish line was in sight; I didn't like approaching it. I had only recently been reminded that work put my life's potholes in perspective, made them almost possible to dodge. I had been reminded how much I liked *any* mystery that wasn't me.

"That was then, this is now." The phrase had galloped through my head from the start of this frustrating, fruitless track. At the outset it had represented twenty years. Now it meant maybe two weeks. The long and short of it unsettled me and I whipped myself to leave. The one phrase I hated in *The Racing Form* was "hung."

I strapped the holster on with a sharp, savage twist of my wrist. They didn't let you wear a gun in the malls.

The fat security guard reminded me only five minutes remained in the day's money grubbing. I reminded him that banks were eating dirt all over the region. He took it personal and patted me down. When I told him who I intended to see, he shrugged as if expecting it. After I showed him the wallet-sized PI photostat he led me to a room on the second floor. The Perm stood in the hall, Italian-elegant, hands on hips. My arrival had already been announced.

He profusely thanked the florid-faced fat man. I suppose a quick frisk and caddy to the second floor constituted "above and beyond."

Prezoil urged me into his office and closed the door. "You don't visit quietly, do you? That's what got you in trouble in the first place."

He took a seat in one oversized wing chair and motioned me to take the other. Sitting there, a table between us, made me feel like an actor in a surrealistic Dreyfus commercial. I gripped the arms of the chair and tried to look like a lion.

"Why did you bring a gun?" he asked. "The way you dress, you probably imagine that no one would notice one more wrinkle."

I smiled. "Okay, I get it. If you weren't a drug-dealing banker, you'd audition for the Borscht Belt. You want to tell me exactly what got me into trouble?"

"Relax, Mr. Jacob. I didn't stay around late to avoid going home."

"You had twenty-four hours to make it plausible, Prezoil. Give it your best shot."

"My only shot." He motioned toward a mahogany cabinet standing in front of a side wall.

"Bourbon straight." I watched as he stepped lightly to the wood, opened it, and deftly poured a couple of Turkeys. He was back in his seat, the drinks on the table, when I asked, "Is this supposed to help you tell the story, or help me to believe it?"

"Neither. From what I've learned about you, one drink isn't going to help with anything."

I lifted my glass and tilted it in his direction. "I'm not surprised you did your homework. But I'd like to know how."

He raised his glass in return. "Don't we all? They say information is everything." He paused to show me his gleaming dental work. "Please don't act the fool. I'm not going to tell you where I get information. But I am going to give you some. I wanted privacy and you were an interference."

I drank half my glass. "Whatever Lonny wants, Lonny gets. There are lots of reasons for privacy, Lonny. Some violent."

He looked genuinely puzzled. "What violence? A large sugar transaction was set to occur and there was no room for a wild card. I wanted you out of The End for a couple of days." He put his glass down on the table. "The reason I'm talking to you is simple. You didn't get hurt, were never meant to. But you know where I live, and I don't want any lingering bad feelings. If you want money for your roll in the snow tell me how much?"

I took another sip and wished the bottle wasn't across the room. "Who drove the truck?"

He looked at me and shrugged. "Darryl Hart. He swore he didn't touch you."

"I don't like the smell of burning rubber next to my face."

"That's why I want to make amends."

I let my voice grow harsh. "Darryl drove the truck, and now Darryl's dead."

He stared at me. "What's that supposed to mean? Darryl was an ass. He fell into a freezing quarry. I told him plenty of times to keep his nose clean."

"How do you know he fell?"

He smiled. "A little bird told me."

"You didn't check yourself?"

"I don't have to check myself." He looked at me with a mixture of disgust and pity. "Let me tell you something. The police believe it was an accident, and I believe it was an accident. Therefore, it was an accident. How much attention is a minor-league grifter worth? You forget The End is a leper colony."

"Nobody cares about a leper, is that it?"

He was growing annoyed. "What do you have besides a big mouth?"

A bigger mouth. "Maybe your organization needed a change."

"My organization?" He squinted into his drink. "Thanks for the promotion. Darryl did something really stupid, that's all." Prezoil made it sound like Darryl owed him an apology.

"Darryl was perfect for me," he said. "He was an inch away from living with a community hero. Why would I want to ruin that fix?"

"Good old J.B."

Prezoil stared at me. "That's right. What are you trying to say?"

I scrambled but couldn't find much ledge. "Maybe he was tired of doing what you told him? Maybe he wanted to work for himself?"

Prezoil rubbed his face with his hand. "You can zip your 'maybes.' Darryl had a monopoly. No other white boys sold sugar in The End. We saw to that." His lips pulled down at the corners. "Darryl wasn't ordinarily stupid. In my book that makes dope stupid."

I wasn't sure whether the exasperation was directed at Darryl's character flaws, or mine. There were enough, I suppose, to go around. "How did you hear about me?"

"You're not the strong silent type."

"Maybe not, but I don't figure you spend much time in 'the leper colony.' Who told you?"

"Another little bird."

I needed a minute to think. I stood, brought our glasses to the cabinet, and tried my hand. It was a heavy hand.

I returned to the corner, handed him his glass, and asked, "What did Emil tell you about me?"

"You're not as stupid as you act, Jacob. He said he heard you were nosing around The End asking a lot of questions."

"He tell you the questions?"

"No."

He was lying. I sat back in the chair and sipped my drink. "It never dawned on you that Blackhead wanted Darryl's patch?"

"Jesus, I haven't heard him called that in twenty years. It still fits." A disgusted look crossed his face. "Emil just wanted a raise, better rates."

"You never wondered whether he did Darryl?"

He turned his disgust in my direction. "Emil hasn't got enough testosterone to think up that kind of idea, let alone do anything about it." He shook his head. "I told you, Darryl Hart's death was an accident."

"It would be easier to buy if you weren't a liar. Hell, do you really expect me to believe you didn't know what I was investigating?"

He started to deny it again, but I had a sudden inspiration. "Let me try it another way, Lonny. You had thrown the party on the night Peter Knight died. You knew I was poking around Peter's death, and you wanted to get rid of me. Isn't that why you had Darryl take a run at me?"

Prezoil looked mean while he thought about his answer. He eyed me with a grimace of resignation. "Okay, I had two reasons to chase you away. So it'll cost me more than laundry."

"Stop counting, I don't want any of your money."

His eyebrows tried to hide in his curly hair.

"That's right. No money. I just want to know why."

He shrugged. "The way you dress I guessed you for new clothes." He stared at me carefully. "On the other hand, I didn't guess you'd find me. What do you want this for?"

I thought about my answer. "It's what brought me back to The End. I don't like leaving loose threads."

Prezoil's eyes were hard as they combed my face. "You understand my offer to make amends is generosity, nothing else? I do not have to bother with you at all."

Connected is connected. "I knew that before I walked through the door."

"We understand each other?"

I understood I wasn't going to use anything against him. Ever. I nodded.

"I don't like my name associated with drugs. Not now, not twenty years ago. There were drugs at that party."

"What kind?"

He seemed surprised by the question then smiled as if remembering a pleasurable experience. "Acid. There was the other usual shit there—alcohol, grass—but it was an acid night." He sipped from his glass. "I hadn't thought about those days for a long time."

"How did you get the drag to walk? You weren't a big-shot back then."

"It didn't take influence, just money. What's the matter with you? No cop ever lost sleep over a drowned punk from The End. Never did, never will. You trip over the police asking about Darryl? At best it scores a two-sentence paragraph in the newspaper. One mention. Then *sayonara*."

"What happened that night?"

"I don't see why you want any of this, but as long as we understand each other?" he repeated.

"We do."

"The same thing that usually happened. Half a dozen kids stoned, listening to head music. Sometime during the night Emil and Peter and Peter's kid sister left. I think everyone else just stayed. It was a pleasure to watch all those hardheads turn to jello."

I was suspicious of his memory. "You're pretty good with details after twenty years."

A moment of anger broke through his calm. "I don't like the sound of 'no.' It's something I don't forget." He saw my frown of incomprehension, and a flash of regret crossed his face. He hesitated, then said, "The Knight girl. I tried to make it with her but it didn't fly. The only guy she ever hung with was her brother." His voice reverberated with contempt.

I wondered why he was so vehement about something that far in the past. But before I could push, he asked, "You know why I'm telling you this?" He curled his fist and didn't wait for an answer.

"I don't want you asking around about business that has to do with me. Even old business. I can tell you myself, and trust you'll be a good boy and forget what you know, or I can take you out of the picture.

"I owe you one. You showed me something I might not have noticed: I was getting sloppy. I'm not saying you weren't good. Hell, I cased the parking lot. But you laying rubber on my driveway was a slap in the face."

He looked at me with friendly eyes. "Let me give you some advice. Take your information and leave The End for another twenty. Don't go back there to work. I owed you, and now you're paid."

He finished his drink and rose. "Time to leave, PI."

I started toward the door, then thought of one last fish to fry. "If Emil is such a jerk, why do you use him?"

He gave me a dirty look. "We were through talking, remember?"

"I'm on my way, aren't I?"

He buried his fingers in his stiff gray curls. "Emil has contact with people who pay high prices for small amounts. I let him make a living selling funny cigarettes. You think he'd be better off on welfare?"

His voice regained its threatening freeze. "I go back a long way with The End and I got sentimental. Once you do serious time there you never really leave. You make war buddies." His look made it clear I wasn't one of the troop.

I had my hand on the door knob. "Tom Belchar another war buddy?"

"Enough, Jacob. It's time to quit while you're ahead."

# 35

I SAT IN MY CAR IN FRONT OF THE BANK, fuming, sorting things through. Prezoil wasn't worried about someone poaching on Darryl's territory—and Darryl's territory was Prezoil's. If I believed him, my idea that Blackhead might have killed Darryl was moot. And I did believe him.

I lit a cigarette and pushed aside old stubs in the ashtray to give it room. Prezoil's memory of Peter's death was a little too polished, though I couldn't put my finger on the embellishments. Or any reason why he'd script them. Malls and all, it was time to head for the wire.

I finished my smoke, started the car, and pulled into the street. At the sound of an angry horn I jumped, glanced into my mirror, and saw a silver Legend all but run into my rear. I waved my appreciation and saw the driver's graphic response. I thought about throwing my car into reverse to smack the front of his Japanese luxury, but the idea was just my frustration swimming to open air.

I got stuck in traffic on my way to Emil's. Just as well—I needed time to find my mantra. The dirty little fucker had hired, then tumbled me to Lonny, looking for points. An idea well within the confines of his cunning sleaze.

The traffic broke before my anger. I wasn't a vegetarian, but didn't want to kill the bastard either. Wisely I decided to speak with Jonathan before my house call to Blackhead. Doing time for hurting Emil was a sobering thought.

An unconscious choice of roads carried me past Boots' apartment building. I glanced up the tall glass face knowing I could see nothing; her apartment was in the back. The end of my work, the beginning of my personal life. "Sixteen tons and what do you get?" I hummed.

The light snow was turning to water the instant it hit the ground, making the road glisten with a metallic sheen under the streetlights. I slowed down as I passed the storefront. I didn't see anyone inside, but thought I saw something move between two parked cars. Probably a cat but it still raised the hair on the back of my neck.

I found a parking space on Barrie's block and sat rethinking my decision to come. I'd only promised to inform him if I found something wrong. I pushed my cigarette into the ashtray, spilling ashes and butts onto the floor. I cleaned up as best I could. But it wasn't until I cursed myself for promising him anything that I opened the door, and was hit immediately with the sloppy wet.

When Jonathan opened the door his eyes seemed unfocused, ripe with shock and sorrow. "Hello, Jacob, come in." He barely looked at me as he ushered us to his kitchen. Like his secret room, the kitchen had a comfortable lived-in feeling.

"Would you care for something to drink? I'm having tea but you're welcome to beer."

"Tea is fine. American, straight up."

He smiled as he poured from a pot. "American, straight up, coming up."

I thanked him and waited until he sat down, looking at the bags under his eyes and imagining they'd be sagging further by the end of my stay. "Jonathan, I finished my work and I've found nothing suspicious about Darryl's death."

I took a deep breath and continued, "He dealt drugs. Coke. But his boss is satisfied it was an accident. Frankly, I believe his boss. I'm sorry, Jonathan, but that's all there is." I heard the flustered rush of my words and bit my lip. There was no reason to tell Barrie that Darryl's desire to move in was drug cover.

Jonathan didn't look like he was hit in the belly. "I'm not terribly surprised. I went to Darryl's funeral; the incurable old romantic is on hold. I appreciate your stopping by. You didn't have to."

"It was lousy, huh?"

Jonathan shook his head. "Lousy doesn't come close. Turns out my soon-to-be partner had been in Vietnam. That made him about ten years older than he claimed." His hand hovered over the black formica table. "That wasn't the worst of it. His father saw fit to bury him in full battle regalia." He looked at me. "Don't say it. Obviously there was plenty about Darryl I didn't know, but I don't think he was a closet hawk." He paused, and in a more somber tone added, "And I still don't think he was suicidal, either."

He stood and retrieved the teapot from the stove, freshened both cups, then sat back down. "But seeing Darryl in a military uniform chopped through my fantasies. I can accept that his death was an accident. But it's hard to let go of the similarity to Peter's."

"The quarry makes it tough?"

He shook his head. "It's not just the quarry. It's me too."

"I don't think anyone who knows you thinks less of you."

"I'm not talking about what anyone else thinks." He looked directly into my eyes. "And I'm not talking about homosexuality. Not even my attraction to younger men. Christ, if my relationships were hetero I'd be a hero."

He rubbed his eyes. "I need glasses. I look right through people I love and see only what I want." His tone filled with disgust, laced with more than a little bitterness. "It was true with Peter, obviously true with Darryl."

"Peter?"

"Yes, Peter. After he died I discovered he'd been a thief as well as a hustler. I thought him frail"—his voice had softened—"like a poet."

I felt sorry for him. Whatever his flaws he deserved better. I thought of Megan and her manipulative phoniness. We all deserved better. "Maybe that was the side of him you brought out."

"Right." He frowned and his voice turned sarcastic. "Darryl too."

"You're not the only fool for love."

He shrugged wearily and sighed. "It depresses me to watch how this affects Melanie. My history with Peter makes it difficult to be much help. That just makes everything worse."

"Help with what?"

"Her moods. They're pretty hard to miss."

"So she's lost her temper a few times," I protested.

"Melanie's volatility is a strong throwback to Peter's death."

I listened as he peeled away the years. "After he died, she was like a cornered animal. Trusted no one, refused everyone's concern or care. Once the shock settled, it got almost worse. She seemed unable to make contact. Now I'm afraid that's happening all over again."

My head filled with a different picture, a picture of Melanie last night. "Jonathan, you're dumping shit on yourself. She hasn't been removed with me."

"Really?" He wanted to believe.

"I wouldn't lie to protect you."

His smile challenged the lines on his face. "No, I guess you wouldn't."

"You don't have to guess."

He heard what I said, but his smile folded back into the worry. "You do care about her, don't you?"

The ambivalences about my attraction to Mel floated to the surface, but all I murmured was, "I care about her."

He peered at me. "There are a couple of things I'd like to ask ..."

I raised my hand. "Don't." I tried to jibe his version of Melanie with my own, but all I said aloud was, "I'll keep your concern in mind, Jonathan. I do care about her." I grinned. "It's been a long time since I've been grilled by a girl's father."

He appreciated my acknowledgment. "Thank you, Matt. She's about all I have left."

I saw an opening. "No, man, she isn't all you have left. Since I've come back here, the one thing I've heard over and over is nobody gives a shit about people in The End. You're the someone who does give a shit. I don't think this neighborhood can afford you giving up on yourself."

A trace of cynicism crept into his tired eyes. "Is there some of your own guilt buried in that? Some question about why you ever left The End?"

I flashed on being led out of The End on Megan's leash. "I left here for the wrong reasons, but I left twenty years ago. I have plenty of regrets, but The End isn't my home. It's yours."

He smiled ruefully. "It's hard to feel at home anywhere now. I look at my affairs and see dead bodies of people I loved but never knew. I see my daughter bending under the weight of my mistakes. Right now, it's difficult to see much else."

I stood up. "Give it a little time, Jonathan. The only person who can crumble under the weight of your life is you."

He pulled himself to his feet. "You're a kind man, Matthew. I understand Melanie's attraction."

I shrugged and thanked him for the tea. Although the conversation was finished, I was reluctant to leave. I didn't expect to come here or even see him again. When I left The End twenty years ago I couldn't wait to get out. I had imagined my leaving was the beginning of a glorious life and marriage. This time there were no dreams. This time I was making up for missed goodbyes.

We stood awkwardly in the kitchen, each waiting for the other to move. Finally I stuck out my hand. "I wish I could have told you something you wanted to hear," I said.

"You have," he said, and led us down the hall. Before he opened the door he looked at me. "I have one last favor to ask."

"What is it?"

"Whatever your relationship with Melanie is, or will be, I hope you say nothing to her about my attachment to Peter. I'll tell her someday, but not now." He showed a resigned but honest grimace. "I want it to come from me."

"Don't worry, Jonathan. I'm not about to interfere. Especially about something I don't understand."

"Thank you, Matthew. I hope we get a chance to meet again."

Barrie's house loomed large and empty behind us. I opened the door and felt a blast of cold air. "Me too, Jonathan. Me too."

# 36

WHILE I BELIEVED JONATHAN'S CONCERN ABOUT MEL had more to do with him than with her, it disturbed me. I didn't want to add to her load. I put out a cigarette and tried to shake my apprehension. Worrying about Melanie came naturally to Jonathan. But Jonathan had an investment in his worry. Caring about others was how he salved his own hurt.

I looked in my side mirror before pulling out into the street. Splotches of water streaked the glass, but again I thought I saw something move behind a parked car. This time I didn't give my hair a chance to rise. I jammed the car into reverse and slammed my foot on the accelerator. The tires spun uselessly, caught, then shot me back to where I'd seen movement. I threw the engine into neutral and jumped out.

Therin was crouched between two parked cars. He tried to squeeze away; but before he got more than a couple of feet I had him.

He started to slap at my hand but went limp when he realized he wasn't going to break my hold.

"Hey man, let go," he complained weakly.

"In a minute." I released his shoulder but, before he could run, I grabbed the front of his light nylon windbreaker. "You're coming with me."

I pulled him back to my car and shoved him inside. He sat dripping and shivering in the corner of the seat. I pulled a rag from the glove compartment and handed it to him.

He wiped his face and hair, keeping me in view all the while. I turned the heater up to high, pulling back into my parking spot. "What the fuck do you think you're doing?" I demanded.

"I'm not doing nothin'," he replied sullenly.

I thought of the times the skin on the back of my neck had twitched. "Don't give me that shit. You've been following me on and off for the last couple weeks. Either tell me what's going on or I'll force it out of you."

"You're a good bully, aren't you?" He didn't meet my eyes.

"Sometimes." I waited, looking pointedly at his averted face.

"Well, you might as well beat me up."

"Therin," I said quietly, "I don't want to beat you up. You're not a very likable guy but I don't want to punish you for that. You've had a mad on at me since we met. What's your problem, kid?"

He shot me a venomous look. "My problem? I don't have a problem. Melanie has the problem, and it's you!"

He paused. I watched his face twist and I waited for him to spill. "You fucking prick," he said, "ever since you showed up, everything has been different!"

Belchar's parting song tinkled in my ears. "She's a little old for you," I said gently. "You were going to find it out sooner or later."

"Don't patronize me. I know how old she is."

I felt tired. "Therin, you're not the first guy to fall in love with a hopeless situation."

His body uncurled as he attacked me. "Fuck you," he shouted, as his hands flailed at my face. "I'm not talking about you ruining things between us. I'm talking about what you do to her!"

I grabbed him to keep from getting smacked. I jammed both his wrists into one of my hands and held tight until he stopped squirming. "Therin, stop. What do you think I'm doing to Melanie?"

"You're a bastard. Since you showed up in The End she's been doing shitty."

Reverberations of Jonathan. I should have stopped while I was behind. "What do you mean?"

"You're tight with her, ask her yourself."

I rubbed my eyes. "Look, I've had a hard day. If you're gonna accuse me of driving someone nuts, you gotta do details."

He hurled his words as if they were rocks: "Is drugs detail enough? What about hour after hour moping alone in her apartment? Is that detail enough for you?"

A dark look contorted his face. His body shook with rage. "Maybe where you live your kind of people can do dope because they have the money. Here, everyone winds up like those guys behind the storefront. I can't stand seeing her mess with that shit." He looked me full in the face. "You brought ghosts back here with you and they're making her sick."

There was no mistaking Therin's sincerity. "Therin, Melanie's upset about Darryl's death and how it affects Jonathan. It doesn't have anything to do with me."

He stopped shaking but there was no acquiescence in his voice. "Like hell! She never even liked Darryl. Anyhow, all this started with you."

"Look, you may not be entirely wrong about the ghosts. I remind Melanie of some painful history and I'm sure that's been disturbing but ..."

"I don't care what the reason is."

We were chasing our tails. You don't blow away someone's Hollywood fantasies and expect them to respond to logic. "Okay, you don't care about reasons, but I do. Why are you following me?"

A secretive look crossed his eyes. "Because I don't like you, and I want to keep you in front of me." He lowered his voice with a hint of pride. "And because I can."

Sometimes any small success in the face of dashed hopes is important. "You dislike a lot of people, Therin. Do you follow all of them?"

"I'd follow anyone who was driving M mad." He clamped his lips and stared stonily out the fogged windshield.

I flipped on the defroster. "You think I'm turning Melanie into a drug addict?"

"I know that since you started coming around she's been using that shit."

"You never saw her use drugs before?" I caught a whiff of my own curiosity.

"Melanie never did things like that. Never!"

The kid was getting to me; I felt guilty. He went back to staring out the window. Then anger seeped into my guilt, providing welcome relief. "I'd like to spank you for being in my business, Therin, but I like your loyalty to Mel, as moonstruck stupid as it is. I don't expect to be around The End much longer ..."

A look of triumph flashed across his face.

"Don't get carried away." I bit off my words. "I didn't say I wasn't going to see Melanie, just that my work is finished." I stared at him with a look of warning. "If you want to play Geronimo when I'm in The End, go ahead. But if I catch you following me anywhere else, you won't get away with a talking.

"Now split." I leaned across his cringing body and unlocked his door. He didn't wait for me to change my mind. I watched as he bolted down the sidewalk. I closed the door, and lit a cigarette. What I really wanted was dope.

I pushed the car into gear, then stopped short. The picture of Melanie, alone with her unpacked cartons, slapped inside my head. I was torn between returning to Jonathan for more information, or beating the crap out of Blackhead for dragging me into this quicksand. I punched the car back into gear and pulled away: I couldn't stand the thought of more talk.

I drove around waiting for my feelings to settle. Whatever heartache my presence created for Melanie wasn't going to be soothed with guilty concern. At the moment, I wasn't even clear what my concerns really were.

I aimed the car toward Emil's apartment. If I couldn't deal with Melanie, I could at least finish up the case. Still, the bare white walls of her apartment evoked a shadow that wouldn't quit.

I passed a public telephone, had an idea, and jerked the car to another stop. I was standing in the half-booth before I realized the sleeting snow had turned into a cold, driving rain. I was having second thoughts. At the other end the phone began to ring, and she answered before I could change my mind.

Her tone was flat and expressionless. "Who is it?"

"It's Matt."

Her voice dropped an octave and she semi-whispered, "Miss me already, love?"

For one rain-soaked moment I distrusted her seductiveness.

"What's the matter Matt, tongue-tied?"

"I guess." Her throaty chuckle made me feel sheepish: I felt pushed off my mark by a lovestruck adolescent and a social worker who needed someone to worry about. "I was calling to see how you were doing."

"Why shouldn't I be fine?"

"No reason, really. I just wanted to check."

"It was a good night, wasn't it?" she asked wistfully.

"Yes, it was." Another question popped out of my mouth before I could think. "Listen, Mel, where did you get the coke?"

There was another delay, then, "I have some left if you want any?"

An easy out, an exciting invitation. "No thanks. I just want to know where you got it."

"This has to do with your work, doesn't it? For someone finished with a job you continue to ask a lot of questions." She didn't sound surprised, or even upset.

"I suppose."

There was yet another wait before I broke the silence. "I'm sorry, Mel. This is the last strand of a loose end. When I'm done with it, I'm done with it all."

"Done with me too?" There was a somber note inside the tease.

"No, Mel, I'm not done with you."

She hesitated, then spoke with a catch in her voice. "Your client Blackhead," she said, her voice conspiratorial. "I bought the cocaine from Emil."

I grunted my shock and stood silent until I couldn't take the outdoors. "Good old Blackhead, huh? Listen, I'm getting drenched. I'll call you, okay?"

"Would you like to come here to dry off?"

"Not now. I've something left to do. I'll call soon."

My adrenaline was pumping; I wondered if its energy would dry my clothes. Emil was more ambitious then Prezoil had imagined. And more stupid than I'd dreamed possible. It pleased me to nail the greasy fucker for more than just dirty tricks.

# 37

AFTER JIMMYING HIS BUILDING'S ENTRANCE DOOR, I arrived at Black-head's apartment, knocked quietly, and waited. He moved behind the door then demanded my identity. Since I'd spent most of my life wondering about the same, I couldn't do the question justice standing in a corridor rancid with cooking grease and ammonia. Emil unbolted and opened the door a chain's width. My shoulder, fresh arm scab and all, powered it the rest of the way.

Blackhead stood staring glassy-eyed at the dangling latch. "I keep forgetting the Nazis won the war." He spoke in a drugged-out drawl.

"What're you high on, Emil?"

He slapped the door closed and sprawled back onto the couch with his legs outstretched. "You called me Emil." His brown, crooked teeth exposed themselves. "You either want me for something, or you're riding the rag. I ain't heard nothing about your 4×4."

I sat down on the ugly purple mohair. "It's impossible for you to tell the truth, isn't it?"

Blackhead's bloodshot eyes drooped into my own. "You want to get high, don't you?" His grin grew wider and his eyes sparkled. "I am smoking some serious Sinsemilla, man." He reached into his pants pocket and tossed a ball of tinfoil at me. "Try not to spill none, okay?"

My fingers searched for the seam to open the foil. I stared down at the large buds but forced myself to set the package gently down on the floor. Something was wrong. Emil was too calm.

Blackhead watched with heavy eyes. "You like being ugly?"

I sat deeper in the chair to get away from the tantalizing aroma. "You sound pretty sure of yourself today, Emil." I kept my tone conversational.

He slouched further into the couch.

"Confident, like you're in the catbird's seat."

He shrugged.

"Like you expect a promotion."

That caught a bit of his attention and his face began to shut down. "What the fuck are you doing here?"

"Well, Lonny said ..." I saw concern flash behind his haze. "How much of that did you smoke, Blackhead? Maybe you don't recognize the name. Lonny Prezoil. Do you recognize it?"

"What do you want?" His high had slipped into sullen.

"Sorry Emil, all that work and you still aren't going to get the job."

I watched him try to connect me and Prezoil. The confusion never left his face, but he realized I wasn't bluffing. "How do you know Lonny?"

I cross-ruffed. "You don't seem concerned about the police catching on to your method of career advancement?"

"Why would the police give a shit about me setting up some private Peeping Tom?" He pulled himself out of his slump and stood. "I'm going to wash my face." He turned sideways and sneered, "Aren't you afraid I'll try to sneak out the back?"

I showed him the gun. "That would give me an excuse to shoot."

He stumbled toward the bathroom, and I heard the water run. Straight or stoned, he should have been more worried about Darryl's death. Or else Emil was made of stronger stuff than I'd credited.

I sat forward in my seat, reached down, and tore a bud from the pack. I'd just put it between my teeth when Emil suddenly appeared over my shoulder.

"You won't get high with me, but you're not above stealing my dope." He walked back to the couch, sat, and said, "Maybe we ain't so different."

"How'd you get the red out of your eyes, Emil?"

"Visine, Bloodhound. You figured I rolled you to Prezoil, huh?" I nodded.

"How'd you get it?"

"Followed you to the parking lot."

He clenched his fist and looked at the tinfoil at my feet. "Goddamnit."

I shrugged, then watched his face crunch with thought. "You fucked my play with him, didn't you?" he accused.

"No. *You* fucked your play with him. I'm fucking your game with me."

A sly look crossed his face. "Maybe you're here for a piece of the action. Maybe you never talked to him."

I smiled at the forlorn hope in his voice. "Sorry, Blackhead. I want a piece of you, not your fantasy action."

"It wouldn't be no fantasy if you had butted out when you were supposed to."

"Don't kid yourself. Prezoil wouldn't give you the time of day."

"Ahh shit." He shook his head. "I got nobody to blame but myself. If I hadn't asked you for help, I might be sitting pretty." All of a sudden his hand sprang up and grabbed at his beard. "Did you tell Lonnie it was me that ... Ahh, I'm fucked."

His face darkened. "You're a bringdown, Jack. Why don't you get out of here? You did your job and saved Lonny a rotten conversation. Just give me back my dope."

I tried to bolster my own sagging spirit. "Does it bother you that Darryl's dead for no damn reason? Or that I intend to turn you in?"

"Turn me in for what?" He started to inhale deeply. "Wait a

minute." His mouth gulped for air. "Wait a minute. You're pissed about me using you, but that's no reason to railroad me."

I nodded. "I got to hand it to you, Emil, you're good. Very good. I took you for a lizard in a leisure suit—no balls, no brain. But you lie real, real good."

He half-rose from the couch. "You vicious prick! I asked you to check something out for me. I was scared and made a mistake." He waved his hands wildly. "Okay, I saw an opportunity to use my mistake and get in good with Lonny. That's all, man. I didn't have any idea they'd pull a runover. Shit, you didn't even get hurt. Now you want to stick me for D's death? No way man, D's death was an accident."

I didn't want to believe him. He'd lied to me since we met. "You have a solid alibi for the night Darryl died, right?"

I watched as he ransacked the musty files in his head. His voice was shrill. "How do I know? I was probably here."

"That ought to go well in court."

This time he made it completely off the couch. "Darryl scared you with a truck so it's okay to run my ass to Walpole?"

Doubt dragged at my determination, but I ignored it. "I don't like you dumping someone into a quarry to get more turf."

He paced through the load of dirty clothes and bags of junk food on the floor. "No way, man. I didn't do anything to Darryl, I'm not gonna do time."

"Blackhead, the only way you could deal coke was to get rid of Darryl. Or so you thought."

He stopped his pacing. "I don't want to sell coke," he pleaded. "I don't even use it; it makes me too jumpy. All I did was take advantage of knowing about the transfer. I knew they'd want you out of the neighborhood. Shit, my reward for turning on you had nothing to do with D's turf. You're chewing on it."

"You want to sell coke, Emil. Darryl wasn't cold before you hustled for his job."

He shook his head vigorously. "Not coke. I want to sell bigger pieces. I got no one to sell coke to. No one I know has that kind of bread."

He looked at me. "I don't know if you believe this shit or you're just trying to get even. But this ain't even ..."

"Why are you so worried if you had nothing to do with it?"

He walked into his dirty kitchen and poured a glass of water, forgetting it as he returned. "I've seen too many people busted for things they didn't do. Pigs want clean records. No one is gonna believe me. They'll use your bullshit to close the book. And if that fucking letter writer shows I'll really be dead meat." He looked at me imploringly. "Why do you want to do this to me, man?"

I brushed aside his words. "I have someone who said you sold coke. You're already dead meat."

"Whoever told you that is lying," he almost shouted.

I bit back the growing dread in my belly. "You lied to me from the beginning. Now I'm supposed to believe you?"

His head bobbed eagerly up and down. "That's right, man. That's exactly right."

"That's exactly wrong." My voice was harsh and flat. If he wasn't lying someone else was.

"Is this payback, Matt?"

A half-formed idea forced its way through my stubbornness, and I didn't trust my voice. I nodded grimly.

"You really believe I did D to take over selling his coke?"

"Sounds right to me," I said tonelessly, my conviction gone.

"You check with Lonny! He'll tell you what I sell!"

Emil's proof wouldn't convince anyone from a jury to a broken-down detective, but he had begun to convince me.

ONE WAY OR ANOTHER, it was time to close the book. But I had to be certain there would be no more lies. I pulled the gun from my holster and placed it on the table. "Were you behind the beating? The one from Sludge and his boys."

He looked at the .38.

"You don't have to worry unless you lie."

He stared at the gun. "Yeah. I hadn't figured the Lonny angle yet and wanted you to go away. Inviting you into the neighborhood was a bad mistake. I tried to talk you out but you wouldn't leave." He looked at me accusatorially. "If you listened I wouldn't have needed Sludge. Shit, the truck thing would'na happened either."

I felt my face blanch as a terribly different picture of the last two weeks finally burst through my resistance. "Emil, I want to know about the letter."

He looked suspicious. "Jesus, man, you jump around like a flea. The letter scared me and when you sprung me from the bounty hunter, I wanted you to check it out, that's all."

"What was in that letter?"

He caught his breath, eyes shifting away. "I already told you."

"You told me *some* of what the letter said."

"I don't know what you're talking about."

I dropped my hand to the gun's grip. My head was splitting, and my stomach was nauseous with heavy foreboding. I scraped the gun along the table.

For a moment I thought he was going to run. Instead, he leaned forward and breathed his garlicky grass breath at me. "Whoever wrote the letter knew things no one shoulda known. I never told nobody this shit before. Nobody. That's what made the letter so fucking weird. Like someone else was at the quarry."

I forced the question out of my mouth. "What happened that night, Emil?"

"Man, it was twenty years ago but it's clearer than yesterday. It was hot, real hot. Lonny tells Pete he's got some very clean acid." Blackhead suddenly stopped short.

"What is it, Blackhead?"

A dirty smile crossed his face. "Lonny. He was a real chicken-hawk."

"Chickenhawk?"

"Young girls. Lonny made sure Pete brought Melanie."

"Peter didn't mind?"

"Why should he mind? She wasn't gonna fuck Lonny. You know her, she don't fuck nothing." Another dirty smile crossed his face. "I always figured she was closet."

I gritted my teeth and nodded.

"Anyhow," he continued, "it was the cleanest acid ever. Lonny said he got it direct from Owsley. He had this fancy stereo and all sorts of good music. We probably listened to Vanilla Fudge fifty times." Blackhead looked at me and raised his eyebrows. "But Pete got bored and wanted to go swimming. So we split."

His face clouded. He had finished the comfortable part of his story. "Keep talking, Emil. What happened at the quarry?"

He surprised me and continued without more prodding, "We left Lonny's ..."

"The three of you?" I interrupted.

He looked confused. "The three of us?"

"You, Peter, and Melanie."

"Melanie didn't come with us. She stayed at Lonny's."

I guessed it coming but it still felt like a knee to my groin. I felt my shoulders slump. "Go on."

"We got to the quarry and went swimming." Emil grew flushed and uncomfortable. "It was hot like I said. So after the swim we were laying on the rocks and Pete told me about the saint."

"The saint?"

"Fucking Jon-a-than. Pete's thing with Barrie was crazy. Pete was top drawer at b&e, but when he worried about getting busted he'd sell his ass." Blackhead shook his head. "He was going down on Barrie for free. Free. I didn't get it. Why the fuck free?"

Homophobia crawled off his skin like a river of maggots. "Then Pete told me he was moving out. He and Melanie were going to move in with the saint." A brooding, hurt look crossed his face and he spoke in a whisper. "Pete said he loved him." Another ugly look, then he sneered, "That's it, man. We're through."

"Finish the story, Blackhead."

"That's it, I'm telling you!"

"You're lying."

He looked at the gun, then forced the next words in a hoarse voice. "He tried to mess with me."

"Mess with you?"

"He tried to go down on me, okay?" All the nervous energy had drained from his body; he almost fell down on the dirty floor.

But I wasn't finished. "What did you do when he tried to fuck you, Emil?"

His head shot up. "I ran, goddamnit! I grabbed my shit and ran." His face worked furiously and, to my shock, I saw tears roll from his eyes. "Don't you see? I fucking ran away! If I stayed he wouldn't be dead! I could have been able to help!"

He tried to stop the flow of tears, failed, and broke into loud heaving sobs. I sat back in the chair numb with the belief that Emil spoke the truth.

He finally stopped crying, staring at me from wet-splashed eyes. "Maybe this is why I hired you in the first place," he panted, chest moving rapidly.

"What do you mean?"

It took him another moment to catch his breath. "I think after I got the note I had to tell somebody about all this. I kept everything inside for a real long time; maybe I couldn't take it no more."

We sat quietly in the middle of his disheveled living room. I actually felt sorry for his twenty years of hidden guilt and grief. Then I felt sorry for myself. Emil's mourning was coming to a close, mine was just beginning.

I waited a few more minutes before I spoke, though my skin was already cringing from answers I didn't want to hear. But the same demand that had pushed Blackhead to hire me, the inexorable drive to finally close old wounds, pushed me to break the silence.

"Emil, you're certain Melanie didn't leave Prezoil's with you and Peter?"

He looked at me. "Sure I'm certain. I told you I can remember every detail. That's what was making me batty."

I felt the perverse lure of a major depression, and almost asked for rolling papers. Instead, I pulled my cigarettes from inside my pocket, lit two, and handed him one. "Where did you go after you left the quarry?"

He took a long drag. "Home. I went home."

"Was Melanie there?" I felt my body tense while I waited for his answer. Everything in the room seemed farther away. Like my eyes had sunk to the back of my head.

"No, she didn't get home 'til after I downed out. I don't know what time." He hunched his body in my direction. "Why do you keep asking me about her? And why do you want to know about that night anyway?"

I skipped the first question and lied about the second. "I'm just curious," I said.

"What the fuck for?"

"I said I'm curious, that's all. Where would she have crashed if she didn't stay at home?"

"You'll have to ask her. We weren't exactly tight, you know. Never really got along. We didn't fight or nothing, mostly stayed away from each other. She never liked that Pete and me were close." He frowned and some of his earlier sadness returned. "After Pete's accident she always blamed me for not coming home with him."

"You ever wonder whether she sent you that letter?"

"How could she? We left her at the party and the letter had details. Anyhow, I think she crashed at Lonny's with everyone else."

"He tell you that?"

"Sort of."

"What do you mean 'sort of'?"

"Look, Matt, you have to understand what was happening. Lonny knew the pigs wouldn't bother too much about Pete. But the less they bothered the better. He said I shouldn't talk to him or no one about that night. He'd see what he could do to quiet things down. By then, the cops had already questioned me once. Anything that would cool things out was fine by me."

His voice dropped. "I figured Lonny didn't want to deal with giving acid to kids. Also, if he did get in Melanie's pants, and she bitched, that would mean more trouble. She was still jail bait."

His words made my skin crawl, but I wasn't getting angry; a wall was building inside, insulating me from my feelings. My body was stiff, cold, and uncomfortable, but my head was clear and alert. "You don't make it sound like Lonny had much of a chance." It was hard to imagine, but I fervently hoped they'd spent the night together.

"Who knows? Lonny don't usually strike out. You never can tell about things, man. Everybody that wants to keep their crap secret, man, you know what I mean? Melanie stuck to Pete like a fly on sugar, but she didn't know he hustled. If people don't want you to know something, they find a way to keep it quiet."

"Pete kept quiet about his hustling?"

"Yeah." Hurt filled his face. "Pete said one of the things that made him decide to move in with Jonathan was that he could stop doing the street. If he needed to lay dead, he could always get bread from Barrie."

I sighed and put the gun back into the holster; it was time to leave. Time to be alone. I stood, shrugged into my leather, and stared at the tinfoil ball of dope. I sighed and lit a cigarette.

"You aren't still gonna set me up, are you?" Blackhead pleaded. "I told you everything, man. More than everything."

I stood by the dangling door-chain and looked at him. There wasn't much to see. I rubbed my eyes and briefly wondered how he had managed to crawl so deeply under my skin. "Don't worry, Emil, you're out of it. Completely out of it."

Skin and all.

# 39

I FOUGHT AGAINST THE WIND as I headed toward my car. As soon as I got inside I tore the stick-on clock off the dashboard and threw it on the floor. I wasn't quitting until everything was done.

Up 'til now I'd seen my time in The End as a fruitless circle of frustration. Now, staring into the night, I knew it to be a sphere of tragedy. And I was somehow part of it.

There was irony here. I'd spent the entire case trying to find out how I was used. At the moment, I knew most everything but that.

I could walk. Drive away from this shithole, go home, shower, get high, watch TV. I could stuff my face with Fritos and call the malls. I could never ask another question, say another word.

I had done it once before.

But different ties bind in different ways. This situation was part of a pattern that extended beyond any single explosion. If I was right, it was only the second act in a lifetime drama.

I leaned forward and started the engine. No matter what other role I might have played, if this was a street opera, it was my job to close it down.

I passed a phone booth and stopped the car. I looked him up in the book, which was miraculously intact and stuffed in its slot. Unfortunately, it didn't cover his home town. Ma Bell figured no one from The End needed to call the rich.

I had better luck with Information. I dialed the number and spoke the moment I heard his voice. "I have a couple of questions to ask you about that party."

"I told you we were through." His quiet voice was strained.

"And I'm telling you we're not."

"You forget who you're talking to." He hung up.

I was too cold and too wired for that kind of crap. I re-dialed the number; when he picked up his receiver I shouted, "You can have my legs broken, my heart cut out, and my ass cemented to the bottom of the fucking harbor. But you can't get it done before I get to your house and find out what I want to know. In front of your fucking family, you understand?"

My intensity froze him. Hell, it surprised me. I took a deep breath and held my steam while he decided what to do.

"Where are you?" he finally said.

"We can do this over the phone."

"I don't want to do anything over the phone. Now where are you?"

"In The End."

"Do you know the Wagon Wheel?"

"Yeah."

"I'll meet you there in a half hour."

I drove around until a parking spot opened with a view of the front door. I didn't think Prezoil was going to bring anyone with him, but I wanted to be certain. Despite my outburst, I valued my legs.

He was early, overdressed, and alone. I waited another five minutes to see if any of his gladiators would follow. All I saw, however, was the usual scum who patronized the joint. As I left the car, I realized that tonight anyone in the Wagon Wheel could break my legs.

I spotted Prezoil in the rear of the cavernous room and cut a path to his table. The stripper's cage was empty. The jukebox's twang was background to the cacophony of raucous, slurred conversations.

He scowled when I sat down at his table. "You need some new clothes, Jacob."

I waved for the waitress and said, "For this barn?"

"Don't like my little club, eh?"

Before I could answer the waitress came by and took our order. I was perversely pleased that it was a double, straight night for him too. "Club?"

"Nothing official."

"Nothing special either." Now I knew why Blackhead was allowed to sit here without drinking.

A look of impatience crossed his face. "I didn't come here to listen to your wise mouth. What is it you want?"

The waitress returned with our drinks and I took a hefty slug. "Lonny, why did you tell me that Emil, Peter, and Melanie left the party together?"

"That's the way I remember it."

"I told you I don't like loose ends."

"You dragged me out for this?"

"I didn't drag you anywhere. I was willing to ask you about your fucking under-age girls anywhere."

He stared right back at me. "You don't mind pushing it, do you? You were right about the things I can have done to you."

"I know."

"You don't care?"

"I'm not suicidal. I know better than to cause you any trouble. I want to know what happened that night, that's all. Only this time I want the damn truth."

"Your curiosity has nothing to do with me?"

"Right."

"No shakedown when you're out of work and get a little hungry?"

"I don't want proof, just truth."

"You want to tell me why?"

"No."

I watched his smooth tilt. "You do got balloons. Okay, she didn't leave with the other two." He stared at me impassively. "I made it with her. If it's truth you want, it wasn't much fun. You ever fuck a corpse?"

"She spend the night?" My voice was calm, but it was nutcracking time at the Wagon Wheel.

"Hell no, she didn't spend the night. More like half an hour. Then out of there like she was late for a fix."

Lonny kept speaking but I hardly heard him. I hardly heard anything. The bar's noise buzzed into the background and the room faded white. I returned to the sound of my name.

"Jacob, Jacob? Jesus, are you all right? What the hell are you involved in? What's going on?"

He was annoyed but I was through with him. I drained the last of my drink and stood up. I gripped the back of the chair until I could negotiate my way to the door. "Thanks, Lonny, that's all I needed to know." I turned and started for the exit.

"Hey, shamus," Lonny called to my back, "aren't you going to pay for the drink?"

"Lay it off on the house," I said without stopping.

Outside, my semi-faint retreated in the nasty weather. I was bone-tired and thought once again about going home. By the time I reached the car I knew I couldn't. "The dread had already occurred."

For me, that is. The dread had already occurred for me. With one eye, his house looked dark and desolate. With the other, quiet and peaceful. Both eyes knew which it was going to be once I got inside. I rang the bell long and hard and, for a second, had the uneasy sense he had moved. I rang the bell again and saw a light flash on the second floor. A few minutes later Jonathan opened the door a quarter of the way, and stood baggy-faced in a red tartan robe.

"What are you doing here?" he asked, as he rubbed sleep from his eyes. "Damn, you look terrible," he added before I could reply.

"We have to talk."

"Now? I was sleeping. Can't it wait until morning?"

*It* probably could, but I couldn't. "No."

He heard the despair in my voice and stepped aside. "I'm not sure what to offer you at this time of night," he said as he led me down the hall to the kitchen.

"Bourbon. And pour one for yourself."

He looked at me; his eyes were suddenly bereft of sleep. "You discovered something?"

"Pour the drinks," I repeated.

"That bad?" He pulled a bottle from one of the cabinets.

"Worse."

It took a hard twenty minutes to lay everything out. He interrupted me in the beginning. I answered his questions and protestations as calmly as I could. The longer I continued with my story, the fewer the interruptions, until he fell into a shocked, stricken silence. I had expected to feel guilty for tearing the remains of his life apart. Instead, I felt a terrible concern for a man who, in his own ragged way, had given so much to so many lost causes.

"I don't believe you," he said at last. "I hardly know you but you expect me to believe your monstrous theory? That's all it is, you know, an outrageous theory." His arms moved in a dismissive motion, as if to make my "theory" disappear.

Deep within was the horror of having heard the truth. He hadn't yet realized it; mostly what he realized was that the life he had so carefully constructed was over. I kept quiet and gave him plenty of time and heart to take the hit.

"What kind of evidence do you have?" he demanded, his denial taking center stage.

I just shrugged. "I'm a detective, Jonathan, not a lawyer."

"I think you're the insane one," he half-shouted as he slammed the kitchen table.

"Not this time, Jonathan, I'm sorry."

He gave no sign he had heard. "Ever since you've returned to The End there have been nothing but disasters. Nothing!" His face was red, and his eyes bulged. "Now you show up in the middle of the night and expect me to accept *this*?"

I waited while his outrage played itself out. He had just finished burying one and I was burying the other. The sadness of it all was that Jonathan knew what I said to be true. He had to know; he had lived with her. He might be blind, but he wasn't stupid. He would have seen signs; but his love, his need, wouldn't let him understand. I knew what that was like; more than once other people had to show me my self-deceptions.

He paced around like a caged animal. "I ought to throw you out. You're nothing but trouble. Are you trying to punish me because of who I am? Maybe you're one of those people who think I can't really love her because I'm just an old queer." Barrie walked over to the table and slammed his fist down again, this time shaking the glasses enough to spill some of their contents.

"I ought to throw you out," he repeated, but his voice had lost its tempest. I watched silently as his years of love and loyalty spat him in the face.

Finally he turned to me and demanded, "What do you want from me? Do you really expect me to throw the one person I have left into *Titicut Follies?* Toss her into Hell for the rest of her life?"

"You can't ignore this anymore, Jonathan."

He interrupted me as an idea crossed his mind. "Are you trying to get money from me? To keep quiet?"

"I'm not a blackmailer," I said gently.

His temper took over again. "You haven't any proof, god-damnit. You've said as much. What if you're wrong? You can't destroy someone's life on speculation. Why the hell come here any-way? A damn courtesy call?"

"I came here because you love her and, in her own way, she loves you." I stood, retrieved the bourbon from the counter, and poured some into both our glasses. "I came here because I can't walk away from this."

He strode to the table and swallowed from his glass. "Why not? Why not go home?"

"Melanie's sick, Jonathan. I think you know that. I don't think you knew how much." I held out my palms. "Maybe her depressions and withdrawals frightened the questions out of you. Maybe it was the intensity of her rage. But you know people too well not to have suspected."

He grunted a short, harsh laugh. "Right, I know people so well. Like Peter, like Darryl and now, you tell me, Melanie."

"That's exactly right. You weren't blind to their flaws; you were attracted to them. That's almost worse than blind. You didn't love them the same way, or even for the same reasons. And you certainly didn't make them who they were—that was fated by the first generation of their family that couldn't find good reason to live." I paused, then added, "I believe you bought them time."

I watched the lines in his face shift, his anger replaced by wracking sobs. He sunk onto his chair, buried his head and cried deeply, the anguish muffled in his arms. Melanie's time was up.

I had no tears. Instead, I waited patiently until he regained control, then asked quietly, "What really went on between Peter and Melanie?"

I expected another flare-up, but he spoke in a voice resonate with sadness and deep resignation. "They were incredibly close. Bonded. It was one of the reasons Peter was willing to move in. He thought it might separate them a little. Though he never said, I think he felt burdened by their relationship."

He stared at me, his face a ravaged set of features and lines. "She had no identity of her own. She'd spent her entire life in Peter's footsteps."

I thought of my first night with her. "Was sex part of their bond?" I asked.

Barrie turned his face away, but the question didn't shock him. He lifted his arms in a gesture of helplessness. "I don't know. I just don't know. Peter never said, and I'd never ask Melanie."

I sat with my melancholy, thinking of what was in store for Jonathan and Melanie. And me. Eventually I reached across the table and placed my hand on his shoulder. "I came here because Melanie is going to need her father."

He lifted his head and stared at me with bleary, guarded eyes.

"You've been good to her, Jonathan. A good father and good friend. There aren't many people who've been lucky enough to have that. Her years with you were the best years of her life."

My words squeezed through his sadness. He raised his hands to his face, rubbing his eyes as if some ugly view might go away. But I didn't go away. I watched as he struggled to regain his breath. "Go get dressed," I said gently.

"Why?" he asked. "What's supposed to happen now?"

I pushed my gut-ache aside and tried to rouse the troops. "As bad as you feel, you're better off than Mel. She needs you in her corner, now more than ever. You need each other."

He rose and left the room as if in a trance. I didn't want him gone long. We would both be spending too much time alone once this was through. I poured more alcohol into my glass, lit a cigarette, and waited for his return.

He reappeared dressed, but shaking his head. "I still don't know what you expect. I won't lie to you. Even if what you say is true, I won't turn her over to the police."

"I don't have a blueprint but Melanie's very sick. She needs help, not benign neglect. We're in a mental and legal minefield that someone's got to navigate."

"I don't understand what you want me to do?"

I took my wallet out of my pocket and rummaged for Simon Roth's card. "I want you to get him. I'm going to speak with Melanie and I want both of you to meet me there. If there is one lawyer in town who can jerryrig the legal end, it's this guy."

He glanced at the card I put in front of him. "This is a business card. No one's going to be at an office this time of night."

I picked up a pen and the card and scribbled Simon's home address. "Tell him I sent you. Then tell him everything. Everything. He'll come and I don't think he'll need persuading. If he does, remind him that he owes me a big one."

He waved the card but shook his head. "I don't know why we have to do this now. Maybe if we sleep on it, it will look different?"

I waited a moment, then said, "Melanie once called herself a shadow person. I thought I understood what she meant, but I didn't. Now I do. It's better that we take care of this. She'd prefer the night."

We sat there for a painfully quiet time. He kept shaking his head and I kept drinking. When the glass ran dry I didn't bother with a refill; I just drank straight from the bottle. Eventually, I found the guts to move and started down the hall.

"Matt."

I turned and watched him fiddle with the card. I waited until he quietly asked the question Boots had only stabbed at. "Do you love her, Matthew?"

"I don't know, Jonathan. I'm afraid I have no love left."

# 40

My head felt heavy as I dragged it up the stairs. Despite the hour, light streamed from her apartment. I rapped softly on her door. For a brief second I felt eyes stab the back of my neck. I sprinted down the steps, peered up and down the street, but saw no one. I knelt quickly and looked under the row of parked cars, but again came up empty. I jogged back to the door when I saw Melanie standing behind the wood and glass. She opened it and signaled me inside. She wore a pair of white jeans and a yellow tank top. Her hair was swept off her face—her fresh lipstick, mascara, and eyeliner a surprise. Melanie's ease at my arrival caught me short. It was as if she had been waiting.

"A funny time of year for those clothes," I said, passing through the doorway.

"I hate the winter. Tonight I'm pretending it's summer, my favorite."

I smiled grimly. The heat in the apartment was turned up high.

For the first time in the long night, my bones began to thaw. I unsnapped my jacket and thrust away a fleeting moment of desire as I caught a whiff of her perfume.

"Did you come to dry off?" she asked.

It took a moment before I remembered our telephone call. *The* telephone call. "No Mel, I'm still working."

"I thought so. Would you like a drink?"

"Bourbon would be fine."

"You drink on the job?" she teased over her shoulder.

"On some more than others."

"And this is one of those?" She held the drink toward me with an outstretched arm, eyes clear and tranquil.

I took the glass and nodded.

She smiled placidly. "You're definitely not here for another night of love."

I sipped at the whiskey and sat down on the couch. She waited until I was seated before moving to the plastic recliner. "We were reversed the last time you visited."

The image of her riding my lap jump started my libido. But I just couldn't afford desire. "Why did you lie to me?"

For an instant she looked like a mischievous teenager.

"Why did you lie about the coke?"

She shrugged. "It was time. And habit."

"Habit?"

Her playfulness evaporated as she leaned forward in her seat. "I'd never admit to a personal relationship with Darryl."

"I don't understand."

"Of course you don't." She stood and smiled down at me but her eyes glanced toward the clock on the mantel. "I want a drink."

As she walked to the liquor cabinet I said, "You expected me to come here tonight."

She poured her drink and turned away. "I didn't know when, but I hoped it would be tonight. I wanted a chance to talk to you before ..."

Her words trailed off to a stop. She swiveled her body back toward the couch and spoke into her glass. "It took you longer than I thought. For a while I imagined you were going to leave everything the way it was." She smiled at me. "I would have been surprised, but it wouldn't have mattered."

"What wouldn't matter?"

She shook her head and lifted the bottle. She poured into her glass, but brought the bottle back to her seat anyway. It was time to cut to the bone.

"Melanie," I said softly, "you need help."

She stared at a point somewhere over my shoulder. "I've already taken care of that." When she saw the question on my face, she frowned. "But you wouldn't know that."

With her eyebrows raised she said, "You stopped at Jonathan's, didn't you?"

It was a statement, not a question. Therin's face popped into my head and I rubbed the back of my neck.

She sounded loving. "Were you kind?"

Something inside me lurched and I felt pity pull against my collar. "Melanie, stop asking questions," I said helplessly.

"First, tell me if you were kind."

I shrugged. "I don't know. I tried."

"What they say is true. 'What you don't know won't hurt you.'" She pushed nonexistent hairs back from her forehead. "I kept many secrets from Jonathan. That's why it's important he learns of things in a gentle way."

There was no lie, no delusion in her concern for Barrie. I heard myself croak, "What secrets, Mel?"

"Don't play now, Matt. I told you about my longing for Peter. And I know you've discovered others."

She rushed on without waiting. "There were secrets between me and Darryl. Secrets that might have devastated Jonathan. It was important that no one knew."

"You were involved with drugs?"

"That was your sixty-four-dollar question, wasn't it? Where did I get the coke?" She smiled sarcastically. "If drugs were all there was I might not have lied." She sipped from her drink. "Darryl and I were lovers."

I felt my skin tingle as I finally understood.

Her eyes flashed and her head snapped up. "Don't stare at me that way! I know what that look means." Her eyes glittered and shone like wet crystal, her words flung like a handful of gravel. "I know what you're thinking, 'a whore like her mother.'" She shook her fist at the dead mother in tight, rapid thrusts. "I was never like her! Never!"

Mel's lips drew tight across her teeth and she sneered. "You and I were lovers too. Were we strangers? Did you leave money on my dresser? I got entangled. I sold nothing! In my life sex was never impersonal!"

Her chest heaved; the liquid shook in her glass. Rocked by her venom, I caught my breath, then asked, "Why the past tense, Melanie? We're still entangled."

The question helped her regain her fragile control. She sighed and looked up at the clock. "Past, present, it doesn't matter." She held out her drink. "Look at us. We started in the past. Are we finishing the past tonight? Or the present?"

She stared back again at the glass in her hand. "If I were alone I might have made a margarita. You know, part of making it summer ..."

The undercurrent of finality hammered against my taut nerves. "Why didn't you make it anyway?"

"I'd rather drink what you're having," she said, looking more thoughtful than angry. "It's funny—I would drink what you're drinking, and I don't even like the taste."

All the textbooks in all the libraries couldn't have summed it up better, I thought.

"I'd never allow the slightest word about Darryl," she offered, changing subjects abruptly. "It would have killed Jonathan to know." She smiled contemptuously and some of her earlier anger reappeared. "If he knew what all of us really were ..."

"He'd have worked at loving you more," I interrupted.

"Oh no." A hard, knowing look shifted the contours of her face. Her fire hadn't abated, only changed form. Now her voice seethed with bitterness. "It doesn't work like that. Not in the real world, Matt. Jonathan is good, but Jonathan is still human. The other two knew what they were doing, and they did it anyway."

"What was it they did, Melanie?"

"They left me." She leaned back further in her seat and raised her glass in my direction. "This is why I'm glad you're here. You can't leave me, and I can make you understand."

Her words put a chill in the hot air.

"You loved them?"

A crooked smile appeared on her face. "Loved them? Perhaps I loved Jonathan, but I don't know much about love. Darryl was a toy." She rubbed her eyes, smearing the makeup. "Even though I want to talk to you, I find it hard to tell my secrets. I never have, you know."

A pause. "What I had with my brother was beyond love. We were actually a part of each other." She struck at the air with her free hand. "Darryl only wanted me. He didn't need anyone. Peter almost understood."

"Understood what?"

"Almost. I said 'almost.' If he had really understood, everything would have been different." Her face twisted into a mixture of rage and torment. "He refused. He refused to understand."

She turned her head sharply, staring at the clock again. I tried to bring her back. "Both of them were going to live with Jonathan. You don't blame him?"

She seemed startled by the suggestion. "Of course not. Jonathan never lies. He always tried to give me what I needed. That's who he is."

Her tone hardened as she shifted focus. "They didn't care about him. Both of them plotted to get what they could." Her voice grew harsh. "They were *liars*." She waved her hand like a brush, painting out the room and the "liars."

"Melanie, you weren't protecting Jonathan twenty years ago?"

She shook her head as a note of shrillness entered her voice. "Different lies. Darryl lied to Jonathan. Peter lied to me. Twenty years ago I was the little one. That's what Peter always said: 'You're the little one.' He told me he lived to protect the little one."

She snorted. "You're always the little one until someone tells you you're not. Then what are you?" She raised her hand questioningly. "He said it would be a good deal. He'd get me in and we would both live swell."

She shook her head. "Can you believe he could use a word like 'swell' after I'd heard him talk about passing his body out to strangers like it was candy? After watching him offer it to Emil? We were supposed to share Peter's body. It was going to complete us."

Her head jerked; she forced herself to drink. "That's when I discovered I was the only believer. I should have seen it earlier. We used to have terrible fights about our mother, and Peter always took her side. I should have realized he was defending the two of them." She refilled her glass from the bottle in her hand, and sat back in her chair.

"It's not like I expected," she said, breathing heavily.

"What's not?"

"This talk. I'd imagined a feeling of peace. I always thought that's why Catholics have last rites."

I smiled despite my tension. "You mean 'confession.'"

She swung her glass absently. "Whatever. It's not important now. Don't misunderstand, he had affection for Jonathan."

I was momentarily confused by her shift. "Who?" I asked.

"Peter, Peter." She sounded exasperated. "Darryl didn't care for Jonathan at all. Darryl actually liked Prezoil." She shook her head disgustedly. "Peter liked J.B." She smiled but it was to someone on the horizon. "That's what I called him, you know."

One person's affectionate nickname had been another's nasty joke.

She reached out her arm to offer the bottle. "Peter cared for Jonathan, but he was a piece of me. Darryl cared for no one but himself. Love, or need, isn't as important to men as plain old greed."

I picked up the bottle and poured while Melanie scoured my face with her eyes. It was sad to see the world through her fractured prisms.

"You agree with me, don't you?" she demanded.

I didn't want to upset her. But this was a night for truth. "I recognize what you see. There's a difference."

A look of hate swept across her face. She nestled the drink to her chest. "No. You just *hope* you're different." She tipped her head toward her drink. "Everyone hopes they're different. But you just talk less."

"Why did you hand me Prezoil?"

She gave a bitter little laugh. "It was time to put an end to everything once and for all." She leaned forward to stare at the clock and then at me. "I knew you wouldn't quit until you had all the answers. I knew it the same way I knew something was going to happen the minute I left Jonathan's."

"When you moved out?"

She looked impatient. "Yes. Please don't be stupid now."

"Why do you keep looking at the clock?"

She ignored my question. "I waited and watched and there was Darryl. I could see his game right from the beginning. He was going to turn Jonathan into a lap dog. I didn't know what I would have to do. Or whether I would have a choice. I had to plan."

It was now a helpless and tortured expression. "You see, Matt, there's that word again—choice. That disgusting, ugly night I overheard Peter and Emil's conversation and watched Peter behave like my mother, I had *no* choice."

The anger had returned, delivered in a voice full of agony. "That whole night was a continuous pornographic movie, one I'd seen since I was a baby. What happened afterward had to happen. I'd felt like that before, but never as totally as I felt it that night." Unconsciously she rubbed more of her makeup around on her face. "It's a, a possession. You watch yourself but feel nothing. You watch yourself act, and it's like watching a movie."

Her drink shook in her hand and she gripped the arm of the plastic chair with the other. She closed her eyes and breathed deeply. "When Darryl insisted upon moving in with Jonathan, I knew I might hurt him but I wasn't sure. I didn't know even after he threatened to tell Jonathan about us. He was afraid I was going to cause trouble."

She smiled grimly. "I don't cause trouble. It isn't up to me."

I started to speak but she ignored my interruption. The glaze in her eyes had gone. They sparkled with a mixture of fear and venom. "I had to make plans in case anything happened. I was afraid of prison. That's why I sent Emil the letter."

"Why Emil?"

"He was the start of everything," she snarled. "He worked at turning Peter against me, taking Peter's innocence. First my mother, then Emil. The two of them. My mother tried to ruin us, but we almost got away. Emil brought Peter right back. Peter never would have offered his body if Emil hadn't seduced him first."

"But Emil refused Peter."

"That was just his manipulation. He made Peter want him. Just like my mother made men want her. That's why I sent that letter. I knew he'd go shooting off his big mouth. If something happened to Darryl I wanted the police to blame Emil. He deserved to have his innocence taken away."

She calmed herself with a few deep breaths and continued, "I didn't expect him to find you. Your appearance was the final sign."

Waves of uneasy responsibility washed through me. "What kind of sign?"

The look in her eyes pleaded with me to understand. "At first it was a sign that something was going to happen. A sign that history rolls like a wheel, always repeating. When you began asking questions I was frightened and tried to stop you. Later, when I realized you wouldn't quit until you had all your answers, I knew it meant something else. A signal to stop resisting, though that came later."

She looked at me wildly. "I know how to stop resisting. After Peter and Emil left the party, Lonny raped me. I stopped resisting then, too."

Prezoil's face jumped in front of me and I wanted to bludgeon it with a shovel. This was why he'd lied.

Melanie jerked her thoughts back to me. "At the end when I stopped resisting, I understood the rest of it. What I had to do. That's why I came to your apartment." She smiled sweetly at me from underneath the mess on her face. "We were good. No one could supply what Peter refused, but we were close. I needed to feel that one last time."

I didn't want to hear anymore. "You wait for betrayal," I said tensely, trying to push her away.

"Of course I wait for it"—she shook her head emphatically—"what choice is there?"

She stood, walked to the window, fiddled with the closed venetian blind, and stepped back toward the mantel. "I can't spend my life waiting for one person after the other to prove the same thing over and over.

"*I'm not like my mother,*" her voice rose a decibel higher, "hurting everyone before they had a chance to hurt her. I'm not like that. I wait and the hurt always happens. Spending my life in helpless circles." Her eyes filled with tears. "I burned parts of me for Peter—and for what? For something I saw every morning when my mother stuck out her hand."

Her face contorted. "That's why I'm telling you this. We were special together, in a way that might help you understand. When I told you the things that I knew you couldn't leave alone, I was telling myself I couldn't keep waiting. I don't want to usher at the same movie my whole life. I'm too tired for that. Too tired."

Her words, coupled with the noise from the front door, gave me room to breathe. I didn't know what would come next, but at least Simon would take charge. I felt my body sag as my own tired took hold. This was finally over.

I kept my eyes on Melanie's face, concerned about her reaction to Jonathan. But I felt my stomach drop when an unexpected voice screeched from the doorway, "Take your jacket off!"

I spun my head and saw Therin, sweat and tears pouring from his face. His long, stringy black hair lay matted and wet on his neck. He stood pointing a .22, holding it stiff-armed in his two hands. Foam had collected at the corners of his mouth: he was overdosing.

"I thought you didn't approve of drugs, Therin." My own sweat rose on my neck and back. Melanie stood watching without surprise.

"I didn't tell you to talk, I said take off your fucking jacket." The barrel twitched.

I raised my hands, "Okay, Therin." I got up slowly and carefully removed my coat.

"Now slide all that shit to me." His voice was stretched with tension. The gun kept jumping around.

I looked at Melanie, but she was staring at the clock again, her hands clenching and letting go. Tears ran down unheeded through rivulets of distorted makeup. I unbuckled the strap and pulled off the holster. I knelt, checked the safety, and slid the bundle toward

Therin's feet. I sat down again and draped my arm over the side of the couch.

Where the fuck were Jonathan and Simon? I glanced at the clock. They should have been here by now. Suddenly I realized that I didn't know whether Simon was in town.

The thought drove my eyes back to the clock. This time Melanie noticed. "Why are *you* looking at the clock?" She spoke quietly through her silent tears. "Everything comes to an end. This will all be over soon. People will wonder for a minute—that's all."

"Killing me isn't going to end anything."

She looked at me and frowned. "Killing you?"

I looked to the door and pleaded with Therin, "Why don't you think for a minute? I don't know how much you understand, but Melanie needs help, she doesn't need you pointing a gun."

Mel stood with her arms at her sides in front of the mantle. "Stay there, Therin. You know what you have to do." I glanced in his direction and saw his grief-stricken face flush, new tears spring into his eyes, but he nodded.

Melanie turned toward me, and at the same time I heard the muffled sound of a car door closing. She heard it too. "Do you have someone coming to get me?" she erupted hysterically.

I tried to sound calm. "Just Jonathan. I asked him to bring a friend of mine who can help us. No police." I heard footsteps on the stairs, saw Therin look desperately at Mel.

Her arms began to shake and she cried, "Damn it!" She stamped her foot. "Now Therin! Now! Before he gets inside. Don't break your promise! Now! Right now if you really love me! Right now!"

Out of the corner of my eye I saw the gun tremble and I jack-knifed over the arm of the couch. I heard two shots explode the screams in the room, but felt no burning metal shatter my back.

I stuck my head out over the side of the couch. Jonathan and Simon were in the doorway, staring white-faced and horrified at the sight on the floor between us. Therin had put his first bullet in Melanie's heart, and then blown his own face out the back of his head.

I sank down on my knees and sobbed.

# 41

SIMON WAS EVERYWHERE ALL AT ONCE. He dragged Jonathan and me onto the porch, went back inside, and reemerged with a large, wet, hot bath towel. He rubbed our faces as if to wake us from a coma. While he wiped at mine he put his lips by my ear and asked if I'd done any shooting. I tried to talk but all I could do was tremble and shake my head. Jonathan sat next to me staring fixedly at the street. Although it was damn near freezing, both of us were oblivious to the cold. Simon told us to stay put as he went back inside.

I jammed the towel into my mouth and bit down hard to keep my stomach from wrenching. Barrie looked at me with dull, lifeless eyes. I wanted to talk, to ease his misery, but my misery had no words. Instead, I grabbed his hand.

Simon reappeared on the porch. "I'm glad you called," he said somberly. "Can you take the towel out of your mouth?"

I nodded dumbly and let the thing fall.

Simon leaned over and pulled it away. "Can you give me a handle for the police?" he asked tersely.

"I'll try."

I thought I'd spoken but Simon shook my shoulder. "I know you're in shock, but if you can talk it will help," he repeated.

"It was a murder, then suicide," I said, then cracked. Blood pumping from Therin and the thought of Melanie sprawled on the floor drove my stomach into a paroxysm, and I grabbed for the towel. Jonathan just sat there holding my hand. I couldn't tell whether he heard anything or not.

I struggled to push the splattered floor from my mind. "The woman was responsible for two deaths. One recent, one twenty years ago. Her murder was really a suicide, induced, something she concocted with the kid."

"With the kid?"

"Yeah. He wasn't wrapped tight and she brought him over the edge. I don't know what else went on between them, but tonight was her idea."

Simon looked at me carefully. "Was your gun used?"

I shook my head. "No. It should be somewhere on the floor, still in the holster."

Simon nodded. "I hoped that was yours. Basically, it's the same story that Jonathan told me?"

"With a different ending. I had him get you to help her with the cops and to get her treatment or something. I didn't guess this was coming."

Talking helped clear my head. Somehow the words distanced me from the pictures, the smells. I thought for a moment then asked, "Can we leave her killings out of it? Say she went nuts about Darryl's death? That it drove her into memories of her brother's accident and she couldn't take it? Or just make something up? The cops have the drownings as accidents, anyhow." I felt Jonathan look at me, but he didn't let go of my hand.

Simon searched my face. "Why?"

"I don't know exactly. Respect for the dead. For all the dead. The less anyone knows, the better they'll be remembered."

I felt Jonathan squeeze my hand. Simon shrugged and said he

would try. He asked if we would rather go inside, but neither of us budged. He stayed with us in our silence until the house was awash in blue and red flashing lights.

Suddenly there were swarms of people everywhere. Blues, plainclothes, medics, and suits from the coroner's office. Simon steered everyone away from us and, almost as suddenly, Jonathan and I were left by ourselves. Out in the cold.

I expected to go downtown, but eventually Simon reappeared alone, holding my jacket, and told us we could leave. They all had questions but understood we were still in shock. Simon had called a couple of his contacts; the cops would leave us alone for at least forty-eight, though they would hang on to my gun. Simon added that they'd bought the double suicide. He suggested we call him early the next day to get the story straight. I tried to grin and nod my head—it was good to see him.

Simon went back inside, and I stood up. I didn't want to be there when they dragged the bodies out in plastic bags. Despite a look of apprehension, Jonathan got up as well.

"I don't think I can be by myself right now," he said.

I nodded and said I'd take him home. He held my arm all the way to the car, reluctant to let go, even to open the door. I sort of pushed him inside and drove to his house, where I parked across the street and shut off the engine.

He made no move to leave. The car smelled like death and I rolled down my window. Tonight there would be no escape from the cold. We sat in the silence of our private horrors for a very long time. Finally Jonathan said, "I don't understand why she is dead."

I expected him to cry; but he sat there rock-faced, waiting. Waiting for what? I couldn't make it any better. "Melanie knew she was out of control. She was afraid she might kill again. Melanie did what she believed needed to be done."

He raised his hands in helpless bewilderment. "I don't understand how she could live with what she did to Peter and keep it secret." The skin on his face was drawn tightly over its bones, magnifying the raw guilt that shone from his eyes.

I reached across the seat and took one of his shaking hands.

"She never really understood that she had killed someone else until she killed Darryl."

His mouth was open and I wasn't sure he got what I said. I tried again, for the two of us.

"Peter wasn't another person to her; he was something she couldn't, then wouldn't, find inside. The night of the party, when she followed Peter and Emil to the quarry, she thought she discovered, in Peter's street life, what she most hated and feared in herself. She thought she found her mother. She had no boundaries with Peter. He was an extension of her insides, the piece of her she could not let exist."

I flashed on Melanie's dead body dripping on the floor. "The hot summer night at the quarry started what she finished tonight."

Someday, with somebody else, I'd finish what happened at the party.

"She didn't trust me to help her at all." Though forlorn, his voice was calm.

"She trusted you as much as she could trust anyone. She might have finished killing herself twenty years ago if it hadn't been for you."

"It might have been better that way," he said bitterly.

I thought for a moment. "Not better, different." I kept guessing. "If we pushed deeper into what really went on when Peter and Melanie were still living in their home, we'd find it was worse than we know."

"Should I push, Matthew?"

I grimaced. "It's over. You were the only separate person she ever really loved. Her desire to stop herself, as insane a way as she chose to do it, came from what little self-respect you gave her. It's time to leave the dead alone; we have our own mourning to do."

I pulled my hand free and lit two cigarettes. Jonathan's face was still midwinter white, but some of the shock had drained. Tears were edging down, but the hand that held the cigarette was steady. I suddenly felt the cold draft, but kept the window open. "Maybe she knew there was no recovery from what happened to her? That she couldn't have that much of her childhood stolen by poverty and abuse, and expect to get well?

"She had no hope for herself or Therin. But she had hope for you. I said it earlier—you were a good father to her, Jonathan. Her years with you were the best and only years of her life. To the end, she knew you to be a good man."

Jonathan sat next to me sobbing. I looked past his head, across the street, to his house. It stood large and gloomy, the porch light scant welcome. I thought about offering him my vacated office couch, but he suddenly reached across and threw his cigarette out the window. "I have to go in there some time, don't I?" he asked.

"Not right away," I replied. "You can stay with me until you're ready."

He shook his head. "No. I'm grateful for the offer, but I want to be alone."

"Are you sure?" An anxious thought skipped through my head.

He looked at me and smiled grimly. "You don't have to worry. There's been too much death." We sat breathing quietly until I lost all track of time. Finally he sighed and opened his door. He had one leg outside before he swung back in, reached over, and kissed me hard on the cheek. "You did right by her. I know that," he said.

I resisted a desire to grab him by the shoulders and pull him toward me. I too was afraid of being alone. He looked at me, made an effort to smile, and pulled himself out into the cold. I rolled up the window.

He was halfway across the street when he turned around and came back. I rolled down the window. "I want to thank you, Matthew," he said, his voice thick. "And to tell you that you don't have to wait around, I'm okay," he said.

I started to tell him he was more than okay, but he was already gone.

THIS TIME THERE WAS NO HOSPITAL in which to recover. No extra-strength painkillers to blot out my memory, dull my interior. No gruff but friendly nurses; no friendly but hostile doctors. No wanted or unwanted visitors. This time there was only me.

I wish I could tell you I drove home, tied one on, tallied the cost of that two way toll, and continued with the rest of my life. I wish I could tell you that, but I can't. It was going to be a long, hurting time before I finished the math.

Drugs and alcohol moved me through the first few days of blurred shock but shortly thereafter they lost their charm. There were always limits, even to trusted old friends.

Simon walked me through the legal system unscathed, our lies intact. We never got much of a chance to talk about the *old* lies between us, but we would. Hell, what I'd discovered about myself left little grip on any moral high ground. It was a relief; we could become friends again.

Even more astonishingly, I no longer suffered breath death when I thought of Lou. With the ache of my history staring me in the face, with Melanie's homelessness ground into my heart, I wanted what little family I had. Like Boots had said, Lou was family; I wouldn't have felt as if I were suffocating if he wasn't.

It still took a while before I called. "Lou."

"Matty." His voice was warm, sympathetic.

"You got grounds to be angry."

He brushed away my suggestion. "You don't need any more *chazarai* from me. You've been through enough."

"I sound that bad?"

"You sound plenty bad, but I heard about what happened from Shoes."

"Boots."

"You call her what you want. I call her 'Shoes.'"

I was glad that someone had called her at all. "Regardless, Lou, I acted like a shmuck. I'm sorry."

"So, Boychik, you acted like a shmuck. It wasn't the first time, won't be the last."

His chuckle eased my embarrassment and I started to speak, but he interrupted. "Look, when things get difficult for you, you close down, refuse to talk. Usually that only makes everything worse."

"I know."

"And *I* know that you think it's impossible to open up when you feel torn up."

"I'm afraid if I let go I'll just get violent," I admitted.

"Nah. You're way past that. Now the hate comes because you keep everything inside."

"Are you sure you've been talking to Boots and not Gloria?"

He laughed. "I don't need a shrink to understand this, Boychik. I live on the other side of that fence. When something's bothering me I can't stop talking. Even when I don't know what it is. Or how my mouth is affecting people."

A trace of sadness had crept into his tone by the sentence's finish. An ache of compassion for the loneliness of his life, for my life, burst into the air. "I want you to move out here, Lou," I blurted. "There's no reason for you to be alone in Chicago. Or me to be alone here."

I ignored his gasp on the other end of the line. "Hell," I added, "if you're going to be a real-estate tycoon in your old age, you oughta be able to inspect the property."

The invitation was as much a surprise to me as to him. Despite the spontaneity, I had no regret. It was what I wanted.

It took a few more telephone conversations—none of them particularly easy. We hashed through the antagonisms of the recent months and finally cleared the air. Lou would move into our building's first available apartment.

The charred rubble of the past few weeks had somehow become foundation stones for relational resurrections.

For some relationships.

I retired the Mall-man. Occasionally I wondered whether the decision reflected a stubborn refusal to repay Harry the Mole for handing me Blackhead, or a gift to myself for being alive. Either way, the malls were history.

But *what* parts of me *were* alive? What *was* my history? Had my attraction to Melanie been a leftover from the me who had stampeded after Megan, attracted to her contempt? Melanie's love had been hotly packaged hate, and I'd run after it, run after it damn near as hard as I'd run after Megan.

Or did the tears I'd been unable to check after Melanie and our first lovemaking reflect a better side of me? The side I'd believed gone since Chana's and Becky's deaths?

Maybe someday, when the shame of who I might be settled into knowledge of who I was, I could talk it over with Boots. When the math was done, the toll tallied and paid.

Sometime deep in the winter bleak, I drove to The End. I hung around on the streets and walked every single block. When I passed Hope House I thought of visiting Jonathan but turned away at the door. I just kept walking until I could leave.